PENGUIN BOOKS

CHAPPY

Patricia Grace is one of New Zealand's most celebrated writers. She is the author of six novels, seven short-story collections and several children's books, as well as non-fiction.

Awards for her work include the Deutz Medal for fiction for the novel *Tu* at the Montana New Zealand Book Awards in 2005, the New Zealand Fiction award for *Potiki* in 1987, the Children's Picture Book of the Year for *The Kuia and the Spider* in 1982 and the Hubert Church Prose Award for the Best First Book for *Waiariki* in 1976. She was also awarded the Literaturpreis from Frankfurt in 1994 for *Potiki*, which has been translated into several languages. *Dogside Story* was longlisted for the Booker Prize and won the Kiriyama Pacific Rim Fiction Prize in 2001.

Grace received the Prime Minister's Award for Literary Achievement in 2006 and was the recipient of the Neustadt International Prize for Literature sponsored by the University of Oklahoma in 2008.

Grace was born in Wellington and lives in Plimmerton on ancestral land, in close proximity to her home marae at Hongoeka Bay.

Chappy

PATRICIA GRACE

PENGUIN BOOKS

PENGUIN

UK | USA | Canada | Ireland | Australia
India | New Zealand | South Africa | China

Penguin is an imprint of the Penguin Random House group of companies,
whose addresses can be found at global.penguinrandomhouse.com.

Penguin
Random House
New Zealand

First published by Penguin Random House New Zealand, 2015

Text design by Megan van Staden © Penguin Random House New Zealand
Typeset in Newzald by Megan van Staden

Printed and bound in Australia by Griffin Press,
an Accredited ISO AS/NZS 14001 Environmental Management Systems Printer

A catalogue record for this book is available from the National Library
of New Zealand.

ISBN 978-0-14-357239-8

ARTS COUNCIL OF NEW ZEALAND TOI AOTEAROA

The assistance of Creative New Zealand towards the production of this book is
gratefully acknowledged by the publisher.

penguinrandomhouse.co.nz

MIX
Paper from
responsible sources
FSC® C009448

Kerehi Waiariki Grace

Whakapiri ki te tini me te mano, e kore te aroha mōu e mimiti.
(Though you have gone, our love for you does not diminish.)

PROLOGUE

I came to this country in the first place needing to piece myself together, hoping there could be attachments. By twenty-one years of age I'd lived in several countries before returning with my mother, father and sister to Switzerland, where I was born. But I didn't think of Switzerland as my country either. Nor was it the home country of my mother or my father. It's where my dad's work base was, and still is – for now. It's where some of the best ski slopes are. It's the home of several international organisations for which my mother works as a translator. Languages are her thing.

What sort of a name is Daniel, I asked my discontented self. A name neither here nor there, pronounced this way or that depending which country you happened to find yourself in.

And what sort of a country was Switzerland anyway, I thought. So neutral. So cuckoo. So heavy with banks and the world's money, it's a wonder the ground didn't crack open beneath it all.

Stones.

There are the mountains, nature's organisation of stones and great for viewing, but there's only so much mountain one can take, only so much skiing one can do unless you are an addict like my father or have ability like my sister. We'd shifted from place to place too many times for me to become a Winter Olympics prospect, too often for me to have made lifelong friends.

What was there to see in Rome, Madrid, Tübingen, Athens, Turin, but stones ancient and dusty, piled one on top of the other, cemented, plastered, corniced in the making of castles, cathedrals, barns, bridges, fortifications, museums, universities – or laid out to make roads. That was my state of mind while studying German literature at one of Germany's ancient universities.

I am a stone, I thought. I am clay. Or I am dust blowing anywhere or nowhere.

Our mother was just our mother once, when we were little, who tucked us into our beds, kissed sore knees, read to us, filled the kitchen with smells of baking, had us up beside her at the benches to cut out and decorate biscuit figures for Christmas. She wrapped us and played outside with us in the snow. And while doing so her voice tinkled all about us like ice crackling, 'Oh I always wanted to do this.' Her pink cheeks. Her shiny eyes. 'Make snowballs, go sledging. We had a sledge, pulled by a horse, but not snow. We had nīkau palm slides which we sat our backsides in, pulling the fronds up between our legs and whooshing down dry-grass hillsides.' When she rocked herself back and forth and said, 'Whoosh,' and 'Whee,' I tried to imagine it all.

But having a mother to ourselves couldn't continue in houses as grand as the ones we lived in. Not that I knew then that they were grand. However, I soon came to understand that there were too many rooms for our mother to take care of, too much fine food to be prepared for too many fine evenings for too many teethy people. There were too many dresses, too much finery to think about. Suits to be sent for cleaning day after day. Shoes. Hairdos. Our mother was already beautiful and didn't need appointments, dresses, sparkly things to make her so.

It became necessary for other people, not our mother, to look after rooms, to cook all day long, to help us dress and take us skating, see us to bed at night, tend to pains and illnesses, watch us riding bicycles, drive us places.

Although I enjoyed our trips to the mountains, it was not so much because I liked to ski. I had no aptitude for it. But I enjoyed our mother staying with us on the slopes, learning along with Janny and me, falling and laughing and getting up again. Our father, too, would stay with us for a day before going off to find elevations more suited to his skill. God of slopes. He has skied all the skiable mountains of the world.

After a while it became inconvenient for him to take Mother, Janny and me along with him, and anyway, by the time we were eleven and twelve my sister and I were ensconced in misery boarding schools, French speaking to improve our language skills.

Though she played the part for several years, the high life didn't suit Mother. High life was no life, she decided. She needed to work, get her teeth into something. In the same year that we went to boarding school, she began her own study of languages. Already competent in three – three I thought then, I didn't know about the fourth, which was really her first – she was determined that she would become a licensed interpreter and translator, contracting to important world organisations. This would be her mission in life.

Why German literature? Well, I didn't choose it. My parents did that for me because they understood that I liked to read, and nothing so far had driven me to choose a course for myself. It was true that I was always compelled to read: light works in spring and summer, heavy in the thick of winter when there's so much dark and snow to hide from. But it was the *reading* of books I enjoyed – whether in English, German, French or Danish – not the study of them. Writers and their subconscious didn't interest me, no matter how involved I became in what they wrote or how interested I became in their manner of telling.

And why the ancient university? My parents chose it for me

because it was old, prestigious, focused, disciplined. Discipline was what I needed.

Stone it was, the university and the university town. I was stone, heart of stone. And alone.

One late night after leaving the city I smashed my car into a wall of stone. Fragments rained down. Metal flew and rained down. I stepped away from all that rain, unscratched and not unhappy.

Prosecution seemed like the beginning of something new, though that came to nothing. But it made me bold enough to tell my mother I was chucking it all in – the stones, the study.

'But you can't,' she said. 'Can't throw your life away.'

I stood like stone.

'Change courses,' she suggested, 'find something you like. You have to do something. The trouble with you is you've had it too easy. You don't know what it's like to have to work. To have work is the important thing in life.'

My father, over the phone, told me to settle down and see sense. But the financier didn't sound as though he cared what I did, being involved in deals with this or that country and taken up with all his affairs. I think he was in Spain at the time.

'You're going to your grandmother's,' my mother said after the enquiries were over.

I thought at first she was talking about Bedstemoder, our father's mother in the city of Copenhagen, where Janny and I had often stayed when neither of our parents could be home with us in the school holidays. Another city of stones. I was not averse to spending a week or two with Bedstemoder Konnie, who was funny and generous and had a wonderful library.

However, my mother was talking about Grandmother Oriwia, her own mother, on the other side of the world. We'd been to see her once when we were little. There had been a mysterious grandfather too, but he wasn't there at the time. My sister and I knew his nationality, the name he was known by, and that was all.

There were aunts, uncles and cousins.

We played in the trees, went swimming in the ocean and skidding in the mud of the estuary.

Grandmother Oriwia sent us cards at Christmas.

Attachments.

'Go there for six months and sort yourself out,' my mother said. 'You'll soon see how the other half lives.'

'Who was he, the grandfather?' I asked my mother as I packed my bags.

'Go and find out,' she said. She too was packing, leaving for somewhere. 'That'll be something for you to do. And remember you've got to pull your weight. You have to work. Whatever they do, you do. You'll find out what life's all about. You'll have to learn how to make their beds. Can't just throw it all together, and there's no one there with time to run round after you.' But she didn't sound upset, seemed to have forgiven me, excited that I was making this journey – which she had already made twice without us. 'I wish I was coming with you,' she said.

When I began thinking about what she'd said about finding out about my grandfather, I became interested by what I now saw ahead of me – an opportunity to piece bits of *myself* together.

But the story that follows is not about me. Even though I've been able to glean a personal history from it, it needn't matter to anyone else who may read this, with the exception perhaps of my sister. There's a much more interesting story than one of a spoilt brat with his own bank account who had to try and kill himself in order to draw attention to his . . . His what? His suffering?

Forget it.

Anyway I'm exaggerating. I didn't want to kill myself, only wanted something to happen. I've never wanted to die, only to live.

When I began the interviews with Grandmother Oriwia and a doubly adopted uncle known as Aki, I didn't intend putting them together as a book. All I wanted to do was set down family stories that I could share with my mother and sister. I thought that asking our grandmother about the man known as Chappy would be a good place to start.

'Your grandfather?' she said. 'If you want to know about your grandfather there's a lot I can tell you. Also there's a lot I can't tell you. My husband was always a mystery to me.'

We were sitting in the garden facing the house, which was built of wood with a low-pitched, corrugated-iron roof painted red, two windows either side of a front door, and creamy-yellow walls with green facings – all a little faded.

One of the things that had made an impression on me when landing in this country was how colourful the houses are. I like the idea that home owners can build their houses in any style they like and paint them any colour they choose. There's freedom in that. On my first day it was the house, more than the garden, which drew my attention.

'Anyway, the best place for you to begin would be to go and talk to Aki, your uncle by double adoption,' my grandmother said. 'If it wasn't for him . . .'

Grandmother, armed with a chocolate cake, took me to meet this uncle, who lived about eight kilometres up a gravel road in the middle of a forest. There was an old weatherboard house there. It was without electricity and running water. He had one tank to catch rainwater, which piped into the kitchen, and another that provided water into the wash-house, an old shed at the back of the house. Cooking was done on a wood stove in the kitchen, or sometimes over a fireplace in the yard.

Aki was seventy-one, tall and thin. He hadn't always been bony, my grandmother said, but she mentioned that he'd always been stubborn, 'hard in the head' was how she put it. When we arrived he made a pot of tea and cut the chocolate cake into large pieces.

He was pleased to be asked to talk about my grandfather, whom he referred to as his brother. We arranged that I would visit him later in the week, and he agreed that I could bring a tape recorder with me.

My grandmother complained about him all the way home. 'He's silly,' she said. 'He doesn't have to live like that, stuck up in the bush all by himself, patching up his roof, chopping wood, making bread, growing corn so he can feed his pig. You have to move on in life. It's not as though he hasn't seen the world.'

There were things I had to do before I could begin my interviews. I needed a car and a recorder. Oriwia advised me to buy overalls, a Swanndri and gumboots. 'It's no use wearing good clothes up there,' she said. It turned out to be good advice. I spent more time out of doors mucking in than I did recording.

Grandmother and I went to Wellington by train. I soon found a car that I liked and went shopping for what I needed. The reason Grandmother had insisted on coming with me was she knew I'd never driven on the left side of the road before. Also I didn't have a New Zealand driver's licence, which she said wouldn't matter round the small town where she lived, but to be without it in the city could mean trouble. I took her word for it. She'd left her tearoom in charge of farmer friend, Dulcie.

Arriving at the house on the arranged day, I set up the recorder and sat down at the table opposite Uncle Aki with my notebook and pen. I had a list of questions, which I didn't get to ask because when I pressed 'record', and before I'd had time to draw breath, Aki began talking.

He spoke four sentences in English – intriguing sentences they were, too – before breaking into a language that I never remembered hearing before. There were two words I recognised as he continued. He ran them together. They were 'moon' and 'face'.

'The fool,' my grandmother said, when I told her what had happened and after I'd played a section of the recording to her. 'Anyone would think he couldn't speak English.' She rattled her baking trays, swiping at them with a cloth. 'Him and his language, what's he trying to prove?' She shoved the trays onto the rack above the oven. 'All right, leave it to me, I'll write it up for you. Tonight. In good English.' She emphasised this last sentence. It wasn't until she made the offer that I realised my grandmother was conversant in this other language too. 'As though I've nothing better to do,' she mumbled. 'Next time, if there's going to be a next time, tell him to speak English.'

I bit my tongue. There *was* going to be a next time. I'd already arranged this, but who was I, a twenty-one-year-old stranger, to tell such an impressive man not to speak his own language.

In what follows, the first lines were spoken in English. The rest is my grandmother's translation from Māori into English. I think Grandmother must have worked on it throughout the night as it was all ready for me, in neat, handwritten pages, by next morning.

| Chapter 1 |
AKI

Every night while I walk the decks of my tub,
I'm seeing a ghose.
No, no. I gotta say that again.
Every night while I walk the decks of my tub
a ghose is seeing me.

At first I thought it might be Moonface come to light, reminding me he was my companion on our journeys to see the world. Silly thing, I thought. I hadn't forgotten him. He's the one I talk to in the lonely hours, out of habit. As long as I am alive he will *be*.

But it wasn't Moonface.

That first time it was just a glimpse I had of that ghost seeing me when some slant of light – brief torchlight perhaps, or a strip from a slit of open-and-shut door, or a roll of the ship – slipped a sliver of moon onto that dark side where I walked.

Anyway, an iris, sitting whole and lit in the outer half of an eye corner, and a section of high, luminous cheekbone is what I saw. But I kept on walking, stepping it out on the dark decks after nightwatch and several hours of making steam, ourselves steaming and intoxicated on steel moving against steel, hot pipes, grease and oil enclosed in an airless, shuddering and lurching cavern.

Blood needs air, and when coming out into it, the first salt and gluttonous skulling is like throwing back highballs one after another, becoming so heady and drunken that a man could pitch to the boards with the weight of it.

It wasn't Moonface whose eye had met with both of mine. The eye that I saw seeing me was a pleading eye, not of a ghost but a man.

What was the plea?

Was the eye asking me not to see? To forget what I had seen? Or to give help?

I walked on by.

We were three days' journey away from my home port of Wellington, New Zealand, where I was looking forward to time with family and friends. What came to mind as I walked while being watched, was that after setting out from San Francisco, we heard that a stowaway had been dragged out of the chain locker and put to work mopping galleys and scrubbing the boards – slow on the job because he had busted ribs or something. I hadn't seen him myself and, the next I heard, he had disappeared. A search was made and the message went out that we must report any sightings. After twenty-four hours the rumour was that the man had gone overboard when we hit rough weather.

Now, I thought, the eye must be telling me to keep walking, keep the secret – which I was more than willing to do. The owner of the eye may have known, as I did, that the way some ships' officials dealt with stowaways was to throw them overboard before docking. In this way the masters were able to avoid all the red tape and responsibilities to do with landing a stowaway. I'd seen it happen once in my travels and had always wondered if that poor fellow made it to shore or not because the weather was so cold that morning. There were whitecaps on the waves of the harbour and it was barely daybreak.

I'd heard of stowaways being thrown to the sharks or the alligators, or dying in a fumigated hold. I'd been told others had gone mad from drinking salt water and ended up in chains with irons on their feet. I'd seen men arrested and taken away on arrival. The latter happened once in Wellington. It was difficult to tell what would happen now if this poor man was discovered. I didn't know what kind of heart sat in the chest of the present red- and hair-faced shipmaster, so it was best to keep the secret. A secret can give you musing as you work, something to bring you forward to a clean-up, a smoke, tots and a decent feed. I walked back the way I had come, felt the eye again – the owner of which was afraid of what I might do – seeing me.

Though the man-not-a-ghost was on my mind as I turned in to my dormitory – where mates were already snoring, muttering, cracking their jaws – nothing kept my eyes from slamming themselves shut for the remaining night hours.

I preferred the work hours to the slack hours, enjoyed using the body, creating steam, and the magic of making ten thousand tons move through vast oceans. But at the tag end of this journey I was distracted by the pleading eye as I worked out my watch. The owner of the eye, I thought, would need water. There had been no rain for over a week.

The eye's owner would be hungry by now. You can't be a man if you let another man go without food and water.

At the end of my shift, and because I had to know I stood upright, walked on two feet and breathed air, I wrapped meat and potatoes in paper, filled my mug with water and placed these as close as I could to where the eye lived. I pressed myself back into an alcove nearby and waited. It was a good half hour before a slow, misshapen being crept from the shadows, reached for the two items and made a painful retreat into the dark. A breath-taking wind had come up, and a fine swell played tricks with my feet as I went on my way, even though I'd had my sea-legs for a few years by then.

I was fifteen when I first, accidentally and luckily, became a seafarer, not knowing what adventures I would have, who I would meet or what new places I would visit. Seeking work, two uncles and I came to the harbour of Wellington to seagull. Having work is the most important thing in life.

The uncles and I had started out the day before, in the dark of a winter morning. Not a penny among us, but we had preserved eels for the train guard, a blanket and towel each, bread and a half packet of tea in a biscuit tin. We had a fishing line in a billy. Our gift of eels got us into the guard's van without tickets, and soon after daybreak – coming out between high hills, which we could see receding as we took turns at the one small window to the rear of the van – we were looking out over grey sea lashing big tails, and the ships and buildings of Wellington Harbour. After leaving the train we went to present ourselves at the waterside.

We were in among a crowd of men, seagulls they called us, all hoping to be selected for a day's work. 'We can try,' Uncle Tad said, 'but not much show for the native man.' There was no queuing those days. No, you took your chances. Though the selectors' eyes passed us by on that first morning we sat out the day hoping to be called on, hoping we could make ourselves useful in some way and earn a coin or two.

In the late afternoon, after an unsuccessful day, we made our way to a sandy beach which lay beyond the wharves and jetties and sheds – round Oriental Parade there.

We took ourselves out of sight behind a rocky outcrop, where we collected kaipūpū – some to cook up in the billy, some to bait the line with. We pulled in a few little carp, cleaned them and cooked them on a fire we made after dark. We slept there on the sand.

After three days' seagulling, eyes having passed over us on all three, the uncles decided we'd be better off at home catching decent-sized fish and growing cabbages. The walk back to Porirua would take several hours.

We were leaving through the main gates when a taxi pulled up and a ship's captain looked out and spoke to us. Well, I thought he was a captain. All these dazzling, uniformed men were captains to me in the days when I didn't know better.

'Gentlemen, I could do with a helping hand, or two, or six,' he said. 'Follow me.'

We followed the cab back through the gates to the wharfside where a ship was being loaded, and with the help of the driver we took from the taxi a bolt of cloth, a small carved table, a supply of whisky and a suitcase. During our three days of wandering the wharves and jetties in the hope of earnings, of all the sights to be seen it was this coal-powered steamship bearing the same name as my home town that had most drawn my attention.

After we had delivered the goods on board, the 'captain' handed over three florins, which we were more than pleased with. He accompanied us off the ship in case we stowed away or stole.

'Wait here,' he said, 'and let's see.'

We waited an hour or more. The man, who wasn't a captain I found out later, didn't return. Instead another grand uniformed man arrived and seemed to sigh within himself as he looked us over. To my uncle he said, 'We can take the young one,' and rattled off a whole lot of information that my untrained ear couldn't catch.

My uncle spoke to me in our own native tongue. They're short-handed because of sickness and unreliability, he told me. They needed a new peggy and could give me work on board, no pay for three months, but I would have food and training. Sailing in an hour. If I proved myself, if I was reliable, they would hire me. Uncle Tad added a few thoughts of his own. 'What if they never pay, just dump you back here when they've got the work out of you? When he says a few crew got sick does he mean they died and got chucked overboard? And what will your parents have to say to me if I allow to you go?'

Go on, go on, go on, Moonface was urging, not that I needed any encouragement.

'Let me go,' I said.

Uncle Tad hesitated before offering the two-shilling pieces, three in a row on his outstretched hand. I took one and began my life as a seafarer, because there was really no other choice for me. When I left my own home a month earlier to live with my uncles closer to the city, my mother told me that if there were no jobs and no money I was to come back.

I wasn't ready to return.

Even though we were in debt to shopkeepers, it wasn't for the sake of money that she thought I should go. The land provided for us. But my mother encouraged me to leave because something had to be done about sorrow.

My first job was to bring the meals from the galley and keep the mess room clean. Later, as junior trimmer, I learned to shovel coal, providing it where needed and shifting it from here to there to keep our ship on an even keel. Later I became a furnace man, stripped to the waist, belt turned to the back so that the iron buckle wouldn't heat up and burn a buckle-shaped hole from belly button to backbone. But SS *Otaki* was one of the last of the coal burners. The work I did later, in the engine rooms of other fine ships, was easy by comparison.

| Chapter 2 |
AKI

Having grown to the height and width of a door, I'm easy enough, once seen, for the eye of a ghost – or any eye – to recognise again. Haunting me it was, this eye. Of someone not a ghost. But what more was to be done for this sick and creeping creature, dead enough to be a ghost anyway?

Along the decks and up I went to where I knew the eye was on me. Again I left a cup and parcel and waited.

Nothing.

No shadow.

No movement other than that of the ship itself, tilling the great waters of the wonderful Pacific, bringing me ever closer to my home shores.

I waited for over an hour, fearing that the poor thing had been lost overboard or simply expired, then as I returned to the boards a twist up ahead caught my eye. It was a breath, a straw, a blur, a soundless echo.

Turning from a dark recess the figment tumbled, a cup of mine hooked on a long, pale finger. It fell into a scrap of light, which swept away and back again from a scrag of rocking moon. Falling with a clatter. Yes, a clatter, for this was nothing but a bag of rattly bones.

'*No ghose, you,*' I said as I stepped towards him and leaned down.

Because I could see that this was not a native man like me, I thought I had to try to speak to him in English. Although I'd seen men like him in various ports and cities and heard their singsong language, I still thought that if I spoke to him in English he would understand me. Ha, ha.

'*No ghose. Chus' a liddle Chap.*'

I pulled him into an alcove – like ice he was – and walked up and down for a while to make sure there was no one about before returning to the dorm for warm clothes and a blanket. My mate Mo was there sitting on his bunk with his foot on a piece of newspaper slicing a bunion with a razor blade. Mo had his own India language but we were learning to understand each other's English. Mo had joined us in San Francisco. How he came to be in that city I don't know, because as far as I understood he had no home or family there. What I did understand was that he needed my protection. We had our own corner.

Others were there, mainly Englishmen who talked a lot, played cards, slept, kept their own loud company.

'*Liddle Chap,*' I said, jerking my head sideways to indicate direction. '*From Chapan.*' I felt I owed Mo an explanation as he had observed me earlier going out with the wrapped pie and the mug of water. Mo shifted his head. He giggled and kept on slicing.

Out in the shadows I stripped this wreckage of his damp clothing, dried him, put him in a jersey, trousers and socks of mine and wrapped him in a blanket, pushing him into the recess because someone was coming. It was Mo. He handed me a cup of hot cocoa.

'*Chap,*' he said.

The little Chap's hands were shaking so much he couldn't hold the cup so I did that for him. Immediately he'd finished he fell asleep.

Back in the dorm I rolled onto my bunk and worked out how I was going to help this Chap ashore. I had already decided that I would take him home with me, 'where he can be our wayfarer,' said Moonface.

We'd always had wayfarers at home. I don't remember them all, only recall that there were hundreds of these men on the roads when we were kids, men walking the highways looking for work. They were men off boats who had jumped ship, or who had been sent to the colonies by wealthy families who didn't want to own them. The latter were earls and dukes, we believed, paid to stay away from their own countries because of shameful incidents or because they were drunkards. Gentry or not, the swaggies would go from place to place in the hope of being given work, a meal and somewhere to sleep. They were from England, Ireland, Scotland, Italy, America or Australia, and apart from the ones we called 'the silent ones', who worked, ate, slept and were gone by morning, they all had stories to tell. Or they had deformities, bad habits, idiosyncrasies, bullet holes or other wounds that impressed us. Some had songs and music.

My parents would give them work, then my father would show them to the wash-house where there was a bed and blankets, and where they could light the copper for hot water and wash themselves and their clothes. At the end of the day they would join us for a meal and conversation.

One had card tricks. One had a monkey on his back that we could see hunching under his clothes. It moved sometimes, but though we watched and followed the man around, the monkey never poked its head out. Well, that was us as kids. Another had a frog in his throat. Most of them had newspapers, catalogues and comics stuffed about their bodies like underclothes. Some had books.

I used to think what great adventures I could have fighting off crocodiles, sharks, pirates and enemies if I, too, were a traveller. I planned how I could survive high seas, run away from having to go up and down chimneys, escape from bombs and plagues.

Once on an icy morning I cut my hand, sliced through the meaty bit of my thumb when I was splitting morning wood with a hatchet. That was embarrassing. I was nine.

Anyway, I took off down to the creek holding it all together, and swished the hand around in the water, but it wouldn't stop bleeding. I went back to the house where I was told off by Mum for not watching what I was doing. She squeezed the bits tight and sent my sisters off to get cobwebs from under the outside windowsills. When they came back she bound the pieces of meat together with the spider web and told my sisters to make me a cup of tea. She was telling me off the whole time.

Dad was out fencing, which was what he did in winter if he could get a contract. He'd leave home in the dark and come home in the dark. But before night I took off to Grandfather's house because I didn't want to explain anything to my father.

Grandfather shook his head at me when he saw my spider-webbed hand, but he didn't say anything except to tell me to sit down and have a feed. I said to him, 'What's blood made of?'

'Air, rain and horseshoes,' he said, and he laughed, throwing his head back. He only had every second tooth. One of them stuck right out, horizontal, and held his pipe in place.

All Dad said when I arrived home was, 'Not much use around the place with a hand like that,' which brought to mind Onehand Alf, a wayfarer who had returned to us several times. He'd been aboard a ship which ran aground on the coast of Africa. After heaving himself out through a porthole, he'd had his hand bitten off by a shark. Sometimes he said crocodile. What remained was a docked limb with a purple stub which, when he was carrying water or the milk bucket in his other hand, would thrust and pull like the jointed metal shafts that drove the wheels of trains. He could do most things, including making three cigarettes at a time by laying his tissue papers, already licked, on his blunt arm, threading his tobacco along and rolling them. He couldn't go back to his own country because the coppers were on his tail. I didn't know what that meant then.

Anyway, I decided that what Alf could do with one hand, I could do also. I'd show my father I wasn't useless. And that's what I did – milked the cow one-handed, split the kindling, carried the buckets, fed the dogs and chooks, lit the copper. My father didn't say anything. The cut soon got better, leaving a scar like a white hair.

And then there was Sharpo, who came along once a year with his steel and whetstone in a sugar bag. Though my grandparents and parents wouldn't let him anywhere near our knives and axes, which they always sharpened themselves, he was so shrunken and withered that my parents felt sorry for him and wouldn't turn him away. They gave him food and a bed and let him hang around until he decided to move on. Money was a problem for us in those days, but we were never short of food.

| *Chapter 3* |
AKI

The next day, which was the day before our arrival in Wellington, I sorted through my sea bag. From it I took a hibiscus shirt and a woven hat which, on our outward journey, I'd bought as gifts to take home. They were the type of clothes passengers liked to wear when disembarking. These I put in a grass basket, adding a towel and soap, a comb, a razor, and Chappy's own cotton trousers which I had washed and laid along hot pipes to dry.

If my plan was to work he would need to gain strength, which meant food and drink. I smuggled what I could to him over the next hours and it did revive him. He stood upright, only stooping again and again to give me his thanks. His fingertips were ash-coloured holding a boiled egg, fingernails bleached the colour of pipeclay, but two red dots appeared high on his cheekbones with the drinking of tea.

Before daylight I took the basket to him, showing him each item and whispering to him in my own language. Though he couldn't understand a word of it, what a relief it was to be speaking my own tongue. There were many things I missed as I journeyed to the various countries of the world – my family, our customs, our food, our singing, the land. But most of all I missed my language. I missed conversation, tricks and jokes, gossip and laughing. I missed listening to grandparents and others whom I considered were speakers and storytellers of great knowledge and skill.

By the time I left, I was confident that Chappy knew what I was asking him to do. On a piece of paper I had drawn a picture of the wharf gates and the road outside, and marked the way to the war memorial where I had drawn a cross to show where he should wait for me. All I could do now was hope for the best and see how events panned out. Perhaps I would never know.

Living up here in Aotearoa, far distant from other countries, and having listened to tales from the likes of dukes and earls and other hobos, you could think of the rest of the world as a wild place and all its oceans as treacherous. There are such places, there are such dangerous seas of course, especially if you're in the wrong kind of tub. Anyway, until you have experienced it for yourself, you wouldn't expect that the rockiest part of a journey, after crossing the marvellous Pacific or the wild Tasman oceans, would be the entrance to the harbour of home, where a fine ship may be biffed from all angles as if in a giant boxing ring. This madcap channel is enough to send passengers who are out on deck and eager to witness the breakthrough to the harbour teetering back to their cabins.

With our work over for the day, Mo and I disembarked, Mo covered by a wicker chair that he'd been asked to carry ashore. It gave him the appearance of an upside-down turtle, pale underbelly and four legs in the air. He sniggered and giggled under there, unable to walk in a straight line. I was taking him home with me during off-duty hours, for what is there to do in a city unfriendly to someone like him. Though I had never asked questions, I realised he'd been signed on at a lower rate of pay than any of us.

Once the chair was deposited with its owner, we crossed the jetties and made our way through the iron gates, along footpaths, across potholed roads and tram tracks to concrete steps where stone lions guarded the war memorial. On high, a bronze horse with a soldier astride it reared above the city. Up the steps we went and, enclosed by walls, found Chappy in Grandmother's shirt and Paa's hat, the grass basket beside him with my clothes and blankets stuffed inside. I laughed. I wrapped my arms about him – which startled him I think. Mo sat himself on a stone bench and laughed too. I'd never known Mo to laugh so heartily, never seen that wide open mouth, the red tongue, the square grey teeth. Never before heard his aa rar rar rar.

We made our way towards the railway station and entered the concourse, where I left my two companions with our luggage and went to the front of the building where there were taxis waiting. What I wanted was a dozen beer for our celebration at home, but since the native man was not allowed in hotels this needed a plan. I approached one of the taxis.

'Waterloo Hotel,' I said to the driver.

'Don't like your chances,' he said. 'Anyway, it's just there, across the road.'

I held up money. 'Take me there. Get me a dozen beer and a bottle of whisky,' I said.

'One man's money's as good as the next's,' he said.

That's how I got my plonk. Back at the railway station I took it out of the box and put it in my swag, along with chocolates, scarves, sarongs and all sorts of things I'd collected from here and there.

I took my companions to the station cafeteria, where we had a meal of pies with peas and mashed potato, all eyes on us. There was a two-hour train journey ahead, followed by a bumpy ride in a taxi, one stop at Jimmy Shop's shop for lollies, then home.

By the time our taxi arrived at the first gate, it had been swung back on its failing hinges by kids who had swarmed from wherever kids swarm from – creek banks, long grass, treetops and bolt holes – and who now decorated every plank of it, vertical, horizontal, upside down, right way up. Attired in cut-down shifts and shorts made from adult cast-offs and flour bags, they came running, hems hanging, holding up britches, batches of black hair flopping in mops.

They were easily able to keep pace with the car, which now had no formed road but only rutted cart tracks, potholes and creek beds to make its way along. The kids cast dead mānuka brush onto mud patches so wheels wouldn't become bogged, or they pulled branches and large stones out of the way as the taxi, one wheel in front of the other, was edged along by Hermie Krauss, who loved an opportunity to show what his cab could do.

All this time, while their scabby arms pulled away rocks and put down branches, the kids' muddy faces, with their excellent teeth on display, were calling out to me through the open windows of the taxi, '*Unca Aki godda lady and a plack man. Uncle Aki godda lolly.*'

Once free of the creek crossings, the holes, ruts and rocks and a second gate, and as the cab crossed the home paddock where the grass had been cropped by house cows and a few sheep, I threw out Minties and toffees, keeping the unwrapped lollies – blackballs, liquorice allsorts, jelly babies and jubes – to be handed round later.

| Chapter 4 |
ORIWIA

When Aki stopped at Jimmy Shop's store in an overloaded taxi, Oriwia said to herself, 'Here comes that husband I'm supposed to have.' Her next thought was that she didn't want a husband who spent more than half his life at sea. Now that Dad Jimmy had had a stroke, and since her sister had left home and married a road digger, all the work of the shop was left to her. What use was a sailor when she needed a man on the spot, someone to carry tins of kerosene, sacks of sugar and bags of flour, a man to collect goods from the railway and heave stuff from here to there. Someone to help lift Father Jimmy. Muscle was no use to her on the other side of the world.

And who were the other two men with him – one blacker than anyone she'd ever seen and with sunburnt eyes, the other dressed-up one a kind of what? Nothing. Or a rabbit. As if he might suddenly run off on a zigzag rabbit path, shot at. Aki had a tooth missing since she'd seen him last.

At the same time as the kids were swinging the first gate open, adults had also received the message, radiating out from the air round Jimmy Shop's store, that Aki was home, and began deciding what they would take to the party. Mostly it would be fry bread, old-man bread, baked eel or rabbit stew. But as soon as the men had gone, Oriwia, an expert baker of cakes, opened the door of the wood range and put her hand inside to test the temperature for duck-egg sponges.

―――

As my grandmother was recounting this – mostly not on tape – she was actually re-enacting the scene of more than forty years earlier. That is, she was mixing sponge cakes but using hen eggs rather than duck eggs. Not that she was doing this to enhance her telling, not at all. It was coincidence. She was making up an order for a reception tea down at the hall and already had trays of butterfly cakes, fruit and vanilla squares, louise cake and ginger drops out on the benches cooling. I was taking notes and jotting my own observations for writing up later, but hoping to catch snippets on tape as she moved about. That was the best I could do. She'd already told me not to expect her 'to talk to that thing'. Grandmother Oriwia has live eyes like bronze bees.

Also she has a man's strength and a broad body. The arm that now beat sugar and eggs in a bowl with a wooden spoon was strongly muscled under a meaty surround. Halfway through the flogging, a pinch of salt went in without pause, and soon the mixture was creamy – full of fluff and air.

Flour and raising agent snowed down from a sifter while the spatula folded it into the egg mixture – under and over in large pearly waves. It poured with satisfying silkiness into prepared baking tins and, opening the oven door carefully so as not to allow heat to disperse, Oriwia placed the tins on the middle rack.

―――

On that long-ago morning, the cakes came from the oven high and porous. Oriwia spread them first with jam, then with cream, which she had skimmed and whipped up from the previous day's milking. After lifting her father into the cart and seating him on a palliasse that had been placed there, she clicked the horse and set out for the home of Taana and Dorothea, Aki's parents.

The outdoor fires had been boosted under mutton stew. Women in floral or palmy sarongs, handed out to them from Aki's swag and which they had tied over the top of their dresses, were dancing like Islanders. Aki was strumming a ukulele and trying to sing up high like an Islander. Singing, drinking, laughing, shouting and thumping of feet continued as Oriwia rode up. Paa and Aki left the yard to lift Jimmy and his mattress down from the cart.

Despite the noise and all that was going on, the main distraction was the two visitors. What was there to know? The people kept the two men's cups full, talking and joking with them in a flow of language that they could all see neither of the men understood, but what did it matter? Talk was the thing.

It wasn't until Aki began telling about the 'ghost seeing him' that the din subsided and people seated themselves about the yard to listen to the stories of the little Hapanihi from Chapan and of the man from India. Food was handed out. The eyes went round and saw that, yes, the Inia man was eating, enjoying the food. They saw that the Chapan man hesitated then, with colourless fingers, began spooning meat into himself and biting into bread. Good. Everyone was eating except for Grandmother Nunu, who ate just once a day at mid-morning. Draped in a sarong, her face lit every now and again by dashes of firelight, she danced holding a ladle. Talk started up again, cups were refilled.

But just as the meal was ending, plates were being scraped off and the singing was starting up again, the Chapan man went to sleep. Poor thing. Aki and Paa lifted him under the arms and knees, carried him to the bedroom, lay him on Aki's bed, removed his clothes and covered him in a red hibiscus cloth. He didn't stir. Perhaps it was the brew.

Later, when the night cooled down, Dorothea called Oriwia to help her put Chappy into the bed. Even without a lamp Oriwia could see the pearly scars on his thighs and the soft, green bruises on his chest and upper arms. On lifting him he was so light she thought the bones that protruded all over his body must be filled with nothing but air, like bird bones which you could blow sounds through or use for breathing underwater. He was a bird. Oriwia imagined him feathered. By morning he could have flown.

Dorothea insisted on keeping Dad Jimmy there for the night and made up a bed for him on the verandah next to one that Aki had put there for himself. So after the fires had been allowed to die and most of the visitors had gone home, Oriwia helped Paa and Grandmother Nunu on the cart to be delivered to their house. With them was Mo, who was to be their wayfarer.

———

'Now, Grandson,' Oriwia said, 'I want to tell you about Chappy's first night at Uncle Taana and Aunty Dorothea's place. We didn't know he was in a fever, just thought he was drunk even though we all knew he'd had no more than two cups of Paa's brew. He told me about it much later, when he could speak our language, but it's better if you have the story now since this is where it belongs. Look here, I'll write it for you. There's no revision with these machines, they put me off. Yes, tell it in my own way and have it ready for you by morning.'

Chappy Wakes
By Oriwia Star

Chappy slept until the afternoon of the next day when he woke naked in a bare, darkened room not knowing where he was. His head was full of hot stones, his stomach riding the waves, and he needed water. Pushing the bedcovers aside he put his flutey, reedy feet to the floor, taking up the red hibiscus sarong as he recalled the events of the previous day.

Or days?

He wasn't sure. He remembered that there had been people crowding, watching, laughing their smoky beer-and-meat breath over him. But at that moment the room was tipping him sideways, and too embarrassed to appear outside the bedroom in scars and bruises and a garment that wouldn't stay attached to his frame, he rolled back on the bed where he lay watching the shadowy ceiling boards, knotholes in the wood spiralling out and back again like springs.

He didn't know how much later it was when he felt his eyelids drag themselves open to see faces leaning, women with water, noiseless, lifting his head, pouring, choking him. Soon afterwards he was being lifted burning, under the armpits, under the knees, and taken along pathways, the whole world rocking, churning in tipsy patches of light and dark. He was lowered to cool ground, stretched out and washed from head to foot. Hands lifted his head and water fingered its way down his throat. There were voices now, faces outlined one moment, fading the next. The stones in his head were spilling forward then back-washing behind his eyes. He didn't know at the time that it was Aunt Dorothea and me who carried and washed him. I had come to collect my father.

Chappy woke several hours later in long grass, looking up into the extended branches of a bush full of tiny red and white birds which were motionless and made no sound.

Nothing moved.

As he became more aware he could see that these were not coloured birds on branches. They were flowers, beaked flowers, poised as if to fly.

He turned his head to see an old woman sitting cross-legged weaving green strands, eyeing him, toothless and smiling, making something. He thought at first it must be his grandmother returned to the world to speak to him, but when this one spoke, her words were incomprehensible to him.

The woman put down the work and came to him with a cup. He sat, leaned himself up against the flower tree, forming his words of gratitude though unable to release them. But from the woman, words were spilling like rivers as he took the cup from her. She spread her arms, which hung out like handlebars, fluttering her old yams of fingers, telling him something joyful before running off and calling.

Yes, he believed she ran, bent and fast, calling. Already there were children who had somehow come unheard out of fernery, heads on sideways, inspecting him. He was aware that there was something stuck on his forehead. In a moment Grandmother Nunu returned, putting her knobbly hands on his brow, laughing because of what these hands told her.

Aunt Dorothea arrived. There followed another torrent of words during which Nunu addressed him, pulling her which-way fingers towards her chest, rolling them out again, pulling them in, 'Speak, speak.' That's what her hands were asking him to do.

So, to the delight of the two women, though they had no idea what he was talking about, he spoke words in a language which seemed to them to come, not from anywhere inside his body but from out of his face. He looked like a little Jesus lying there half naked, battered, wearing his crown without thorns. Grandmother offered him water again and Aunt Dorothea peeled away the damp leaves of kawakawa from his head. They were turning to look towards a sound coming from the track.

The children, also alerted, climbed the nearest mānuka tree, threading themselves in it to see who was coming. 'Unca Aki come, got that Chapanee pants, gotta bread and a water and a Unca Mo.'

Chappy was pleased to see his clothes and his friends. All he could do was smile, incline himself in gratitude then attempt to stand, but Aki motioned him down again. Aki would take him home before the sun went down.

Chappy buttoned his shirt, but when he stood to pull on his trousers the sky and trees began turning and his legs softened, so he leaned himself against a tree trunk and breathed deeply while the world righted itself and the sun descended. The women had gone. Kids had dropped from branches and run home before the ghosts came, before you got stole. Aki came from the spring where he had filled a cream can with water. He was telling Chappy something in a swarm of words which came from his stomach and rolled out of such a mobile face it seemed his round eyes could fall from it. 'Lean on me,' his words and arms were saying. Chappy stood away from the tree, the world remained still.

'No, no, my friend. I can walk.' Though Aki could only guess at what he might be saying to him, Chappy took steps, showing what he could do.

There was a smell of smoke and of food cooking. At the outdoor fire people had gathered again. Kids were already munching, bread in one hand, a piece of eel in the other. Chappy was given a chair to sit on and handed a plate of food. He kept his eyes lowered, aware that he was being watched, thinking that he could've done without the spoon, could've picked bones from the fish and eaten with his fingers like everyone else. He could've sat on the ground like everyone else, could've dipped bread in eel juice just like everyone else. Being a man who was without goods, without money, without a country, he felt foolish being treated like a man of wealth and power. He began to eat using the spoon and the tips of his fingers to flake the white flesh away from the thin ladder of bones.

End

'It's marvellous,' I said, and truly meant it. I could see that my grandmother was proud of her efforts. Taking one of her cakes or a tray of biscuits from the oven always gives her satisfaction and a moment of pride; that is, of course, unless there happens to be some little element that doesn't please her with the bake. Then she will complain that it could have done with this, that or the other. But as she handed me the written piece I detected more than satisfaction and pride. She was excited by what she had done.

'Aki can go on from there,' she said.

'Yes,' I said, 'but before he does there are a couple of things I'm curious about. Maybe you can tell me: who is Moonface? And what was that about sorrow?'

'Moonface, Moonface,' my grandmother said. 'It was a name people gave to his little brother because of something Aki said at the time of the little one's birth. People converted what Aki had said into English, because it was funnier in English. Also it was easier to run two English words together than to repeat a much longer phrase in Māori. For once it was English that slid more easily from between people's lips. It was a fonder, sweeter expression somehow. Marama was his real name.

'Now that you mention it, what comes to mind is something Chappy told me. It was to do with what the ghost saw, the ghose, the liddle Chap, on the night aboard ship when his eye met with the eyes of brother Aki. According to Chappy, on the moonlit night of shadows when Aki walked the decks, the dark shape of a giant appeared and eyed him, too late for the ghost to hide himself. But the ghost slid himself down, out of sight. He watched in fear as the giant passed by. He saw that this creature was a large man, given extra height by a child he carried on his shoulders. Later, after the placement of water and food, Chappy, who had been contemplating going overboard, knew that he owed it to the giant and the child to survive.

'Also, at the end of the journey he believed he owed it to the giant, the child and the cocoa man to dress and mingle and ghost his way to the city memorial, which he did, unchallenged.

'As for sorrow. Yes, it's right isn't it? The word "sorrow" strikes. It hits much more than the word "happiness" does. You can't allow a word like "sorrow" to pass by without wanting to know.

'Ask Aki about Moonface and sorrow. He might think that's nothing to do with the story of Chappy, but everything's connected. It's all intertwined. If it hadn't been for the theft of his little brother, Aki would not have left home and gone to sea in the first place. If Aki had not gone to sea we would never have come to know Chappy.

'Grandson, if it hadn't been for Moonface and sorrow you would never have been born. You wouldn't be here talking to me now. Or you would've been someone else, not this international grandson. Perhaps a more local and ordinary one. Tell him to speak English. I've got better things to do than stay up all night.'

When I visited Aki the next day, I was hesitant when asking him to tell me about Moonface and sorrow. However, he agreed, saying he'd never spoken about those things before and it could be time to do so. This was the only occasion when I did get to put my prepared questions to him. In all subsequent recording sessions he was ahead of me, as though he had already put thought to what he wanted to say. He would settle himself when he was ready, press 'record' and begin. It was as though he couldn't wait to tell his stories. Anyway it didn't matter about my questions. They became redundant as time went on.

There were no preliminary sentences in English this time and, when I brought the tape back and played it for my grandmother, she listened to all of it intently without complaint and said, 'Leave it to me.'

| Chapter 5 |
AKI

I was the only one home with Mum when Moonface was born. When I found out I was being left at home I was so mad that a clawed demon grew inside me, pulling and tearing and punching all my insides, trying to make a big scream come out of my mouth. Because I had my teeth barred and wouldn't let out any sound, it shoved itself up into my head and began pounding. Tears poured – not that anyone noticed or would've cared, there in the kitchen discussing this and that, making all their plans and laughing their heads off.

Every year I'd been part of that planning and laughing and getting ready, part of it all my life, right up until Dad turned to me that afternoon and said, 'You can't come this year, Aki, you have to stay home with Mum,' and went on discussing grinders with Paa. I didn't even know until then that Mum wasn't going. I went out in the dark where I sat against the chimney stones and sniffed and snorted.

All through autumn, all through the cold months, all through spring you looked ahead to shearing season – so much looking forward it made you sick. And when I went out to feed Pet and Kipi and saw that the puddles in front of the kennels had dried up and the ground was getting hard, I knew the time was near. By the time the sun got round to blasting against the shed so the tin of it could burn a hole in your hand it was all under way.

Already there'd been stuff set aside from last year's garden. Now the tents needed a shake out, camp ovens needed a count up, blankets needed sorting.

One day the shed doors were hooked open and the gear unwrapped from cloth or taken out of boxes and off shelves. There was the oil and grease smell in your nose. Out of rags in the big hands of my father, grandfather or uncle came the shearing handpieces – all the separate bits that had been loosened or taken apart, waiting until the new season came round. They were clean and sharp already, but it was done all over again – the washing, oiling, greasing, doing up combs, examining; the touching up and putting together, while you waited to grow up enough.

But that year when I was ten, I was struck down at the last minute, with everything ready to go. And how could Mum not be going? She was the best fleeco for miles.

All right, Mum was about to have a baby. I could see that for myself, though no one had mentioned it. And, yes, someone had to stay with Mum, but why not one of my two older sisters? The answer to that question, which I worked out later, was that Mina and Ti were needed to take Mum's place in the shed, although I couldn't remember them being any good at wool-handling.

'Look here, Aki,' Mum said when she found me snotting by the chimney, 'when the season's on everyone helps with the shearing whether they're at the sheds or at home. It's the whole family.'

'Bunkum,' I said to myself.

'There's the shearers, the sheepos, the sweepers, the fleecos, the pressers, the cooks. And there's the ones at home keeping everything going while they're gone, getting the wood and the water, feeding the animals. Or having a baby. So what's the difference?'

'All bunkum.'

'Every year it's been Grandmother and Uncle Harry staying home, looking after our houses and all our dogs and pigs and chooks. Well, now Uncle Harry's not here. You know that. Nunu has to have a helper and I have to have someone in the house to run and get her if I pop, so don't be silly, Aki.'

And she left me there. I had to boil down, pull my lip in and find myself a new face.

I didn't get up to see them off in the early morning, but I heard them joking, laughing, loading up and clopping off, the horses snorting in the dark. When they'd gone, I upped and went out to milk Tui. As I undid the leg-rope to let her off, I gave her a good hard whack. Some of the milk in the bucket slopped over my leg.

Mum was in the kitchen. She was frying eggs and vegetables – quite a good smell. Nevertheless, she went on from where she'd left off the night before: 'We're lucky to have these shearing jobs you know. There's plenty with no work, living on eels and watercress. Can't paint their house. Can't pay their shop bill. Got no cow. Can't go to the doctor. Clothes made out of sugar bags. So think yourself lucky, Aki.'

It was two days later when I came into the kitchen after milking Tui that I found Mum walking round the kitchen in her nightie, bending and sighing. She said, 'Go and get your grandmother, Aki. Run.'

'I got to feed the dogs, let the chooks out,' I said.

'No more of your lip,' Mum said. 'Get your grandmother.'

All right.

I turned to go out the door but heard this big groan behind me and Mum was telling me to wait.

'I left it too late Son,' she said, and she put some wood in the fire. 'Get me a blanket, Son. Get me a sheet, Son. Spread them on the floor.' I was 'Son' now. So I did what she told me and she sat with her back to the concrete fire-surround, puffing and agonising while Moonface came slithering into our lives. It was awful. I wanted to run away, but I couldn't because in among all the sweating and groaning Mum was saying, 'Don't you dare run off and leave me, Aki.'

I had to bring her string and a pair of scissors, and when she'd finished tying and cutting I had to sit down by her and hold this squeaky, slimy, fishy-looking thing wrapped in a nappy.

I didn't expect it to be warm.

The squeaking stopped, the face screwed itself and I nearly dropped the whole bundle when eyelids opened and two marbles rolled between them before they shut again.

You find glass marbles buried in the garden sometimes, or coming out of the ground round Grandfather's place. These glassies are from the necks of old bottles and there's a trick when you look at them. Sometimes they look green but other times there's no colour at all.

These eyes had a trick, too. There was colour but you couldn't tell what it was, couldn't name it. It could've been bottle-brown, navy-blue, red, purple, chocolate or orange.

There was a little round face – white and sticky, as though it had been painted with Lane's Emulsion. A patch of black hair. Two slicked eyebrows. Blue lips. Blood.

'Who does he look like?' Mum asked. She was wrapping the leftover mess in newspaper, full of happiness.

'Like the moon,' I said. Mum took this moon baby from me and placed him in the bassinet. Mum was wet and bloody and, taking a little container of hot water with her, went out to the wash-house holding her stomach together with her other hand.

Though Grandfather's mouth had every second tooth, Grandmother's had none. She was sitting under her plum tree making butter when I arrived. She smiled her gums and eyes at me, and when I told her what had happened she asked a few questions and decided there was no big reason to hurry.

'I'll just finish this and get my things,' she said. 'Won't be long Aki. Go feed my pig. Take this milk across the river. Call my cow.'

I fed the pig and took the billy of milk across the river, leaving it on a post for Daisy Biscuit to collect. Grandmother finished making her butter and collected a bundle of clothes into a blanket.

Mumu wouldn't come when I called her. When I whacked her on the stomach, she looked at me, dribbled and didn't move, but she set out after Grandmother when we started on the track home. Mumu had the same kind of walk as Grandmother: head going from side to side, body swinging from side to side in the opposite direction to her head, and at the same time managing to move forward. I had to slow right down to walk with them.

By the time we arrived, Mum had washed and dressed. She'd tidied the kitchen while Moonface slept on in his little bed. My baby stuff had been given away long ago, and this was a brand-new canvas bassinet that we'd bought a month before. New nappies and blankets, too. Mum and my sisters had made gowns, knitted jackets, hats and bootees. That was another part of Mum's nagging: 'There's people got no hope in life, babies wrapped in rags, so don't forget that, Aki.'

What Grandmother did was take the baby from his bed and lay him across her arm with his head tilted a little. Placing two crookedy fingers on his chest she began to move them round and round, and soon bubbles and fluid were flowing from the nose and mouth of this squeaky brother who had looked at me with coloured-glass eyes. It was all very interesting, but soon I had to get out and feed the pig, let the dogs off and open up the chookhouse door. I was looking forward to breakfast. The boil-up smelled pretty good.

But there was a further task before I came to the table. Grandmother and I had to go and bury the contents of the newspaper parcel, which was still sitting there on the hearth. We took it over to the edge of the cemetery where all our placentas are buried. I dug the hole, Grandmother tipped all the mess into it and recited for quite a long time. We went home for a feed.

Though Grandmother milked her own cow, I had a double lot of chooks, pigs and dogs to attend to. There was wood to chop and stack on the hearth, water to carry and milk to deliver. But in the afternoons I would go in and Mum and Grandmother would give me Moonface to hold – upright, he and I with our hearts together – where he would wriggle, burp, and keck on my shoulder. Though the oozing from the first day had now stopped, this baby had all gaps working and one day when I was bending over him, he pissed in my eye. I was told it was good luck.

Right after that he gave me a reverse wink. That is, he opened one eye at me just for a moment. I believe he liked what he saw, both times – first when he rolled his glassies at me on the day he was born, and then when he backwards winked. The reason I believe he liked what he saw is because, right from the beginning, he chose me.

His first smile was for me, and once he learned to slide about on his backside he tried to follow me everywhere, crying when I had to go somewhere without him. Such a wail, like torture.

I had my own dog who went nearly everywhere with me, too, but who I had to leave at the gate on school days. She was a black bitzer with red eyes, bandy in front and knock-kneed behind, who was always smiling. But at least she understood and did what she was told. Moonface? What a performance. What heart-break.

But also what welcomes I received every day when I came home from school. First there was Kata, waiting at the far gate laughing and jumping, then Moonface back at the house or over in the garden or creek with Mum, also laughing, holding out fat arms.

On the third night after the birth of Moonface, Dad came riding home in the dark, stood in the doorway with a side of mutton and a pleased face, put the meat on the table, walked across the kitchen to where the bassinet was and took the sleeping baby from it. He brought Moonface into the lamplight where he observed him closely for some time while Mum looked on as though amused, and Grandmother smiled her gums. I wanted to say something about the eyes of Moonface but I didn't.

'What is it?' my father asked.

'A boy,' said Grandmother.

My father put the boy against his shoulder and walked backwards and forwards across the front of the stove. He did this for quite a long time. I wondered if he had ever walked like that with me. I tried to remember.

'And what's he called?' he asked.

'Marama,' my mother said.

It was the first I'd heard of it, and I wondered if Mum had just thought of it at that moment. It was a very good name.

Apart from the full-lung bawl that Moonface let out anytime I left him, he was the easiest of babies, according to Mum. A few weeks after he was born he was sleeping the whole night through. He was never sick or feverish, hardly ever cried and began taking solid food at an early age. When the time came, his teeth popped through his gums uncomplaining. I told Mum he should sleep in my bedroom as no one except for me had to sleep in a room by themselves. So when he was six months old we shifted his cot.

In the mornings when Mum or Dad came to wake me, Moonface would already be sitting up looking through the bars. What a yell went up as I threw on my cow clothes and ran off to milk Tui. It was bad enough being booted in the heart by his big-mouth bellow when I went off to school in the mornings. I couldn't do anything about that. However, I made up my mind that it would be easier if I took him with me everywhere else I went.

The school we attended was four miles away by road, but there were shortcuts we could take through the trees. One afternoon I had to take the long way home so I could call in to the store for Mum, who wanted a packet of tea. I walked with the storekeeper's daughters – Moana-Rose who was dark and skinny and Oriwia, who was fat and walnut. (Yes.) They were our adopted sisters. Very pretty. (Okay?) Oriwia was a year older than me and wore her hair in one long plait that went down to her backside. I intended to marry her. Gave her hair a good pull on the way and she hit me with her bag.

Unlike the rest of us, Oriwia and Moana-Rose had a school bag. I happened to know that they both had shoes too, but they hid them in the bushes on their way to school and put them back on before they arrived home. (Because you didn't want to be skites.)

After I'd bought the tea, Uncle Jimmy Shop asked me to help him unload a cartful of goods before it rained. The cart was out in the yard where there was also firewood, old iron, broken washboards and wringers, holey pots and pans, bits of canvas, animal pelts, horns, rusty tins and a broken box. Jimmy Shop let anyone help themselves to anything in the yard except the firewood.

We unloaded dried goods, brooms and scrubbing brushes, sandsoap, boxes of tea, milk powder and condensed milk, Vicks, Lane's Emulsion and canned peas.

When we'd finished, Jimmy Shop offered me a handful of lollies but I asked if I could have the box instead.

'That's not a box, it's firewood,' he said. But he let me have it. Lollies as well.

The only thing left at home from my own babyhood was a set of pram wheels, which I sometimes pulled along by a rope with a load of wood on top. I fixed the box as best I could and tied it on top of the wheels to make a cart for Moonface.

In the dark or half-dark, I'd lift Moonface out of his cot, pull off his night nappy, wrap him in his blanket and take him in the cart to let Kata off his chain before going on through the house gate calling the cow. Moonface would sit there while I milked Tui, talking his sounds at Kata and me, his face luminous above the edges of the box. Mum was impressed with the cart.

The day I turned twelve – that was in August 1925 – Mum mentioned to my sisters, Mina and Ti, that it was my birthday, reminding them to give me their good wishes. Mina had part-time work helping at Jimmy Shop's store, and Ti was helping Mum at home while the men were bringing in new ground so that we could extend our gardens.

On the way to school, and all morning while sitting in the classroom, I thought about this day being my birthday. The desk where I sat and which used to fit me was now resting on my knees so that its feet came up off the floor. This made me understand that anything to do with school was now unsuitable for me.

At lunchtime I started for home, chewing my bread as I made my way through the trees, at first running, but then slowing down to a walk, captured by the penetrating smell of damp leaves, spores and mosses, the mordant, chilled air, the running water, the black and the green. Also there were the warm, mottled patches where sun was being sieved through the fronds of fern trees. A journey through bush fills your lungs and frees you.

Instead of going to the house after coming into the open, I went down towards the flats where I knew Dad and others were stumping in the burn-off.

I came over a mound which overlooked the slope where they were working – Dad, Grandfather, and several uncles from across the creek. On the flat there was a fire going, also a sledge with wood piled on it. I could see that my cousin Noddy had the job of salvaging any good wood from the pulled-out stumps to put on the sledge. The men were stripped down to trousers and boots – though not all had footwear – and if it hadn't been for what I knew about the different shapes and sizes of my relatives as I drew near I would not have been able to tell one from another. They were covered top to bottom in fire-black.

I went closer and stood at a short distance from my father.

'Dad,' I said. 'I've left school now.'

None of the men had stopped working when they saw me coming. Except for Dad they didn't stop now, though it was easy to see that Grandfather and others nearby were listening to what I had to say. My father stood straight and looked at me, waiting for me to go on.

'I don't go to school any more,' I told him. 'I've learned enough.'

His head moved to one side a little. He was looking at me as though I were a stranger, his eyes set in his blackened face, sweeping me, beginning from my toes and moving slowly upward. 'Stranger' is the wrong word. He was looking at me as though at someone new, as though I had become somebody different he hadn't noticed before.

'Thank you, Son,' he said after what seemed a long time of standing still eyeing me.

I noticed that Paa was smiling at the stump he was working on, whacking a spade through the clinging roots of it. This was not one of Grandfather's big-grin smiles, just a wrinkling upwards of his smeared face that didn't let any of the teeth show.

My father handed me the lever he'd been using. It was his way of letting me know that he understood I could do a man's job now, or perhaps it was his way of telling me I *had* to do men's work now and that there was no going back to childhood. Whatever it was, I felt honoured that this implement had been put in my hands.

The lever was a good, strong mānuka pole, hewn to a blunt point at one end. I was to push this down beneath the severed roots and work it back and forth until the stump came free. My father took the spade from Grandfather, who straightened his back and took his pipe from his pocket. I discarded my school shirt and began work.

There was a time that I'd heard about when land was fought over and died for. Peacetime arrangements were negotiated on its behalf. There was a more recent time I'd heard of when land and people were thriving. During this time there was an abundance of crops, of work, of workers, of land, of produce and overseas markets, but all this was interrupted by wars and laws and the pen.

The 'pen' was how Grandfather described various signings – land taken away by the tyranny of the pen. The pen was a personality of fierce omnipotence, a greedy chief of might and potency.

It was the pen which made his father, grandfather of my mother, one of only three lawful property owners of lands which in the lore of the people truly belonged to everyone – the life-blood of an extensive group of kin.

Following those good days people became poor, lucky if some could get work cutting flax, or fencing and scrub-cutting on other men's lands, or work on the railways or the making of roads.

For those of us who had been able to hold on to land, the dream was to amalgamate properties and give rights and lands back to all true inheritors, but it was a struggle. There was no market for anything we could produce, and no money for farm development. Grandfather had time to tell about these things because he smoked a pipe. That's what I thought then. I didn't think I'd ever be parted from any of it.

Moonface took fright when he saw me that evening. He didn't like me at all when Ti brought him out in the half-dark to meet us. Mum handed Dad a tin of hot water and a lantern, which he took across the yard to the wash-shed for his bath. He got me to wash his back for him, and then we changed places. Moonface was happy with me once all the fire-black was removed.

My little brother's cot had been given to one of our relatives across the creek and he slept with me now. He didn't use nappies any more and had given up his titty bottle. Because he had become used to my coming and going, he didn't set up such a wail every time I left. Now that he could walk and because he liked to play about in the wood chips, or the mud or the water, we didn't use the cart so much, though sometimes he used it himself, wheeling sticks and stones or kittens or invisible companions.

I don't know why he always slept sideways in our narrow bed. Each night my sisters bathed him and gave him his tea early so he wouldn't drop off to sleep at the table. One of us would carry him to bed, putting him close to the wall, but when I went in later I'd find him lying crossways. I'd lift him and place him against the wall again, knowing that his head would be on my stomach by morning. I'd ease myself from under him or just scramble out and let his head flop. It made no difference. Nothing in the world woke him until he was ready to wake.

Once outside he waddled, he played, he talked his funny talk, he bit down on his front teeth and grinned up at the sky. Sometimes I rode round with him perched in front of me on the horse. Being on the horse gave us enough height to pick a handful of Christmas plums once they had ripened on the trees. He was a happy boy, a good boy and a great joy to all of us. He smiled on us in all his awake moments.

Ma Minnie died. My cousin Noddy said his mother just dropped carrying a billy of eggs. Our work was put aside for a few days while we gathered at the marae for the ceremonies. As usual I was expected to remain in the sleeping house with the elders, held by the ear, listening to all the speeches, whakapapa, waiata. That's how it had been ever since I could remember.

It was afternoon when we arrived home, four days later, to an empty house. There had been no rain and there was little water in the tank, so I was sent to the spring for drinking water.

Though Moonface was tired after the long walk home, he wanted to come with me, and to show his determination picked up an empty billy to carry water in. The spring was a ferny hole in a large patch of swampy ground where chilled water bubbled up from some dark place.

As soon as we arrived, Moonface lay down among the fern and went to sleep. This meant I would have to fill the container, leave it there, carry my brother home and then come back for it. The day was getting on, the sun beginning its slide. Down at the edge of the spring I used the billy to fill the water tin.

Because the land round the spring was uneven, I wedged a piece of wood and a handful of dry fern under the tin to make sure it wouldn't topple.

When I'd finished I turned to where my brother was sleeping, and he was gone. I stared at the indentations where he had lain. Nothing in my head was connecting with what I was looking at.

Knowing that once asleep, Moonface would stay that way, my first thought was that he'd been stolen. But perhaps I'd been mistaken about the place where he'd lain down? I called his name, looking here and there, but always came back to the spot where I'd seen his eyes slap shut, where I knew he would be until I picked him up to carry him home.

Well, he's up to his tricks, I thought. One of his latest games was to hide from me, but up until now this had been when I was coming home from work. It was difficult to believe he'd stood from his sleeping spot without me noticing. Bracken is noisy. Birds tell. Grass whispers. And Moonface was not the most careful of four-year-olds. I went into the trees, calling him, starting to panic and swear. I ran home, calling him.

Everyone for miles took part in the search. Tin torches on long poles were set around the edge of the swamp. While some searched the bracken and flax bushes, others went up through the trees. I wanted to believe what Mum said, that he'd be asleep somewhere and wouldn't wake until morning. Kata, though he is no kind of tracking dog, can always find Moonface or me, but on this night he stayed by us, as anxious as we all were.

'Nothing'll wake him once he's gone off,' Mum kept saying. 'And he can't have gone far. He never does go far.' She was already crying.

I don't know how many days or weeks it was before we stopped searching. 'We'll have to wait for him to come back to us,' people were saying. By that they meant Moonface was dead and someday we would find what was left of him. Land or water would deliver him and then there would be answers. But how could he be dead? I hadn't seen him dead. We hadn't buried him, so how could he be dead? When I went to sleep, the boards of the house were cracking down on me.

I didn't accept that we should give up our search. My mind could not be free of what had happened – the cold spring water, the silver tin, water silvered, the creaking birds, the pouring, the boy invisible, the unspeaking leaves, the trail of torches, the voices calling, the crying, the wailing of all the grandmothers in the world, the waiting, the ferny nest. Because I couldn't sleep in my room any more, Nunu took me to stay with Paa and her. Though I couldn't bear to get up in the mornings, my grandparents talked me from my bed. Though I found it difficult to swallow, they pushed food into me, and Paa took me out with him. 'Work's the best thing,' he said.

Memories, or what should have been memories, were instead ever-present realities in a time that was standing still. They were realities that moved when I moved, as when an opponent is blocking your way to the score line, facing you, moving when you move, side-stepping when you side-step, jinking when you jink, double-jinking when you double-jink, all the time reading you, all the time staring you down. There is no way through, no way past, no way ahead, no way of seeing beyond. You can only go down, only to be dragged up again, dirt in your mouth, by those who you only wish would leave you alone.

'I killed him.'

'Look here Aki,' my mother said, 'you think you're the only one. You think everything's to do with you. Who let him go with you when he'd already walked for an hour? Who was it who said not to worry, he'll be asleep somewhere? The trouble with you Aki you think only of yourself.' She banged open the flaps on the range, threw wood inside and the chimney was rumbling. 'Everyone else has to get on with life, which at the moment, includes running around after you.'

I shut my mouth. I went to sleep for a while. The timbers were clapping like big hands.

One morning my father and grandfather were gone. 'They've gone to find your brother,' my grandmother said when I asked after them. A sense of dread came over me. I knew they'd gone into the ranges where no one goes.

Some days went by. I don't know how many. What I remember is going to the outhouse in the dark one night and seeing the torch flames moving, strung out along the forest track. These were lights belonging to the people who had been waiting for the return of father and grandfather.

'The torches are coming,' I said when I went inside. Did I feel some kind of hope just then? If so, what was that hope?

People arrived bringing our horse with two men wrapped in blankets on its back, the man behind holding the front man collapsed against him. People helped the front man down, a formless individual. It was as if they were retrieving only the blanket. In it was my bearded and stinking grandfather, who they carried by me into the kitchen. I thought he was dead. The other man they helped inside was my father, though I hardly recognised him. He was bearded, matted, and half his usual size.

The two men were stripped of their clothes, wrapped in blankets, propped up on pillows and given pot water from the meat and vegetables cooking. My grandmother and aunties were filling vinegar bottles with hot water, wrapping them and placing them here and there, close to the bodies of my father and grandfather, who were fed at intervals all the night through. People were coming and going. It was noisy and warm in the kitchen while the two men slept. I sat there and waited, not wanting to go to bed, where recently I had spent nights on end seeing through my eyelids.

The next afternoon, the men were taken out to the wash-house to bathe and dress. There was a question on the edge of my tongue, but I knew better than to ask it.

When they returned, my father stood behind my grandfather, a hand on the back of my grandfather's chair. The hand on the chair was to show everyone that he was not being disrespectful in standing to speak ahead of his elder, but that it was his intention to take the burden from the older man. These are the protocols I learned little by little during my life, without even knowing what I knew.

My father gave an account of their journey from the campsite towards the mountain and how they'd had to break their way through heavy bush as there were no pathways. It was a whole day before they came to the place where the creek runs at the base of the mountain, and that is where they camped for the night, moving into the trees to sleep where the ground was dry.

The next morning, because they didn't know what they should do next, they began exploring, looking for what? They were not sure. Listening for what? They were not sure. It was on the third morning that they found what they didn't know they'd been looking for. It was an indentation in soft ground, ahead of it another and then another. They were long, thin footprints, pointed at the heel and splayed towards the front in the shape of mussel shells but not hollow. Light, as if those who had made them had little weight to speak of. They followed this trail through soft earth. These were the footprints of the patupaiarehe.

I felt like crying. My father didn't believe in the fairy people. He was lying. Whenever our mother and aunties had warned us against going into the bush because we would get stolen by little green-eyed people with copper hair, he would say something like: 'That's all humbug, just don't go there, you'll get lost, you'll die. Do what you're told.'

But Mum and the aunties would continue.

'Because they themselves are small they want to steal children.'

'Enticing them with melodies, coloured fruits and promises.'

'Once they take you, there's no way home.'

On and on, the story getting bigger and better every time, and scary enough to keep us away from the trees. It kept us safe in the same way that the taniwha kept us safe from certain known dangers in the rivers and sea.

My grandfather spoke. His words were for me. 'The reason your little brother is no longer with us', he said, 'is because he never belonged to us in the first place. They came for him. Now he is where he belongs, with his own people. There are other worlds. Little Marama was always of a different world.'

Yes, I thought, other worlds, like heaven and hell and Hawaiki, but you've got to be dead to get there. I didn't believe any of them. They were all liars, traitors. My brother was dead. I killed him.

'This way you have him with you always,' Grandmother Nunu said, tapping all her kindling-wood fingers on her chest with a sound of pecking chooks.

My father went on talking, describing the density of trees, the tameness of birds, the changing light, being watched by the kēhua, all the time keeping his eye on me.

Footprints, footprints, footprints, I thought. How do we know your minds didn't go walking, putting those footprints down in front of you as you made your way? What else did you see? What else did you find? A discarded jersey? Isn't it true that the patupaiarehe run naked, dance naked, their bodies incandescent in the dark forest light, their lustrous hair flowing like the night-time fish which weave green light in and out along the backs of darkened ripples? Did you see?

You were there.

Did you see the tail-light gleam that each of the fairy people carries? Did you watch them do the dance of the fireflies?

My father looked at me. He knew the questions I had in my mind.

'We saw no more than the footprints,' he said. 'But . . .' He paused for a long time. 'But we heard the singing. We heard laughter, like the laughter of children.' He was looking straight at me, right into my eyes, telling me this from his heart.

In a way it was a happy story, a potent image, this one of my little brother dancing with his kin, laughing with children, playing forever in the night-time forest.

Over the next weeks, with much on my mind, I decided I had to believe. That was the best thing to do. It was a question of locking one door and opening another, which is what my father had had to do as well. And wasn't it true after all, on looking down at the ferny bed on that late afternoon, that my first thought was that my brother had been stolen?

Now I was obligated. My father and grandfather had risked their lives for *me*. There was no doubt in my mind that they did what they did because of me. My father in particular had gone from not believing in something, to thinking of possibility – because it was the only thing left to do. He did it for love.

After that, I could eat without choking and sleep most of a night through. Returning to me were words that my grandparents had aimed at me that afternoon: 'There are other worlds,' and, 'This way you have him with you always.' It seemed to be permission to leave the place of my birth and go out to experience other worlds, though on my grandfather's tongue the word 'worlds' had many meanings.

I stood before my parents and grandparents one day and told them I was going away to find work. I journeyed down the line to live with relatives who turned me into a seagull and waved me out to sea where I came across a little ghost man from Japan.

| *Chapter 6* |

ORIWIA

The morning after giving me the piece entitled 'Chappy Wakes', my grandmother explained that though Aki had arrived home in time to bring Chappy back to the house from the spring that evening, he and Mo had been away since daybreak. They had returned to the harbour by the early morning train to do their shifts on board. Sailing was to be delayed for a week, they were told. So while Mo stayed on board during that time, Aki was able to arrange for a few days off in this, his home port.

When Oriwia arrived to collect her father early the next morning, Aki and Mo were preparing to leave for the railway station. There were children about, and Mo, using a few words of English, was asking Aki if any of the kids were his. Oriwia could see why Mo thought that some of the children belonged to Aki, as apart from Paa, there were no other men about. Aki's father and uncles were out back of a farmer's property making fences. They'd be there for another month.

Mo was holding the flax basket woven by Grandmother Nunu as she watched over Chappy at the spring. In it were a round of bread, one jar of jam and one of pickle. It was a gift for his wife, the gift-givers said, which was just their nosey way of finding out whether Mo was married or not. It seemed he was a single man.

Two boys arrived with the horse, and it was time to go. Mo stood there rigored like a dead man as he was hugged and kissed, and though the women were aware of his discomfort at this close contact, it amused rather than deterred them.

Dorothea and Grandmother Nunu were one each side of Chappy, holding an arm each. Oriwia wondered how he felt about that, and wasn't sure how he took to being left behind. He thought he would be accompanying his friends, that this would be the end of his stay. But since Aki had explained Chappy's situation, the women wouldn't let him go. Chappy spread his hands towards them. Empty. He was a man who had nothing.

'Hands,' Dorothea said. 'We can all work. Hands.' She grabbed his, held them. Poor Chappy. 'Work's the most important thing.'

———

One evening, when Oriwia was collecting eggs from Dorothea, she went into the house to shelter from the rain. The downpour cooled the air but, because the stove fire was going and the heat of the day still circled in the kitchen, Dorothea had opened out the door and windows. Moths came in, dizzying themselves round the lamps and candles. They were followed by a whirring swarm of clumsy huhu, also attracted by the light, hurtling in as though they'd been thrown. They crash-landed against the walls, buckling their long feelers and knocking themselves silly. One of these dizzy beetles landed in Chappy's hair. He flinched and tried to brush it away, but it was caught there by its jointed antennae.

Grandmother Nunu reached, put her hand over the beetle and removed it from Chappy's head, receiving a nip on her finger for her trouble. She placed it on the windowsill.

Because these were the first huhu seen this summer season, conversation stopped for a moment. Everyone waited to see what Grandmother Nunu would have to say to this envoy. They were eager to find out what she believed significant about the singling out of Chappy.

'Come in, come in,' she said. 'So you come to welcome our visitor? So you grab him by the hair and fix him here in this kitchen, in this family, in this place? So, you're telling us this is his whānau now? All right, all right, we believe you.' She waved her nipped finger at them and everyone laughed.

Conversation began again as people attempted to convey this message to Chappy who, though he didn't understand, smiled and nodded his head. Dorothea and Grandmother Nunu ladled food onto plates and passed them from the stove to the table. It was then that they heard Chappy speak his first word of their language.

'Kai,' he said.

Though the word seemed to be sung from somewhere in his head, it was instantly recognised. What a shout went up. There was back-patting and words of congratulation, after which Chappy was taught another word. Dorothea placed a cup of water by him.

'Wai,' she said.

Food and water. Every day he added to his vocabulary and was soon stringing words together.

Before long, Chappy was well enough to do light work. While men were away fencing on rich men's land, home fences were in need of repair. Some of this Chappy was able to help with. Otherwise he assisted round the houses, keeping wood supplied to fires, carrying water, sweeping verandahs. Once he found his feet, he was never still. He learned to milk Nunu's cow, and every morning at daybreak he'd be there with the milk bucket. All this Oriwia observed as she went to and fro. When he stood, though Chappy was no taller than Nunu, his body had straightened, his skin had a new glow, his face a new ease.

Chapter 7

AKI

I wanted to go and see my father before I returned to the sea and decided that Chappy was well enough to come with me. On the way I would call in to see Oriwia so I could pay off some of the family's shop bill. Also there was something I needed to discuss with her. I didn't know how I was going to approach the subject of Ela.

'I'll make a cup of tea,' Oriwia said when we arrived. 'Stay and talk to Dad while I bake something for you to take to those fellows working on the line.'

So Chappy and I went out to the yard where her father was sitting on his chair in the shade by a little table with a brick under one leg. Jimmy smiled his half smile, lifted his good hand, spoke a slurred greeting and began questioning, wanting to know all about this Chap. Though he'd heard the story on the night of the party, I went through it again – the story of the seeing ghost. I told all I knew.

Uncle Jimmy, with his good hand gripping my forearm, rattling it and looking Chappy up and down with his one open eye, was disappointed when the story came to an end.

'*Who's he's mountain?*' he garbled and puffed from his mouth-side, speaking in English because there was a stranger present.

'I don't know,' I said in my own language. 'I know his country, but not his land.'

'*Who's he's river?*'

'I don't know.'

'*Who's he's ancestors?*'

'I don't know.'

'*Who's he's name? Who he is?*'

'I don't know.'

'*Ahh, ahh. You going to marry my daughter?*'

These last were the jumbled words that Oriwia overheard as she came out with four mugs of tea and a plate of pikelets on a tray. She laughed and, while we helped ourselves, sat down, alternating between drinking her own tea and helping her father with sips from his. One eye of Jimmy's was fixed on me, waiting for an answer, but it was Oriwia who spoke. She'll tell about that. Instead, I'll talk about my tooth.

What I knew about love was to do with normal things. Connections. Past and present. People. Land. Your own stuff, your food, what makes you laugh. A brother. Moonface. Home things. But as for that other condition? I wasn't prepared. That other thing that jumps on your face, cracks you sideways, sends you spinning to the sky.

Ah, the tooth.

What most seamen want when hitting shore in foreign countries is either to be with a woman or be drunk, preferably both. For me, being a little backward when it came to women, I'd have to hit the bottle first and hold out hope that somewhere along the way there would be a woman. Never stone cold sober. No no.

However, the port of Honolulu was different. What I liked to do in Hawai'i, which I didn't do in other countries, was to leave shipmates to whatever they wanted to do, and go off on my own.

On the first day I would shop for gifts to take home, walking the pavements and wandering about the marketplaces, where there were coloured fabrics, patterned shirts, shell necklets, and many other souvenir items for sale.

On the next day I would venture out, hoping to come across native men whose language was similar to my own. They were often from families who, a generation before, had been forced to leave their lands when large companies had come in and diverted water away from their gardens to use on their own ever-expanding cash crops. The native men had to leave most of their uplands and plantations and move shoreward, where they attempted to live on fish and coconuts and whatever they could grow. Before long they would be moved on again. The few who were able to get work had to travel many miles by truck to the city and back each day.

In the town, I would come across them raking leaves in the grounds of large hotels or sweeping pavements down in Waikiki. What I came to look forward to at the end of the day during shore leave in Hawai'i was spending time with these men who seemed to be my kin, learning to speak with them, getting to know about their lives, sharing a cigarette, sharing stories, comparing life's circumstances.

Late at night, after a few hours of good company, I'd go down to the beach, find a comfortable place, and with sea rolling in and a warm wind blowing, I'd sleep out under the stars, sometimes with a big moon for company. It was what I enjoyed doing after so many days and nights of confinement aboard.

Sometimes, if time allowed, I would leave the towns and seek out the fishermen.

On the day of the tooth, as soon as I'd finished my watch in the early morning, I hitched a ride on a delivery lorry heading off for Ka'a'awa, Waiahole and some of those places. I'd never explored the North Shore. I was ignoring my tooth.

In my bag I had a bottle of rum and packets of cigarettes, which are a good lead-in to conversation, and which I intended sharing with a native man who I would find fishing from a beach or pulling up a canoe.

Once the truck had reached its destination I left and made my way down onto the sand where I walked for an hour. The tooth was beginning to thump, so I found a sheltered spot and took what I thought would be enough swallows from the bottle to douse it. It made no difference. Feeling annoyed at having to concentrate so fully on one small bit of such a large-sized self, I gave myself a hefty punch in the jaw, which made matters no worse and no better. What I needed was a pair of pliers and someone to help me.

I walked the morning through. The sun was high by the time I came across a native man pulling in a fish. Behind him in the trees was a shelter, where I guess he slept or rested. I greeted him and sat with him in the shade, taking the bottle and the cigarettes from the bag and placing them between us.

'From the boats?' he asked.

I told him which ship I was from, and which country, using his language as best I could, and for a while we compared our languages. Then I pointed to my jaw and said I needed pliers, showing with a gripping fist and a down-jerk of my elbow, what I wanted to do with the pliers. He laughed and blew smoke.

'Soon,' he said.

It was a long 'soon', but I realised why we were waiting when two little boys appeared from in the palms.

'Two very bad boys,' he said by way of introduction. 'Should stay home with their aunty, but they run away after school and come to sleep by me.' He turned to them. 'Bad boys,' he said, 'this is your uncle.'

I wished I had brought chewing gum with me.

Their grandfather cut a triangle from each of two coconuts with the tip of his fishing knife and the boys drank, facing the sea with their moon eyes looking sideways at me. He cut fruit for them.

'Go home to Aunty,' he said, but they didn't move. They bit into their fruit.

'I'm taking Uncle for his tooth. Go home to Aunty until Mummy wakes up.' They remained turned towards the sea, expressionless, as though he hadn't spoken.

'If you come with me, you get nothing,' he said. 'I don't carry you, you get no food.' He picked up the bottle of rum. Their eyelids lowered and their mouths tightened to prevent too much smiling. They jumped up to come with us.

Beyond the old man's shelter, back through the vegetation, was a compacted road just wide enough for a vehicle. It was where a truck would pick up workers – including the mother of the bad boys – in the middle of the night. We took the road, which became no more than a walking track as we made our way further along it, me with my shore bag, the old man with the bottle, and fish on a string.

At a certain point, the old fellow left the boys and me and went inland calling out a name. It was some time before he returned, accompanied by a companion of about his own age who carried the rum and a pair of ancient pliers, which I was happy to see. The two were having a great time in each other's company. We were to go back down to the beach for the operation.

The two men smoked for a while, we had a few swallows from the bottle and, after I'd removed my shirt and stretched out in the shade, the owner of the pliers began working the tooth out of its socket.

'How many you want out?' he asked, and he laughed. In a moment, to great shouts of triumph, there the tooth was waving in front of my eyes in the beak of the pliers.

'This the right one?'

I took off my trousers and went to wallow in the sea where I rinsed and spat enough blood and poison to attract sharks, though all I came across were little green turtles bubbling.

After that I went to sleep in the trees, waking some time later with the two bad boys looking down at me. I guessed they'd been sent to get me. They took me by the hands and pulled me towards the track. The waves were heaving onto the shore, and in the dusk the white fringes of them drew down their own light.

Outside a small house several people were eating fish. Among them were the fisherman, a woman whom I found out later was his wife – though I guessed she was ten or more years younger than he was – the aunty of the bad boys and her husband, and the dentist with my tooth still in the grip of his pliers. Also there, not saying a word, was a venerable elder, 'A'makualenalena.

'And here comes the rest of him,' shouted the tooth-puller, waving my fang as I appeared. I soon understood that this tooth of mine had been the topic of conversation throughout the meal.

I was welcomed all round and, once seated, another woman came from the back of the house bringing a large platter, on it a fish which was hand to elbow in length and as thick as my thigh, smothered in the milk of coconut, fruits and poi. When the dish was placed in my hands I offered it round, but it was obviously meant just for me. I broke off pieces, dipping and eating, knowing I could eat the lot. One less tooth was no disadvantage to that.

About the woman who brought the fish, which is the whole point of this story. I could've begun where we are now, with the fish on a plate, instead of going on about the tooth. But I must give honour to the tooth. It was the tooth, that rotten thing, which found me love. What would my life have been otherwise? On that night there was the distraction of food and so many questions to answer about home and family and travels that I didn't realise I'd been bowled, even though I knew there was something making me breathless.

It was getting late and I explained that I needed to leave as I had to be on board by morning. I intended finding my way back to the road, just hoping there would still be vehicles going my way at this time of night.

'Go with Ela,' people said. 'On the workers' lorry, leaving at midnight.'

I mean, you did see beauty there in Hawai'i. Girls. Dancers. You could look at these beauties and be struck. Looking at them you could feel oiled and ignited. They were the postcard girls who loved the whole world. Not on beaches really, that's not where you saw them. Not dancing under palm trees or anything like that. No, but on the arms of sailors who were not as backward as me, or occasionally in restaurants waiting on tables. But I'm not talking postcards when I mention Ela. Postcards didn't show you the dark-skinned ones, the ones over thirty with crooked teeth, the big ones with their hair tied back for work.

Beside me in the lorry, skin touching, Ela was telling her companions that this was a new brother, giving them my history and geography. Not getting it right from what I was hearing. She told them about the tooth.

When this was through and the workers, mainly women, turned to other conversations, I broke the silence between us by mentioning the two boys.

'Their fathers were bastards,' she said. 'I don't know how I could've fallen for the same old story from blue-eyed boatmen twice in a row.'

I thought I should shut up about the boys.

We sat in silence until she said, 'They're filthy pigs.'

I didn't know what to say.

'That last one, father of the younger one, pissed on my cooking fire. What do you think of that?'

I was stabbed. In the core of me, I knew what an unspeakable insult had been given to a beautiful woman and how mortified she would feel to have brought someone like that to the family. I wanted to put my arms round her.

'The cooking was done,' she said, 'the fire dying . . . but still . . .'

I knew men like that, I wanted to tell her – hearty, ignorant, drunk, full of themselves.

'What's more, he did it in front of my father, brother and uncle.'

We were on the edge of town, the road had straightened and widened. Lights were on along the distant streets and in the tall buildings.

'What did they do?' I asked.

'They took him and threw him in the sea.' She laughed.

'Did they stand on him?'

'I think they did.' She laughed again. 'Maybe not long enough.'

'Come again next time,' she said as we parted. 'I'll cook another fish.'

As I went over these parting words, which I did again and again in the days to come, I could make nothing more of them than words of friendship, of a host to a departing visitor, or at most words of a sister to a new brother who would be welcome to return.

I went about my work and, as I walked the decks looking out over the endlessly deep and endlessly wide ocean, I couldn't put our conversation, her face, her shame, her laughter out of my mind.

How could Ela have spoken to me about something so dreadful, so personal and shaming, when she hardly knew me? My head couldn't get rid of it all, and in some ways I was thankful on the home run to have the distraction of the seeing ghost.

That's my tooth story.

When it was time to go, Chappy believed he would be leaving with me.

'You're stopping here,' Mum told him once she understood his thoughts. 'You're not going off working on any boats until you get meat on your bones,' she said, growling as though he were a son of hers.

What I understood, as he and I attempted to converse with each other by means of signs and antics and a word here and there, was that though Chappy didn't want to work on the boats and didn't want to leave the country, he thought he would try to get a job at the waterside. He didn't want to impose any longer on our family. Several new words had been added to 'kai' and 'wai', learned mainly from the gummy mouth of Grandmother Nunu, who had taken him in hand because of his affection for her cow.

Grandmother came in during our conversation and had her say. 'Your work is here,' she said. Up on her feet was Grandmother, milking a cow, feeding hens, bringing wood, pulling weeds, watering plants, digging potatoes, scraping corn, demonstrating to him.

It was true that the women needed help, especially when the men were away and now that my sisters and I had left home. And anyway, paid work was too difficult to find during those hard times. For Chappy it would have been impossible. Any effort on his part to find employment could have led to enquiries that would land him in trouble.

| Chapter 8 |
ORIWIA

'I never knew all that before,' my grandmother said with some indignation, coming into the tearoom kitchen just as I finished reading the new translation she had given me. She took up the kettle, filled the teapot amid a feathery pillow of steam, and dressed the pot with a scorched knitted beehive. She embraced it with her big hands, shifting it in circles, her mind elsewhere because of the information that hadn't been shared with her all these years.

My grandmother had given me so much of her time already that I didn't intend asking her any more questions that morning though there was one burning a hole in my tongue. I was there to help.

On the bench beside me was a tray of cream and raspberry doughnuts which she was about to carry through to the glass case at the shop front. Beside it was a marble cake ready to be iced. 'He never told any of it.'

'Any of . . .?' I put the pages down so I could fill sugar bowls for the tables.

'That stuff. About the bus ride, the fisherman, little Eric and Lani. His tooth and the fish.'

Oriwia went out with the doughnuts and returned with the empty tray.

'Or that awful story about Lani's father. I suppose he didn't want us to know about that. So why tell it now?' She was in a huff, sifting icing sugar and cocoa into a bowl. I noticed that she sometimes made pink icing for marble cake, but today it was to be chocolate. I poured tea for her from the beehive pot, wondering if she would have time to drink it. Pushing the cup towards her, and wanting to distract her from her present train of thought, I let the question out.

'But what about –?'

'What about what?' With the bowl hugged against her, she whipped its contents, scowling down into it. With it almost time for the tearoom to open, Grandmother slapped icing over the cake and smoothed it, stopping every so often to take a mouthful of tea. When she'd finished, she went out front to unlock the door.

'What about what?' she asked again as she came back in.

'The question. Great-grandfather's question?' I washed the bowl and baking tins and wiped down the bench.

'Which question was that?' she asked, filling little metal teapots with hot water to warm them, pouring milk into small jugs.

'"Are you going to marry my daughter?"'

'Ah, that?' Her mood changed. She laughed but turned to go out again. Her first customers of the day had come in.

While she was away, I opened my notebook and turned on the tape recorder. I had learned to be ready at all times. As we worked my grandmother would talk. I would catch what I could, jot down when I could, remember what I could. At the end of a day I'd gather the bits and pieces from tape, jottings and memory, and type them up.

———

'I don't want to marry you, Aki,' she said on that morning. 'With the place falling down around us, goods to collect, unloading, stacking and packing to be done and deliveries to make, an absent husband is the last thing I need.'

With little money coming in and people's debts building, Oriwia thought it would've made sense to stop trading and shut up shop, but knew Dad Jimmy wouldn't like it. Here he had friends and relatives who came and sat with him, got him laughing, shifted him about when he needed it, pushed a whisky into him if they had any. In the good times the shop had been a meeting place for everyone, a lively gossipy place full of life and laughter. She believed the good times would come again, people would have regular work or there'd be markets for what they produced and their debts would be paid. She'd get her roof fixed. She'd make tea and scones for customers.

Anyway, she felt that if she walked away from it all she'd be walking away from her mother's land and the memory of her mother. That made her afraid.

'Muscle on the other side of the world is of no use to me,' she'd said to Aki as she poured tea and began helping Jimmy with his cup. Aki had nothing to say, but she noticed he could hardly keep the smile off his face. 'If I was in love with you,' she'd said, 'nothing I've said just now would matter. And if you were in love with me, you would've left the boats long ago and we'd have a couple of kids by now. And, if you were in love with me,' she added, 'you wouldn't be sitting there looking so relieved.'

Aki burst out laughing and so did Oriwia. Even Jimmy joined in, dribbling, choking and nearly coming out of his chair. Chappy was sitting there smiling without understanding a thing. What Oriwia could see was that Aki was in love with someone, somewhere in the world. She didn't ask him about that, but did envy him because she believed in love. She saw that she had somehow freed him.

Oriwia wiped tears from Jimmy's face and went to find a tin to put the baking in that Aki and Chappy would take to Taana and others out on the fenceline.

One day, that year or next, Oriwia believed, Aki would bring a bride home, someone new to live among them. She would bring new skills and ideas with her, just as others had. Her father Jimmy had brought his shop and his trading. Taana had come from the south to marry Dorothea, bringing his building skills. Others had brought their own weaving techniques or dress-making abilities, or knew how to sharpen saws. They'd have this new bride to themselves while Aki was away – that is, if he didn't leave the boats altogether.

Chappy, sitting on a tree stump and resting his forehead against the hot flanks of Mu, would reach in and thumb down diagonal teats, straps of milk frothing into the bucket held lightly between his knees. As he milked he sang – to the animal, Oriwia believed. Or he could've been speaking for all she knew, reciting poetry, telling stories.

When he'd finished, he would take the milk to the kitchen, return, untie the leg-rope and lead the cow off to the spring where the grass was good and long. Mu had become used to these daily treats, denied to her before as there had been no one with time to attend her in the boggy area. Sometimes, instead of taking Mu to the swamp, he would take her to the back of Dorothea's flower garden where a stand of bamboo had taken over and where he would feed her with bamboo shoots. He would stand Mu in the creek and brush her down in the way he had seen Taana wash the horses.

At the spring he'd fill the water can and lead Mu back to the enclosure next to the house. She was a jelly-eyed Jersey, Mu the fourth.

From mid-morning there were other tasks he gave himself, such as splitting kindling, carrying wood, skimming cream and taking skimmed milk to the pigs. He was ruled by women who wouldn't allow him to go and work with men, even though he was strong enough by then. He was there to do their bidding, but also he was their orphan, someone who had come into their care and on whose behalf they felt wounded.

In the gardens where everyone worked together, they soon had him hoeing between rows, watering, harvesting, or whatever the seasonal task might be. There was plenty to occupy him until evening milking, when he would tap the side of the bucket and Mu would swing her way towards him.

Oriwia shut the shop once a fortnight and delivered her father to Dorothea. She would settle Jimmy in the kitchen in cold weather, or under the coral tree in Dorothea's garden when the weather was warm.

Dorothea insisted on these arrangements for Jimmy after her sister Moana-Rose left home and there was no one to look after him on market days. Though these were still called 'market days', they were nothing like the days of Oriwia's childhood, when Jimmy would sit her and her sister in the dray and they'd set out in the dark of early morning to the market ten miles away. There they would stock up on grain, seeds, groceries, produce, haberdashery and hardware. They were times of fun, talk, little girls petted by everyone in the town.

Now it was just a five-mile journey to the depot in the village to pick up goods she'd booked the week before. What she ordered was only what she had money for, which was becoming less and less as time went by. She could see she was going to end up with an empty shop that was falling down round her, a kitchen full of rotten duck eggs, milk going down the drain, potatoes she couldn't hope to sell because everyone grew and stored their own. This was the type of produce people gave her in exchange for tobacco, matches, candles and household needs.

These thoughts occupied Oriwia as she delivered Jimmy, had a cup of tea in Dorothea's kitchen and set out on her way to the depot with her cart empty except for a bucket, a knife wrapped in a cloth, a piece of rope and whatever she was taking to her sister, whom she would visit once she'd collected her goods.

On this particular day, Oriwia arrived at the railway station before the depot opened, so she released the horse from the shafts and tethered it in a shady place where there was grass growing. In the cart she had watermelons, fruit cake in a tin, two large jars of shortbread and a basin of eggs to take to Moana-Rose. As she waited she was greeted by people on foot or on horseback.

Occasionally a vehicle passed by creating dust, and it was coming through this screen, wheezing like a train, that she recognised The Duke, a wayfarer she remembered from when he'd stayed with Dorothea and Taana many years before. Later, he'd married a local widow. However, The Duke remained a wanderer and the marriage didn't last. He was often in the area and was known to all the people of the town.

Oriwia gave him a wave and he saluted her in a tired fashion. He blew his webby cheeks out and propped himself against the wheel of her cart to remove broken boots and peel off mangy socks. Leaving his footwear on the ground, he turned and leaned into her cart.

'You selling watermelons Moana-Rose?' he asked.

'I'm Oriwia,' she said. 'No, not selling, taking them to my sister.'

'You want to sell them, that's what you want to do,' he said. He fished in his pocket and brought out a penny. 'Look, I could do with a bit.'

'Put your money away,' she said. 'Cut yourself a piece. Knife in the cloth.'

So he unwrapped the knife, cut himself a slice and took great bites. With eyes sticking out like pickled onions, he sent black pips flying, first from one corner of his mouth then the other. He shoved the awful socks into his boots, tied the laces together and slung them round his neck, walking away on pale, tender feet that flapped through the dust like two landed tarakihi, off to get a free ride on the train.

'Beauties they are. You want to sell them, Moana-Rose.'

As he went, she thought about setting up a stall somewhere and selling people's produce for them. She could take a portion of the price and people would have a little cash to pay against their shop accounts.

Across the road from the station was a small bakery, quite run down. Oriwia remembered her father stopping there on market days when they were little and buying ginger kisses for Moana-Rose and her to eat on the way home. What she looked forward to most on those days was going into this place of delicious smells and peering under lace-edged covers which had pink, blue and yellow flowers fancyworked on them. Plated under the covers were butterfly cakes, peanut brownies, vanilla slices, fruit squares, melting moments and the ginger kisses.

Oriwia had been told about the fancy stitching and fancy baking her mother did. It was all true. On a shelf at home were embroidered cloths, runners and three sets of worked pillow-cases. These were all so precious to her that she never used them.

And in a kitchen drawer was a notebook, taken from a small suitcase which their father had opened for them one day. It contained her mother's notes and recipes collected from Maori Women's Welfare League meetings. From the notebook, and with advice from one aunty and another, her mother had taught herself to bake. It made Oriwia happy, when she was complimented on her baking, to be told she took after her mother.

These days the bakery was dilapidated, paint peeling, boards warped and shelving all lopsided, as though the whole little building had been given a shove and with the next push might topple sideways. No worse than her own shop, she reminded herself. Her own place was also making its way back into the ground. There were no cakes in the bakery these days, only bread, pies and buns, and most of those done to order.

Anyway, now coming towards her was the daughter of the

woman who had sold her father ginger kisses all those years ago. Dulcie was two years older than Oriwia. They had attended the same school. She came across the road pushing a barrow of bread. Dulcie had a dough face and raisin eyes. Of course it was unkind to think of Dulcie in that way, Oriwia thought. However, Dulcie's face was pale, round and pliable with dark eyes, pressed in. Here was someone else who had come to nose into her cart.

'You got eggs for sale Oriwia?'

'Not for sale. Taking them to my sister.'

'But you have plenty? Plenty of eggs?'

'For Moana-Rose.'

'And butter. You have butter for shortbread?'

'Home-made butter.'

'What's in the tin?'

'Fruit cake.'

'Hmm.'

Dulcie continued to stare in at the goods while Oriwia went to get her horse.

'I miss the cakes,' Dulcie said when Oriwia returned. 'I want to get cakes back on the shelves. Times are getting better since the government brought in the Christmas bonus. I reckon I could sell cakes again now the old folks have got their pensions back and farmers have guaranteed dairy prices.' Dulcie was prattling on. 'They say there's going to be a forty-hour week. And there's people around, like these bachelor farmers, who wouldn't mind a large cake or a few small ones. But we got a couple of problems. First, one oven has had it. Kerplunk. Second, no supply of butter and eggs, or cream.' The train was coming. 'Wait here Oriwia.'

Dulcie went off to deliver her bread to the train. Oriwia returned the horse between the shafts, thinking that she probably could supply eggs and butter to Dulcie.

But it wasn't really raw goods that Dulcie wanted.

'With Mum sick, Dad and I don't have time. And only one oven.

But people do ask about cakes. I do a wedding cake occasionally as long as they give me butter and eggs.'

What Dulcie wanted, once a fortnight, was three jars of shortbread, 'because it keeps', and a large cake – Madeira, caraway or gingerbread – that she could cut into quarters for sale. Perhaps eighths. The raisin eyes were glittering. She took up one of the jars, unscrewed the lid, sniffed into it, then took out a piece of the shortbread, broke it in half, examined it and tasted it.

'Oh,' she said, noticing Oriwia's disapproval, 'they're perfect. Look, don't worry, I'll take this jarful and sell them for you. I'll give you pies and currant buns for your sister instead.'

Despite her irritation, the idea of having orders for her baking excited Oriwia. She tethered the horse and followed Dulcie across the street, thinking that instead of coming to town with an empty cart, she could supply the bakery with whatever was wanted. It seemed to be true that there were more people about these days. As well as that, maybe she could load up with watermelons, potatoes, corn, cabbage, whatever could be spared from people's gardens, and sell it by the roadside.

'I give you flour and sugar,' Dulcie said. 'You supply butter and eggs and whatever else. You bake. I sell. We go halves.' There were people in the shop waiting for bread. Harry Krauss was coming in from the bakery with fresh loaves. 'Also I could give you special orders for Sale Day.'

After loading her few supplies from the depot, Oriwia continued on her way to her sister's place, noting with increasing excitement different spots where she might, in future, stop with goods for sale. She didn't know how her father would feel about her selling by the roadside. They were shop owners, not hawkers. He was proud of that. But by now she was prepared to give anything a try. In a place like this where most people had their own gardens it wasn't likely she'd have many sales, but there was nothing to lose.

She could smell the pies and buns that Dulcie had given her hot from the oven, and couldn't wait to see the kids' faces when she unloaded them from the cart.

But it was her sister's face that struck her when she arrived at Moana-Rose's place. There was something different about her sister's face; some light from deep within her eyes had surfaced, some heaviness that had recently invaded her sister's limbs had exited. Her fingers and toes were twitching because of it.

'Benny's got work on the tramlines in Wellington,' she breathed. 'Forty-hour week. Staying with his sister and coming home some weekends until we save a bit and move down there.'

Oriwia refused to let her sense of imminent loss become obvious.

Her sister and children would go, Jimmy would die, and she would founder in debt with her home and shop falling down round her. But this was no time to dwell on such things.

She set the table with an embroidered cloth, the one that their father had told them their mother kept for special occasions and which had been passed on to Moana-Rose on her wedding day. She cut up pie and cake, arranged the buns on a dish, sliced the watermelon and they all had a greedy feast.

With her husband away in Wellington, Moana-Rose pleaded with Oriwia to stay the night, and since she wouldn't be collecting Jimmy until morning Oriwia agreed, realising that it could be a long time before she and her sister would be together again.

Getting into bed beside her sister, despite the lingering oil and tobacco smell of a man and the milky baby smell of Moana-Rose, despite dried-out timber and rancid air and the stink of soak water, there was still the familiar, comforting smell of sister. There were memories of talking, arguing, sneaking into the store to dip their fingers in sugar. At night in bed there was always Moana-Rose's plea, 'Tell me about our mother,' who in those days Oriwia was adamant she could remember.

'She was very beautiful,' she would say.

'But how? What like?'

'Her face was pretty.'

'What like?'

'Like the angel of the Lord who cometh nigh.'

'What about her hair?'

'Two plaits, one at each side, taken up and crossed on top of her head. Long at the back, formed into ringlets and tied in a bunch. She had a long, blue dress from her neck to the floor. Velvet.'

'Blue, like what?'

'Like the eyes of the Son of God made Man in the church of Saint Michael. A large white collar covering her shoulders. Long sleeves.'

When her parents married, they'd gone to live in Jimmy's village, which is where Oriwia and Moana-Rose were born. But not long after Moana-Rose's birth, when Oriwia was two, their mother had become ill with typhoid fever. The people of that village earned money through trading in flax, and Jimmy was away carting when his wife fell ill. On his return, she begged him to take their daughters back to her own village until the outbreak had come under control. 'Take the children to my relations,' she said. 'Dorothea will be able to feed Moana-Rose. Take them away, there's something bad in the water here. Go now. Don't touch the water.'

Jimmy agreed that he would take the children to his wife's village. It was a four-hour journey and, with the baby slung against his chest and Oriwia seated in front of him on the horse, he set out along the beaches before making his way inland through the creek beds and up over the hills by way of the bush tracks. He arrived in the early afternoon with Oriwia asleep over the horse's neck and Moana-Rose wet, hungry and crying.

For the next year, Dorothea had two babies to nurse, her own newly born Tiakiwhenua, and now Moana-Rose.

'Grandson,' Oriwia said, 'I told you that Aki was your uncle by double adoption. That first adoption was when Dorothea became mother to Moana-Rose and me, and we became his sisters.'

———

Besides asking Jimmy to take the children back to her village, his wife instructed him that if she died he was to remain there. He was to sell some of her land and put the money into a general store. 'You're a trader, not a farmer, Jimmy,' she said. His wife died a month later, and a year after that Jimmy began trading out of a hastily built storage shed next door to a blacksmith's. With the help of others, he sawed timber and stored corrugated iron to build a house. Oriwia was five and Moana-Rose three by the time they moved away from Dorothea and Taana's with their few belongings, which included a small suitcase of their mother's things that had been delivered to Jimmy after his wife's death.

Now, Moana-Rose said it again. 'Tell me about our mother. The blue dress.'

Oriwia laughed. 'Sister, you know I made it all up. We found out what she looked like, didn't we, once we opened the suitcase? There was the wedding photo wrapped in brown paper. There was no blue dress.

'Not that the photo was taken on her wedding day. There weren't any wedding photos, but at some time later when a photographer came to the area wanting Māori subjects to photograph, the people dressed her up in her wedding gown and put her in front of the camera. You know all this, my sister.'

'Well, tell me about the suitcase.'

'Nineteen twenty. I was nine and you were seven when Dad gave us the suitcase to open. In it were the embroidered cloths, the photo and the notebook. Although the notebook had the word 'Recipes' written on it, what was inside were mainly notes, anecdotes and hints to do with cooking and the kitchen.

'They were stories about how Aunty Pahemata went about making her blood pudding, beginning from the catching of blood from the throat of a pig, or about how Mrs Calder achieved a perfect set and colour to her quince jelly. There were hints on how to prepare a cloth for a boiled pudding and what a difference a pinch of baking soda could make to tough meat. There were variations on queen cakes and three different fruit-cake recipes with information on what made one suitable for a christening, another for Christmas and a third for a wedding. All sorts of things, my sister, which you already know about. Our mother's basic recipes, I figured out later, were actually in her head.'

When Oriwia arrived back from Moana-Rose's to collect her father, Taana was lathering him up for a shave. She hurried forward onto the verandah, casting her arms about him, eager to give him the good news of her brother-in-law's forty-hour week, the baking orders and the idea of taking people's produce for sale. But as she stood back from him to explain it all, her chest and stomach slumped against her backbone, forcing a long gasp to come from her mouth and a stream of tears to shoot from her eyes. The gasp turned to a wail and a howl. Dorothea came rushing from the kitchen.

'What's happened, Girl?' Taana asked, sitting her down, wiping shaving soap from her face and hair. Jimmy's tears were making tracks down through the remaining lather.

'Don't cry, Father,' she said, her words twanging unoiled from her throat. 'Don't. No. I have good news.'

Dorothea placed a cup of water in her hand and sat beside her. Taana began razoring in long strokes down the unfelt side of Jimmy's face.

'Benny has permanent work, forty hours a week. I have orders for baking. Times are getting better. The town is becoming busier because Pākehā farmers have money for land development, and I could take a cart of vegetables for sale.'

The three listeners took this news in silence. Chappy came, leading Nunu's cow. Dorothea went inside to make tea. When she came out again, Jimmy had fallen asleep. She said to Oriwia, 'But your heart is aching.'

'The shop won't survive, our heritage from our mother,' Oriwia said. 'My sister and my nieces and nephew will move away. My father won't last forever.'

'And you're carrying all our debts,' Dorothea said.

'No. No. It's not that. It's not that. You saved our lives when we were little. And times are getting better.'

'Only for some.'

Jimmy woke as Taana lifted him and seated him in the cart.

'There,' Taana said. 'Take Chappy with you. Chap? Help them when they get home?'

'He's no weight really,' Oriwia said. 'Are you Dad?'

'No weight, only a load,' were the words Jimmy managed to press bit by bit from out of one side of his mouth.

Chappy was wearing a large shirt that had belonged to Aki, and cotton shorts that had been made for him from sarongs. For a moment his eyebrows meandered as the eyes beneath them fixed in concentration, but they pricked like pins as understanding came to him.

Oriwia, trying to remember back to that time, thought perhaps he had vaulted himself into the cart or somehow landed in it without sound and without touching the sides. But then maybe he climbed in just like anyone else. It could have been the baggy shirt, the coloured pants, the thin ankles and the bony feet which made him seem like an acrobat.

Though Chappy was a quietly spoken man, he wasn't shy. All the way back to the shop, he asked about this and that, and wanted to know the word for one thing and another which he pointed out on the way. Oriwia couldn't help laughing from time to time at how her language came out of him.

Mystery man.

Even after he became fluent in their language, the questions they put to him – Who is your mountain? Who is your river? Who are your ancestors? Who is your name? – were never answered.

A few days after her two conversations – the first with The Duke, the second with Dulcie – Oriwia went about on horseback, visiting customers, telling them of her plan to sell garden produce from the roadside if they would give her their surplus. Also, with their eggs and butter she would bake cakes for sale at the Krausses' shop, taking account of everything they gave her. If it worked out the way she hoped, they would be able to pay their shop bills, perhaps even have a little cash left over. People were enthusiastic about the idea of being free of debt, of being able to stay on the land instead of selling land or moving away to find work. Experience had already told them there was no work. They began planning.

On the day when Oriwia first arrived to collect goods, Grandmother Nunu and Ma Girlie were sitting to one side of the gardens making loosely woven baskets suitable for carrying vegetables. There was a shortage of sacks and sugar bags since these were in demand for the making of clothing, curtains and floor mats.

Chappy was among others in the garden picking corn but stopped what he was doing to watch the women weaving using strands of leaves cut from the harakeke bushes. He didn't know the word 'harakeke' then. Though he had seen the criss-crossing hands of Nunu when he pulled himself up to sit against the bird tree on the day after his arrival, he had not witnessed the whole basket-making process before.

He watched the women divide the leaves into strips and flick the green from the ends with mussel shells, leaving just the strands of fibre. He watched them plait these ends to form a base from which they began to weave upwards to make large airy baskets. After observing for some time he went off to the bamboo grove, returning with a load of trimmed canes.

The grandmothers stopped what they were doing to watch a miracle occur – to witness the long hands lay the bamboo stalks down, to see the threading, the tying, the shaping, the binding, the trimming, the finishing, and finally the placing of this new thing on the pile with the other baskets.

No, no, it could not go on the pile.

This new object would not be used as a spud bag. It was a treasure and mustn't be sold. It was so unique that it could only be given away. From that time on, whenever there was a gathering of people for a celebration, such as a wedding or a special birthday, Chappy's baskets would be part of the gift-giving. The mothers would place him prominently as their group was called on to the marae, baskets hooked onto his arms. As gifts they were unmatched. They were referred to in speeches.

The next morning, her cart loaded with goods, Oriwia set out early, arriving at the bakery just after sunrise. Dulcie took the cakes from her and decided she would be the first customer for vegetables.

From there Oriwia led the horse across the road to the sheltered area in front of the railway station. Business was slow, but she kept reminding herself that even one sale, paid for in cash, was better than a day at the shop in which she might see a pair of boots walk out the door with money owing on them and that was all.

Sales increased over the next months, but eventually someone from the town authority, who said he was acting on behalf of complaining railway passengers, told her that she could no longer bring her wares to that site. It was a picnic area, not a commercial one.

'Business was just picking up a little,' she told Taana and Dorothea that afternoon. They took her to talk to Paa.

'You know that chimney?' the old man asked. He was talking about a stone chimney standing not far from the railway station, which was all that remained of his own parents' house. When large tracts of land had been taken from people for a road, his father had refused to move. According to Paa, no one could shift him from it because they were all afraid of him. He had yellow eyes that caused those who dared look into them to fall face down on the ground. On falling they broke their teeth, broke their noses, got mouthfuls of stones and went crazy in the head.

Because of him, this portion of his property was not included in the grab, and the road had to be built around it. Instead the land was made part of the 'tenths' – the portion that the government had decided should be left to Māori when they took the other ninety per cent. Although this small pocket could have been leased to farmers for ninety-nine years with right of renewal, Paa's father refused to allow it.

'Go there,' Paa said. 'It's a good spot.'

'I'll wipe your shop book clean,' she said.

'If you like.'

However, it wasn't all straightforward after Oriwia and Paa tidied up the site and she took her cart there. The farmer leasing the adjoining land thought that his entitlement included Paa's land and had been grazing cattle there. He came and asked her to move, and when she refused, he arrived with the policeman, Gary Couper, who seemed embarrassed. He'd been to school with Oriwia. The matter was eventually settled in a council office when the plans were produced and proved Paa to be right. The farmer withdrew his opposition under Paa's threat to charge him for many years of free grazing.

Gradually people's shop debts lessened, but this was not entirely due to Oriwia's enterprise. As Dulcie had predicted, times were becoming better and contract work easier to come by. Pākehā farmers were able to obtain finance for developing their land, which enabled them to employ Māori who were not.

It wasn't long after Oriwia set up in the new site that her father died.

After his death, loneliness was like a needle that entered somewhere at the base of her throat, was how she described it, a rod of steel piercing heart, lungs, stomach – bleeding them.

It was about eighteen months later that the world returned Aki to them. It was the first time he'd been home since he'd come bringing Chappy with him. One day, Oriwia asked him if he remembered the day she'd told him she didn't want to marry him, and that muscle on the other side of the world was of no use to her.

———

'You see, we'd had this understanding since he first proposed to me out of the side of his mouth during arithmetic one morning at school, when he was ten and I was going on for twelve,' Oriwia said. 'In our own language of course, even though it was strictly forbidden at school. But Aki would never speak English apart from Yes Sir, No Sir, Thank you Sir and when he had to read aloud from a class book. He hardly spoke at all, only surreptitiously to one of us. "We should get married one day," he said. "*All right*," I replied in English, "*don't forget.*" I always thought he should have asked Moana-Rose, who was the same age as him, and prettier than me.

'Grandson,' Oriwia said to me as she locked the shop door and we set off along the road to the house, 'you should've seen his face. His mouth was lopping open and popping shut as if he were blowing smoke rings. He thought I was about to hold him to our childhood agreement. "Well I still don't," I told him. "I still don't want to marry you, but I do want to marry Chappy. You have to go and ask him for me.'"

Oriwia became silent, not speaking until we came to the house. 'Now I've something to show you,' she said as we went inside.

While she was away looking for whatever it was, I removed my jacket and went through the notes I'd taken, wishing my grandmother didn't have a habit of leaving stories in mid-air. I'd already begun typing by the time she returned with three bamboo baskets. These so entranced me that I forgot about unfinished stories for the moment.

One was a simple carrying basket, wide and shallow, suitable for shopping. Another, tall and elegantly shaped, was meant for the display of flowers. A third, which I could see had been well used, was a baby's cradle. I imagined the 'long hands' which had threaded and tied, shaped and bound these. I thought of the young mother taking up a shopping basket and stepping out, saw her at a bench arranging flowers, or in a room placing a sleeping baby – my mother or my aunt. I thought of how objects can call to us from across time.

Chapter 9

AKI

When I first brought Chappy home he was shaky and pale with bones like clothesline props lifting skin away from flesh. On coming home after being away at sea for two years, I could see his face had rounded and his body had filled out. His skin was clear, beige, glowing as though polished.

I found him making a bicycle. He had collected parts, mainly from Jimmy's yard, and was now working on getting wheel rims into shape – not that he had tyres to go on the rims he told me. That was a problem for another day.

'Oriwia wants you to marry her,' I said. His progress in our language was impressive, so I'm sure he understood what I said. It was just that he couldn't believe what he was hearing. He turned away from me so that I couldn't see his face, but too late. I'd already glimpsed, in his half-moon eyes, sudden joy.

'Wants me to bring? Take? Do? Make?' He turned to face me again.

'No, no, no. Oriwia wants to have a wedding with you.' One of my hands was Oriwia, one was Chappy. I brought my hands together to make a wedding. The bike wheel and the spanner clattered to the ground. A long sigh came from him. He sat down. I sat beside him.

'I'm a man without a country, without a family, without a name, without goods or money, without papers,' he told me. 'I'm from a disgraced family, except I no longer have a family. Because of war. My father didn't believe in Japan's expansion across China, but he had to keep his views secret. I was taken into the army anyway. We were kicked and thumped and brutalised to make us into killers. But I knew I couldn't be a killer. They tried to indoctrinate us into hatred. But I was unable to hate.'

As one among many thousands of troops following into cities that had been bombarded by Japanese planes, Chappy witnessed decimation of populations and destruction of homes and buildings. Fires raged through the city. Innocents were killed, injured, violated, orphaned, made homeless. Rather than be part of this, he decided he would take his own life. 'In our first foray I broke ranks, running forward to throw myself into a burning building, but sniper fire got me at the edge of flame. Bullet wounds, burns, hoping for death, but I survived and got shipped to hospital in Japan.'

One night Chappy left the hospital and made the long journey on foot back to his father's house, knowing that he could be caught and imprisoned or executed for running from army authority. He didn't care that he might be detained or killed as long as he wasn't sent back to war.

He travelled by night and hid during daytime, searching out any fruit or plant that he could eat.

When he arrived home it was to find that his father and brothers had been taken away for speaking out against the war. His family were now living in poverty. Although Chappy was ill and starving, his grandmother said he couldn't stay because he would be caught, too, and they'd never see him again. Guards had already been there looking for him. Chappy wanted to give himself up, but his grandmother wouldn't allow it.

Late the next night, she told him he was to accompany her to the port at Hinode. It was a long foot journey, which took until daylight. There she introduced him to an elderly basket-maker, but didn't tell the basket-maker Chappy's true name. She told Chappy that his old name did not exist any more, his family did not exist, his country did not exist and he was to go and make a new life in America.

The basket-maker made a living by making and mending containers for ships' cargoes. In secret he arranged working passage for those needing to escape.

At home, the basket-maker's daughter made a variety of small baskets, which she took to market. She taught the skills to Chappy, and that was how he earned his keep. While the daughter was away during the day, he stayed hidden and kept her supplied with goods. He lived there for half a year, and one night was taken aboard a cargo boat where he would work his passage to San Francisco. He had a little money given to him by the basket-maker, and an address of people who would help him once at his destination.

Chappy never reached the address. In San Francisco he was beaten and robbed and thrown into the harbour where, because of injuries, it was all he could do to keep himself afloat. About him, in the dark, were the steep shapes of large ships. The tide brought him up against one of these, and though he was too exhausted to swim any further, he managed to climb the anchor chain, enter the ship through the hawsehole and make his way into the chain locker, where he was found after the ship had left port. He was given a meal and put to work.

We sat in silence. I thought through all that Chappy had told me. As far as marriage to Oriwia was concerned, none of what he feared mattered except perhaps his being 'without papers'. If caught, he could be jailed and deported, a risk he had been prepared to take as a single man. Filling out documents could incriminate him.

'We'll think of something,' I said, though I didn't know what. In former times a marriage was made in the eyes of the people; now only the eyes of God and the state were good enough.

The other thing he said, which he seemed to think was another reason he couldn't marry Oriwia, was that she was thunder and lightning and large. I think he meant high above him socially, and fiery. It was all nothing. He was in love.

[High above and fiery? I've never known Aki to be tactful before. He really meant uppity and bossy – but I suppose he's chosen words carefully for a change because he knew Chappy didn't mean it that way. Large? Well, I was quite a normal size then, but I'm not butter. Strong, not small. Girls like me, in books I read, were called 'strapping'. That's a word I've never heard spoken in that context. Anyway it's ridiculous. Girls like my sister were 'petite' and 'dainty', silly words. But maybe Chappy was thinking of those pikelets I made when Aki first brought him into the shop – the size of bread plates. I don't like mean baking, or mean anything. I had a surplus of eggs and milk. Anyway that's enough interruption. Leave all this out when you type it up. Sometimes I get hostile with that Aki. O.S.]

That evening, before we finished work in the gardens, I went away and came back with Oriwia, who sat herself down on a log beside the corn rows without speaking to anyone – an unusual thing for her. I asked Chappy to go and sit beside her, but he wouldn't do it at first. I had to take him there. Neither of them said a word or even looked at each other. I went to speak to my parents and grandparents, who were already wondering what was going on.

It was getting dark.

The minute I opened my mouth, and before I'd finished outlining the proposal and the problem, my mother was running over the garden, jumping rows, zigzagging, and announcing a wedding. Never mind what difficulties there might be. There was a hullabaloo as the sun made its drop.

Getting Oriwia and Chappy married in the eyes of God and the state was not as difficult as I thought. There were many Māori in those days who were without birth certificates. The Māori Birth Register didn't open until 1913 – the year Moana-Rose and I were born – when our registration became compulsory. We had already spoken about Chappy as our adopted brother, but now Paa and Nunu decided he could become their unregistered youngest son, Chappy Star, our mother's sibling. In a way, this made him my uncle, though Chappy has always been brother to me.

The name Star was not one which my mother's family had plucked from the heavens. Our yellow-eyed great-grandfather who killed with his eyes had chosen it at the time when Māori were required to have surnames. Whetū, the word for star, was already part of his name, so he added the English equivalent. He became Whetū Star, or Star Star, or Whetū Whetū – however you liked to look at it. I've been told it was one big joke to him.

There were no problems to do with filling out and signing papers and the announcement of banns of marriage. There were no questions asked by authorities about the little pale-skinned man who spoke our language but couldn't speak or write English. They were used to that.

Oriwia and Chappy were married by my mother's cousin, who was the Māori pastor for the Wellington diocese. Paa's wedding gift to Chappy and Oriwia was the piece of land handed down from the yellow-eyed great-grandfather, and from where Oriwia had been selling her fruit and vegetables. Amid all the speech-making, singing, dancing and gift-giving, I had to leave. To tell the truth, I couldn't wait to get back on board to fire up the fires (so to speak) which would see us breaking through the seas to Hawai'i, to Ela.

The second time I went there, that is after the tooth time, I'd planned how I was going to see my Ela again. I was to be in port for a day.

My Ela. That's how I was thinking of her, moon talking as I walked the boards. Whatever she thought of me, which was probably nothing at all, in my heart she was already my Ela. The trouble was I didn't know anything about love. Not that kind. Of falling in. I knew how I felt about a family, a place, a people. I knew that I had a special affection for my grandfather and an everlasting love for a sibling. I had felt love for Oriwia too, but it was brotherly. It was the kind of love you grew into, not the falling in kind which made you feel sick.

The ship berthed early in the morning at a time when Ela would still be at work. I put on new clothes. Yes, new clothes – white shirt, grey slacks, brown shoes – in a manner unsuitable for hot sun. It's how I thought I should present myself. In my shore bag I had rum and whisky, jars of plum jam and green pickle. These last two items were gifts from my mother for the people who had pulled my tooth and fed me. I had gathered other things on my way. There were lollies, chewing gum, cigarettes and souvenirs. Shirts, balls for the bad boys. Scent in a bottle shaped like a church, only it was, you know, tiny. It had little flowers painted on it. I pretended to myself that I had bought it for my mother.

I waited in the street outside the hotel where Ela worked in the night kitchens. But she could've changed jobs, I thought. After a while I went into the hotel grounds to sit under the trees. No one bothered me. Eventually the work truck pulled in by the back entrance with two women already on board. I went to talk to the driver, surprised that he remembered me.

Anyway, Ela came out of the hotel with others and straight away saw me, immediately came running, threw her arms around me. 'Come, come,' she said, lifting my half-ton, clinking shore bag onto the truck with her. So I followed and the lorry rattled off. I had to be back on board by evening, but would have to solve that problem later. We talked about her father, my absent tooth, the bad boys, my travels. The conversation was like a lot of small stabs.

'Fish and gardens,' I said, by way of showing my appreciation of the place where she lived. Her face changed for a moment. Her eyelids drooped. I wanted to wrap her against anything that would hurt her. 'Not our place forever,' she said. That was when I saw a ghost walk through her, changing the bones of her face and tingeing her complexion with concrete. I wanted to reach out to her, protect her from whatever it was. I wanted to lay down my life.

She put away whatever her thoughts were and spoke to the truckload.

'You remember our new brother?'

They laughed.

'Come to see Dad.'

They laughed again. 'Dressed like that?' Laughing.

'Fishing.'

'*Fishing, ah.*' Laughing, speaking in English sometimes.

'Hanging about at the back of the hotel like a sick seagull.'

'*He's bag, glassing on the ground.*'

Some of the things they said I won't repeat. Rude just like the old women at home. Worse. The two men on board weren't saying a thing, just grinning as if they had cut faces.

The only thing you can do in this kind of situation is go along with it. Ela was being told by all of them what was in my heart, and she knew people well enough to know their observations wouldn't be wrong. I'd been planning a declaration, but it was all out of my hands in a way. I couldn't look at her to see how she was taking it, not in front of all those ones with eyes all round their heads. As a distraction I opened the bag, handed round cigarettes, but this did nothing to keep them quiet.

Ela went home to sleep. I went to sit with her father, who was sousing fish in coconut. Later, back at the house with Ela and her family, I disembowelled the shore bag, putting everything out on a log step for them. I left the little bottle of scent where it was because it was impossible. It was an announcement. I had crabs in my throat.

Then I did. I gave it to her before all those flickering eyes and flicking eyebrows. Old eyes, young eyes, kids' eyes. Well, why not? The worst that could happen was that her uncles and cousins would throw me in the sea and not even wait to hold my head under.

Ela didn't smile like the postcard girls. Much less. Her eyelids drooped as her smile formed, but the thing is that the eyelids would lift a little, and when they did you knew that she saw only you – or whoever the smile was meant for. That's how I felt. It was a moment, a witnessed moment. Then she kissed my cheek and went about dabbing the grandmothers and aunties behind the ears. And dabbing the bad boys. And the cousins of the bad boys.

'I don't know,' she said on the way to the work lorry. So I waited. I had no words, nothing to offer, no promises I could make except those that I knew would have been made to her before, by bastards. Why should she trust me to be different? I was a stranger. For all she knew I could be married, could have a tribe of kids already, all over the world. 'My life has been full of mistakes so far,' she said.

'And what use –?' I changed my mind about using the word 'muscle'. 'What use is a man on the other side of the world?' I had to leave it at that, but remember feeling encouraged rather than discouraged because of the frowning, thinking way she looked at me when we parted.

'Why me?' she asked as the truck arrived.

I answered truthfully. 'I don't know.'

The next time I arrived in O'ahu I went to the hotel and asked for her. There were only two hours before I would be required on board. It was early morning. The woman I spoke to said that domestics had a break in half an hour and that she would give Ela the message.

I thought Ela was relieved rather than surprised to see me.

'I want you to know,' I said, 'that I'm not married and don't have any children.' She took my arm and we went across the road to a breakfast place where we ordered coffee. 'I could change my home port from Wellington to Honolulu.' I'd had so much time to moontalk as I walked the boards, it was now all coming out in one go. 'We'd have to get married,' I said, 'for me to be able to change my home port.' That wasn't well said but she seemed to take it how it was meant.

'I'd like to get married one day,' she said, but looked despondent.

'To me?' My asking this reminded me of Chappy when I had put Oriwia's proposal to him.

Ela didn't answer. She stirred, looking down at her coffee.

'And after a while, say six months, I'd try for coastal runs with time off every fortnight.'

Still she said nothing. Her expression remained serious, and I was beginning to feel discouraged.

'Or, I could take you home with me, you and the boys.' She shook her head at this suggestion, but there it was. I'd laid it all out. There was no more for me to say. I watched her, drank my coffee.

'They want me to marry you,' she said in a low voice that had me leaning forward. My coffee went flying.

'The family? You asked them?'

'I asked them nothing. They told me. They've been telling me ever since last time.'

'What did you say?'

'I said nothing.'

The waiter was there with a cloth cleaning up the spill. Ela smiled at me. 'We'll take it slow,' she said. 'Like taking a long, slow walk up the mountains of Hawai'i.' My Ela said things like that.

It's what we did. I called in as often as I could over the next year. I think that's all she wanted from me at the time – to know that I would return. I was signed on to a ship taking tourists on Pacific cruises. One day I turned up with a ring, which I gave to her in front of everyone. She put it on her little finger. It was too small for the ring finger. We were married, with a right-sized ring, on my next extended leave. I left journeying and found work round the coastal routes of the Hawaiian Islands.

But seafaring changed when we went to war.

Chapter 10

ORIWIA

Aki rang his parents late at night. He hadn't been home for two years because he'd changed ships, and though the family guessed his reasons for doing this, they didn't know why he was being secretive. Because they were all on telephone party lines in those days, Oriwia heard the 'long, short, short, long' grind which was Taana and Dorothea's ring. Toll operators tried it three times before the phone was picked up.

Oriwia wondered who had died, this being the first thought when a phone rang in the middle of the night. It was a quarter of an hour or more before the 'ring-off' signal sounded, which meant a long conversation had taken place. The 'ring-off' was followed by Paa's 'short, long, short' call, which would be Dorothea ringing her father. Another long conversation took place, but Oriwia knew that local calls in the middle of the night were most often brief, and if someone had died Dorothea would have let them all know immediately.

It wasn't difficult to guess that the phone call was from Aki – not unexpected – to say he was going to be married. Oriwia lay in bed thinking about collecting the ingredients together for the wedding cake. She spent the rest of the night planning it, wondering who the woman was and where she was from. She was bound to be beautiful.

What Oriwia discovered next day when she went to visit Dorothea was a mother in tears who told her that her son was to marry a Hawaiian woman who already had two sons, that the wedding would take place in Hawai'i, and that Aki would be living there permanently.

'When I encouraged him to leave here, he wasn't meant to stay away forever,' Dorothea said. 'He's been given responsibilities. He's been given the old knowledge. There's the house, the land.'

'What happened to her first husband?' Oriwia asked.

'She never had one,' Dorothea replied.

So, who was this woman, this Ela? A woman keeping a man from his family, a man with obligations who would now be giving his name to illegitimate children. Struck by Hawaiian beauty, the fool. Well, it wouldn't last. Aki was not one who could stay away from his land, his people, his language, for too long. This woman was a schemer who had taken advantage of Aki's backwardness. Oriwia felt a resentment towards this Ela, even after Dorothea had dried her eyes and said, 'These things happen.'

———

It was a Saturday. The Star Tearoom was shut for business, and while my grandmother and I were having a leisurely breakfast, she told me about Aki's midnight phone call. Although it had been a busy week, she'd spent many hours translating the tapes from Uncle Aki. I would wake at night to hear the drone of the tape, the playback, over and over, of some sections. From her draft she had done a corrected copy, and finally handed to me perfect pages in her own fine handwriting. Although I told her that roughs were good enough for me to type up from, she would have none of that. Even the word 'rough' seemed to offend her, so I tried not to use it.

'Despite what I said earlier,' she said that morning, 'when I complained about Aki not speaking English on your tapes, I'm now pleased he's doing this in his own language, otherwise he wouldn't do it half so well. Very good, aren't they? To tell the truth, I love doing the translations. They're full of surprises. This latest one was so interesting. Aki's never talked before about his courtship days. Maybe he finds it easier to say things to a machine.'

I wanted to give the interviews a rest for the day. I suggested we could drive somewhere.

'Maybe this afternoon,' she said. 'I've got shelves to wash down. Come with me and bring your notebook. As Aki said, the war came along, and that leads us back to Chappy.'

————

People reorganised their gardens so that they were growing what they needed for themselves with surplus for sale; they soon learned to grow extra of what sold best. Chappy worked in the gardens, too, loading up the cart once a week with goods for sale. He had now completed the bike – joining a chain, making a pair of wooden pedals, rubbing down the frame and painting it khaki. 'That's the colour you get, Grandson, when you mix together scraps of paint from old tins,' Oriwia said. 'He bought a new set of tyres and inner tubes. The bike had straight handlebars made from a piece of pipe, both ends plugged with corks from medicine bottles.'

Oriwia still looked after the shop and did the baking, but much of her time was now spent on the books, adding and deducting, watching people's debts reduce, putting in her orders and, little by little, paying off her own creditors.

A year after their marriage, their daughter Daphne was born, and a year later came another daughter, Virginia, known to everyone as Binnie. By then, Oriwia and Chappy had decided to pull down the old house and shop and use the timber and corrugated iron to build a new house and a vegetable stand on the roadside property given to them by Paa.

The land was more than they needed for the little house and

veggie stall. Behind the house they planted fruit trees. Taana and Chappy fenced off a paddock and put sheep there, enough to keep them all in meat from season to season.

'That house we built,' Oriwia said, 'you wouldn't call it a house these days. Just one big room to live in and an open veggie stand out front. Fruit as well as vegetables. But we did have a wooden floor in the new place. There were plenty of homes those days had only a dirt floor. And oh, you know, it was watertight and comfortable and we were happy there.'

Once war began there was a demand for fresh produce. Oriwia and Chappy soon found it difficult to keep up supplies. Adding to the problem of supply was a diminishing workforce as young men left the land to go off and fight. Other men and many women went to work in the cities, in the clothing mills and munitions factories.

The home gardens were left mainly to older people – Paa and Nunu, Taana and Dorothea, uncles and aunts. They needed Chappy's help. He would leave the vegetable stall to Oriwia and make the eight-k journey each day to work in the gardens, setting out early on his bike, his repair kit wrapped in canvas. Chappy and his bike became a familiar sight going back and forth through the township, sometimes bringing home a load of bamboo, held on his shoulder.

———

'Grandson,' Oriwia said, 'the main reason he built that bike was because he didn't get on with horses. I didn't know that it was this same bike that was going to take my Chappy away from me.

'What Chappy enjoyed most was to work alongside Paa, who he revered. I mean it Grandson. He loved Paa with all his heart. Grandmother Nunu, too, but she'd died by the time war started. They were the ones who had adopted Chappy, giving him a name and a new life. Remember I talked about Aki being your uncle by double adoption, the first adoption being when my sister and I became his siblings? The second adoption was when Aki's grandparents made your grandfather their whāngai. It was a true adoption in the eyes of the people. Chappy became Paa and Nunu's true son, to be treated equally with Dorothea and her brothers.'

———

While working alongside each other, whether it was in the gardens, eel trapping in the creek, or hauling and cutting wood, Paa would tell Chappy – and others within earshot – the news of the world. This was a retelling of the BBC news from London of the night before, which Paa tuned in to each evening on his battery radio. In those days the news was all about the war in Europe, though Oriwia said it didn't tell it by half.

———

Though what I've written up in this chapter has taken just a few pages it was a whole day in the telling, because every so often my grandmother would remember a photograph or some item, go off to find them, and we'd peruse them together.

There was a faded newspaper photograph of Oriwia driving the horse and cart through the township. Underneath was the caption: 'Maori woman with her cartload of vegetables.' Another photograph shows her posing at her stand, a baby in one arm, a cabbage in the other. When I asked where Chappy was when the photo was taken, she told me he would never allow himself to be photographed in case it led to his deportation.

Other photographs were studio ones that I had seen before, of my grandmother and the little girls.

'Look closely,' Oriwia said. 'If you want to know what Chappy looked like, have a good look at your mother and aunt. My little Japanese daughters.' To please her I studied the photographs, though it was plain to see that neither of the girls took after their mother. They were small and delicate looking. Oriwia was big boned with a broad face and strong features. Her hair was thick and curly, her hands, clasped in front of her, were large and veiny.

'I've often wondered,' Oriwia said, 'if anything would have turned out differently if my daughters had taken after me.'

She went on to tell me what had been happening to her friends at Krauss's Bakery – which to my disappointment was taking us away from our present discussion and didn't seem relevant. I wanted to get back to my grandfather and the khaki-coloured bike which, it seemed, had something to do with his disappearance.

———

After the beginning of World War Two there was a radio announcement that all enemy aliens were to report to their local police stations so that they could be put on a register. Though Harry Krauss heard the call, he didn't believe he fitted the description of either 'enemy' or 'alien'. He had become a British citizen many years earlier, and was married to a New Zealander.

Harry was well known in the town and proud of his reputation, not only as an excellent baker but as a staunch supporter of the local rugby club, where his sons Hermie and Kurt had been chosen for provincial and regional representative sides every year since they left school. Why should he register? He was against Hitler, who was a maniac. He told anyone who cared to listen that if he were living in Germany right then, his sons would have been taken off to the youth camps to be trained for Hitler's army.

But attitudes towards him were changing in the town. People he'd known for years were avoiding him, some long-standing baking orders were cancelled, daily custom declined and he awoke one morning to find a swastika painted on the garage wall. A day later Gary Couper paid him a visit and advised him to register. 'We all know you,' Gary said. 'Don't worry, they're not going to lock you up.'

So Harry took the train to Wellington, upset at having to come under enemy alien regulations. 'This is my country,' he kept trying to explain when interviewed. 'Today's Germany is not my Germany. The flag of Germany is not my flag. I would fight for my adopted country if I could.'

In the following days he had to give up his .202 rifle which his sons used for rabbiting. His radio was sealed so that it could not be used to transmit messages, and the telephone was disconnected. His taxi licence was taken from him, and he was not permitted to move out of town.

After several trips to Wellington to present himself to the Aliens Authority, Harry was given permission to report to the local policeman instead. Although this made life easier for him in one way, he sensed growing hostility towards him, and was becoming more reclusive as time went by. He spent most of his day away from the shop-front and more time with his drawings and making cake decorations, which he would wrap in tissue paper and store in tins. He was worried about family in Germany and wrote regularly to his mother in Berlin.

His situation worsened when a letter to a local paper demanded to know why a family of Germans was being tolerated in their midst and why mail was blatantly being sent to Germany on a regular basis via 'our own Post Office'. Here was a man, as free as the breeze, running a business and becoming rich while young New Zealanders were away spilling their blood on foreign soil. This was a man who had openly said that if he were in Germany right now his sons would be training up with Hitler.

A week later detectives turned up to search the house, bakery and garage. From the house they took a bundle of drawings, cuttings from German newspapers that had been sent to Harry by his mother, other cuttings belonging to his wife – which were mainly recipes and photos of rugby games – an address book, letters, and his passport, which had been renewed the previous year. Also there was a souvenir banner from when the Olympic Games had been held in Germany three years before the start of the war.

From the garage the detectives took a bundle of *People's Voice* papers which they found in a box under a bench and of which Harry knew nothing. Two days later he was taken in for questioning, when he attempted to account for these items now displayed before him.

The souvenir pennant had on it all the emblems of the nations which had taken part in the Games, including the swastika. On the other hand there was the bundle of *People's Voice* papers.

So, was he a Nazi or a Communist?

'I'm a Christian,' said Harry. 'I'm against the Nazis. The banner was sent by my mother to my wife. I'm against the Communists.'

'The papers?'

'I know nothing of the papers.'

'But you hid them in your garage all the same.'

Realising that the papers had been put there by his sons – hidden away because they knew their father would disapprove of them – there was little Harry could say. Hermie and Kurt had registered as enemy aliens along with their father, but were not under investigation. By the way the questioning went, Harry soon realised that in the eyes of the inquisitors it was far worse to be a Communist than a Nazi.

A week later the detectives came for him with an internment order. He was taken by train under escort and handed over to the military on arrival at the Wellington railway station, soon to end up as a prisoner on Somes Island in the middle of Wellington Harbour.

When Oriwia arrived at the bakery on the day Harry was arrested, she found Dulcie and her mother in tears and the bakery in disarray. Oriwia, who had come to discuss an order for a wedding cake, didn't know what to do except to say that there must be some mistake, that the authorities would find out what kind of man Harry was and he'd soon be home. She made tea for them and said she would go and see Gary Couper, who should be able to help.

'Nothing to do with me,' Gary Couper said. 'They're grabbing all these enemies.'

'He's not an enemy. He's Harry.'

'It's the military. Grabbing the German and Itie spies.'

'He's not a spy, he's –'

'Sticking them all on the island.'

In Harry's absence, Oriwia went in at night to help Dulcie set the loaves, but the bakery business was in sharp decline, as was the workshop. A year later, because of agitation within the town, Dulcie's brothers were also taken and imprisoned.

| Chapter 11 |
AKI

I was in Pearl Harbor the morning of the bombing, looking forward to a Sunday with Ela and the family. Though the world was at war, life at that time was good, I thought. Ela had day work in a military canteen, and I had joined the US Navy.

When we first married, I rented a small house near to the port so that Ela would be close to her new place of work and I could be home within five minutes of leaving my ship. But the house was a mistake. It was too lonely for Ela, and the bad boys wouldn't live there. When they were persuaded to stay for a while, they refused to attend a new school.

I couldn't live there either. Besides, we were needed in Ela's village to tend the kalo and yams, to gather food and catch fish. As in my own home area, family health was tied to the land and sea. Though times were changing and a certain amount of money had become a necessity in these times, the old ways were important for keeping families together and the culture alive.

We cancelled the lease. I bought a car so that Ela could get to and from her village where we had taken over one of the little unoccupied houses. It was a much better place for us to live. The boys returned to school, which, I was told, they attended most of the time. While I was in port they stayed home with me, or they went to catch a fish for *me*. That's what they told me, evil boys.

I don't want to say much about my war except that I enlisted in the navy along with Ela's brother and cousins – not straightforward for me, as I was not naturalised. I didn't want to join up in my own country, which would have meant training at home and going to England, Africa, Italy – other people's countries – while US marines, many soon to be encamped in Aotearoa, were preparing to defend the Pacific. It was my wife's country that was endangered should there be war in the region, which could mean that my own country was vulnerable as well.

We came into port on that soundless early morning of quiet sea. The dark mountains stood sharp against a clear sky and we were out on deck fastening the hatches, our last duty for the night. After another week of intensive training out at sea all our ships were in port for the day of rest, ships of all descriptions – battleships, ten in all, heavy and light cruisers, destroyers and others, all lined up – like skittles as it turned out. The only part of the fleet not in port were the aircraft carriers, which were away on a mission.

At first, the sound was like something felt more than something heard, a sensation, incongruous, which didn't quite register on this peaceful day.

It was a sound which was soon to become defined as aircraft coming our way. It could've been our B17s coming in. Banter started up among us as we kept to our task of dogging down. Don't they know it's a day of rest, someone said. Here come the Japs, someone else said, not for a moment believing it.

Even when the first torpedo planes swooped, we didn't give our attention until one of them came at us and we heard the splash of what we soon knew to be a live torpedo. There was a shout from above, and on looking up we saw the underbelly of the yellow plane as it roared upwards, the red eyes of the rising sun on its underwings. It seemed only an arm's length away as we flattened ourselves on the deck. There was an enormous jolt, which concussed us all for a moment. There was a stink of oil, and banks of heavy smoke rolled along the deck. Soon the decks were wrapped in fire and the ship was rolling on its side. Some of us jumped overboard into water, but that was also on fire. Bombers, high above the torpedo planes, were dropping their loads.

I swam along underwater as much as I could, wiping oil from round my nose and mouth and away from my eyes with one hand as I came up for breath, flame driving me under again. In this manner I made my way, half-blinded, to one of the harbour islands. I was lucky to make it to shore. Hundreds died trapped on board their ships. Hundreds more drowned in the burning sea. Others were blown skyward, falling to earth in bits and pieces.

Ships were aflame, men on fire leaping overboard, seas ablaze. Billowing black smoke, shrapnel and lumps of debris flying, bombs falling, vessels sinking. Screaming and shouting, roaring planes.

The sky was dotted with the black puffs of anti-aircraft smoke. Machine-gun fire was coming from our ships, the ones not hit. But to no avail.

There was nothing I could do to help in the way of counter-attack, but I stripped off, wiped myself down and went to help rescue men struggling ashore, many burned, wounded, and throwing up oil and sea water. At first I just waded out and pulled men in, but after a while took charge of a liferaft and ferried the wounded to the nearby naval base. I had no time then to think how the raid might have affected the rest of O'ahu.

The planes roared away after about half an hour, but the fires and explosions and flying debris continued as we went to and fro, bringing in the wounded and the half-drowned. The dead had to wait.

It wasn't until I was given a truck to drive and we began moving out from the over-filled Naval Hospital to take the wounded to the general hospitals and emergency sites that I saw the devastation in the city. The roads to the port had been strafed, houses were on fire, trees had been beheaded, shops had been annihilated and there was glass everywhere. There were bomb holes you could stand to your neck in. People lay dead or wounded in the streets. Wrecked cars had been blown from the roads with people inside. Everywhere there were people crying, carrying the dead and wounded or doing their best to put out fires and clear the roads. Trucks and vehicles of all descriptions had become ambulances.

As I drove back and forth all I could think about was my family. I knew that Ela and the boys would have driven in to pick me up. Though I couldn't abandon the work I was doing, my worries were making me sick. My eyes traversed the wreckage of the streets, trusting not to see what I was looking for.

Eventually I did see our car, safely parked at Queen's Hospital. While volunteers assisted the wounded, I went to look for my wife. Sometimes there's an advantage in being head and shoulders above most people. I walked into an open area where hundreds of people were queuing to give blood. Ela spotted me. I heard her call out and she came towards me, crying, hurrying through the crowd.

Ela and the boys had been a mile or two from the port when the planes came over and the attack began. They drove off the road and huddled together until the planes left. Since she was unable to get to the port, Ela turned round and took the boys home, later returning to the city to find me. It was such an impossible scene that she decided to go to her sister's house where she could listen to the radio. Luckily, Malia and Ishy's house had survived the attack. It was when Ela, her sister and brother-in-law heard the call for blood donors that they made their way to the hospital, where they'd been waiting in queues for several hours by the time I arrived.

'You need to go to Emergency,' Ela said. I didn't know why she was telling me this until she took me to Ishy and Malia, who were keeping their places in the queue. I could see they were horrified at the sight of me, streaked in oil as I was and wearing only a greasy piece of cloth about my loins. It turned out I had burns to my neck and back, and my hair and eyebrows had gone.

'Emergency's overflowing', I said, 'with those who've lost limbs, stomachs and faces blown away, lungs full of smoke, vomiting oil, suffering deep burns. Have to get back to my ambulance.'

Then I passed out.

That was useless. By the time I had properly come to, Ishy had spoken to some people who had finished giving blood. He came back with a young man who would take over my driving job. I went outside and sat in the shade until Ela and the others came out.

How relieved I was, on the journey home, to know that we had all survived. On this terrible day it didn't seem right that I should suddenly feel happy. Ela was talking about me needing a doctor. 'One of your mum's cures will be fine,' I said, and it was.

Ela's mother trekked back along the paths towards the mountains, taking the boys with her. They returned with a bundle of leaves. My mother-in-law made a healing salve and gave me water from a special spring. The moment it passed my lips I felt the goodness of it.

We learned later that nearby airfields and bases were bombed, too. Hangars were destroyed and rows and rows of planes, on their knees as though awaiting Sunday blessings, were annihilated.

Chapter 12

ORIWIA

When night came and Chappy hadn't returned from the gardens, Oriwia thought he was probably having trouble with his bike. The girls were asleep and she was waiting for him to come home so she could go along and help at the bakery.

An hour later, which gave him plenty of time to walk home, her husband still hadn't returned. Had he had an accident? Could he be lying hurt by the track somewhere?

Coming downhill, flying home, bike chain snapping and wrapping his leg, hurling him.

Headlong into a tree.

She felt tears in her chest, but she choked those. If the bike had broken down not too far along the way and he had bamboo to carry he could've gone back to Paa's to borrow the horse. When he arrived there, Paa wouldn't stop talking. Talk, talk, talk. Chappy too respectful to interrupt. The horse was way out back. The horse was unwilling. Yes, that horse didn't like Chappy. And Chappy? He was no horseman.

Oriwia put the lamp on the sill and made a cup of tea, which she carried back to the window. Couldn't ring anyone because Post and Telegraph still hadn't connected the phone line to the new house. Wouldn't mind betting that horse had deliberately gone under a low branch and Chappy had been knocked to the ground. Couldn't leave the girls to go and look. Dulcie would have guessed by now she wasn't coming to help at the bakery. P&T needed a good shake-up. That evil horse.

Oriwia lay down on her bed and watched shadows that were unmoving, listened for horse hooves clubbing the verge, the clatter and tick of an old bicycle, quick footsteps. What she could hear instead were frog croaks, and faraway ruru calling each other. There were at least four.

She thought of blood.

Perhaps she slept, listening, and thinking of blood.

Then as the flame in the lamp turned pale, her ears caught the pad, pad, pad of hooves. She stumbled from the bed and opened the door to see Paa coming towards her on that swank of an upstart horse. Not that she thought about the horse in those terms at the time, but that's what she said about it in telling the story. Though the horse didn't like Chappy, it gave Paa no trouble. It was swell-headed and choosy, despite being just a workhorse like everybody else.

'Where is he? Where is he?' she called as she ran out to meet Paa.

'I came to see if he's all right,' Paa said.

———

'Years had passed by the time I got to ask Chappy about that day,' Grandmother Oriwia said. 'Instead of trying to remember everything now, I'll write it up tonight and have it ready in the morning.'

'There's no hurry,' I said, knowing she'd been up late doing Aki's Pearl Harbor translation. 'Leave it for another day.'

'All right, I will,' she said. 'Another day. But this is the time, the right place for it. I might just do some of it tonight.'

The next morning she handed this to me:

Chappy on the Run
By Oriwia Star

Before leaving to come home that evening, Chappy went with Paa to listen to the news, which Paa translated into our language for him. Coming across on the airwaves that night was the story of the bombing of the American navy base in Hawai'i by Japanese bombers. 'When he heard what I was recounting,' Paa said, 'Chappy couldn't move or speak. His blood stopped. He was a post. He was a ghost. I thought he would drop to the ground. I put my arm round him, holding him up. There was no blood in his head and I thought he would fold over. "It's not your war," I told him, but nothing was coming out of him. Nothing. Nothing. No word, no movement. Like spiked. Impaled. "Wars come from kings," I said. "Men on high. Presidents."

'The post moved. The ghost reddened. It was already dark. Ghost got on the bike and loosed out. "Don't worry," I called after him. "They all think you're a China Man."'

It was a rough track that Chappy, crouched over the cork-tipped handlebars, flew along in the patch of light that his bike lamp cast over the front wheel. He had to get home to Oriwia, had to see his daughters before the detectives came for him.

Wheels.

Through the rough, over and around stones, under the overhangs, by rocks and humps and stumps and debris. Off the bike at the creek, carrying it through the water on the run. On again. There were two miles to go to the gravel road and the last bump hurtled him onto it, flat.

He was on fire.

Missiles, bullets, sabres. Blood. Moving forward over severed heads and gouting bodies. Screams. Crying. City

*burning. Himself on fire awaiting death. Instead waking
bandaged in a place of screams.*

Dreams.

Chappy sat and spat dust and stones. He was not on
fire or dead, but remembered he had to escape. He stood,
brushed himself down, collected scattered belongings,
tested the bike and sat by the roadside with his knees drawn
up, thinking that he must get home and speak to his wife. In
the morning he would go.

But morning could be too late. The detectives could be
at his door right now. His greatest fear was that his children
could be harmed, but even if not he wouldn't want his
daughters or his wife to watch him being taken away. If he
were to leave it would have to be now, but how far would an
old bike get him?

Instead of going north, which would take him through
the township and past his house, he decided first to go south.
With the help of Mina's husband Piki, who worked in the
railyards at Paekakariki, he could board the morning train
and be away north before most people were up and about.

After a two-hour bike ride and a wait for daylight, Chappy
found Piki in the railyards shovelling coal and asked to be
put on the train, which he could see was already pulling in.
With no time for questions, Piki led Chappy through the
crowd of people rushing for the refreshment counter, to the
luggage van, where he told the guard his brother-in-law and
his bike needed a ride home. The guard shuffled Chappy
and his bike in with the luggage, pleased to do this favour
because he knew that at the end of the day Piki would leave a
good bucketful of best-lump coal on his doorstep.

Piki went to the food counter and came back with a cup
of tea and a hot pie, which the guard passed in to his stowed
passenger. Funny-looking brother-in-law.

If the guard was surprised that his passenger was still on board four hours later when it was time for him to swap trains for the journey home, he asked no questions. None of his beeswax.

'You better hide,' he said, and when he saw that Chappy hadn't understood what he was saying he gave him a shove. 'Dumb cluck. Get in behind your bike.' He pushed Chappy to the floor and rolled him into a dark corner where, as the train pulled out and the new guard clicked his way through the carriages, he went to sleep.

'He's gone, he's gone, without even a goodbye,' I said to Paa. 'He's afraid he'll be put away like Harry Krauss. He thinks they'll take our daughters. Give me the horse. He won't be far.' I went into the house and changed into a pair of overalls. The little girls, coming from their beds and seeing my fright and hurry, shaped their mouths like two bantam eggs and howled.

'Stay here with Paa,' I said, 'he'll cook you an egg. No money, no clothes, no roof, not a word of English.'

I rode off, returning at dusk without finding any sign of Chappy. No tyre marks in the dust. No one I asked had seen him.

When Chappy woke it was to the sound of the van being unloaded. The luggage handlers may have been surprised when he hurried past them wheeling his bike. But maybe they weren't surprised. What the guards got up to, what backhanders were delivered to them, was none of their bizniz. One of them Chows, wheeling.

Chappy went on his way as night was falling. He soon realised that the train had not brought him to the big city of Auckland which he had heard about and where he thought he might be safe. This was not the end of the line. The roads were unsealed, no different from the ones he'd left behind.

The train continued on as he turned into a side road where he found himself in flat country. He could smell earth. Turned dirt.

He realised he was thirsty and decided to return to the railway station for water. His light had gone out.

The platform was empty and the drinking fountain out of order, but at the end of a row of shops opposite the station was a public lavatory and a water tap. In a rubbish bin on a lamp-post, he found an empty whisky bottle, which he filled before finding his way back to the dark side road and the smell of earth. He found a sheltered spot, spread the canvas and lay down thinking about what he had left behind, sure that he'd done the right thing. At least now he'd have a chance of avoiding capture, but most important of all was that the little girls would be safe.

Would they?

There were children alone in streets they had rampaged through, crying, dead, shot, blood streams. Screams. Dreams.

All through the warm night, he lay awake until one by one the birds blinked, voiced, rustled in the few low trees that had begun to be outlined against a sky becoming plum-coloured. There were sounds in the distance – of roosters, hooves and a chain rattling.

Comforted by the familiar noises, he fell asleep.

What woke him later in the morning was the sound of voices, a word here and there, in a language he'd heard before. He covered his head with his hands and rolled himself into the undergrowth.

Bullets. The sabre. Bodies. Fire.

That language, of the China Man.

He opened his eyes. He could see them now, close by, making their way along the ploughed rows – men of China, women of China with their children of China, stooping, gathering handfuls of potatoes and putting them in sling bags which dragged their necks down. Beyond them, in jagged lines, were others in a shambling march, stooping and picking. He waited, trembling and hidden, until the potato pickers had gone from that part of the extensive field. He went on his way.

Gradually his fear left him as he realised he was in a market-garden area. Perhaps he'd be able to find work.

At about the same time as Chappy woke that morning, Paa leaned from his horse to knock on Gary Couper's window.

'Look here, Gary Couper,' he said when the policeman came to the door. Gary opened his mouth but nothing came out of it. He shut it again. 'Chus letting you know Chappy Star gone. My son, Chappy Star. So don't you go saying a word. Was you put Harry Krauss's pot on.'

'I never –'

'Anyone come snooping round asking about my son, you keep your mouth shut.' Paa clicked his horse and rode off.

Later that day Chappy, wheeling his bike, walked into one of the packing sheds and showed the boss his hands, which he guessed would be language to show he wanted work.

'You want a job?' the boss shouted. He knew homelessness and hunger when he saw it and thought this could be to his advantage. He gave Chappy work sewing the tops of full sacks, making it clear he wouldn't get paid. 'Food,' the man shouted, 'and a place to sleep.'

Chappy got the idea. Though he feared the Chinese workers at first, they behaved as though he didn't exist. All they wanted was to work and be paid. Whether he was believed to be an enemy of China or not, he was invisible to them.

At the end of each day, by way of food promised, Chappy was allowed to help himself to discarded vegetables before the pig man came. He was allowed to sleep among the sacks and boxes. In the hour before dark, he would ride his bike to the bridge, dismount and wheel it along the river bank to a sheltered spot where he would wash before riding back to his sleeping place.

It was this riding back and forth that first caught the attention of the people of the town. Already uncomfortable with the seasonal workers who came into the district from all over the place, they were now disturbed to discover there was one hanging about making a nuisance of himself. Children were told they weren't to go playing down by the bridge, instructions which only served to encourage the kids to go and find out what the problem might be. When they'd finished their spying, chanted their Ching Chong Chinaman rhymes, thrown stones and run off without waiting to see if any of the stones hit their target, the kids went home and said they'd seen the man by the river taking off his clothes. He had cockabullies sticking out of his mouth.

Chappy decided to leave. It wasn't the stones that bothered him, most of which were well off target. It was being noticed. The eyes of the town were on him, and anyway the harvest season was coming to an end.

(To be continued)

————

[Daniel, Grandson, it was immensely satisfying to write down the story of Chappy on the run. But now I've read it through I have doubts. I'm wondering if I got carried away. Let me try to explain. If I had married someone I'd known all my life (like Aki), I'd have understood almost everything about him. But the man I married was exotic. The unfathomable core, the unknown of him, was what made my heart beat. What I did know was that he loved and adored his daughters and me, that he knew how to work hard and that he had a clever mind and clever hands. That was enough. He never spoke of his childhood or his former life except for what he told to Aki at the time we became engaged to be married. I didn't mind. I wasn't in the least concerned that I didn't know the name he was given when he was born. He was so delighted to be Chappy Star. If there was anything else I discovered about him, it was not because he told me. I knew that he moaned in the night, sometimes yelled and struggled. Yes, I knew about dreams and screams. The bits I've added about the war in China I made up from Chappy's night terrors, from little hints here and there, what I've seen in movies and read in books and papers. You should be allowed to do that when you're the owner of the script. When he told me how he'd ridden off on his bike and knocked himself out on the road, all he said was that he had 'bad visions' which led him to decide that he must quickly get as far away from us as he could.

While I was writing this up last night, the words to describe the visions came to me because I felt them. Other descriptions and details came because I believed them. They lifted themselves out and put themselves on the page. I admit I surmised some of what I have written. I mean, I don't really know for sure what the kids were chanting to Chappy while they were hurling stones, but I could guess because I'd heard it all before. I don't know if they went home and told their parents about the naked man and the cockabullies. All I know is Chappy was catching tiny fish and eating them and that kids threw mud at him when he was standing in the creek washing. He rushed out of the water to grab his clothes because boys were running down the bank to snatch them. I don't really know how the townspeople felt or what they said to their kids. It's conjecture. So those are my doubts, Grandson. When you go to type this up, you can edit some of it out if it seems like humbug. Later I did proper research into the rest of Chappy's journey. We'll catch up with that later. O.S.]

Oriwia kept all her daily activities going at once, moving from one job to another and back again, talking all the while, going from topic to topic, weaving the threads of her stories together. Aki, however, did one thing at a time, his pace leisurely. After a full breakfast of meat, potatoes, vegetables, bread and tea, he didn't stop to eat throughout the day, though he took a moment here and there to make a cigarette and drink a cup of tea. One task was completed before another was begun. Once all else was done, the recorder was turned on and telling his stories became his sole task until he decided enough had been said.

He was seldom indoors when I arrived. I would look for him on one of the pathways he'd made for his tractor and pickup, and find him in the bush cutting wood for the fire, up the creek checking his hīnaki for eels, or he'd be closer to home, scrubbing his dunny, clearing the spring, mending a fence, shearing a sheep or even killing and butchering one.

My grandmother was always scornful of his lifestyle. 'Only the ghosts to talk to. He could stay here with me if he wished. No, I'm all right he says. Just leave a space in your freezer for our meat. So he comes with his parcels of mutton and pork, enough for both of us, enough for our families, and we pack them away. He's silly. His garden's big enough to feed an army.'

Though my grandmother was dismissive, I admired the way the grand-uncle existed. Living off the land was something so far different from what I'd ever known that I had all these romantic notions about it, that is, until I had to get my own hands dirty. Even so, I found physical work was something I enjoyed. This grand-uncle by double adoption, once he saw that I was willing and eager to learn, seemed happy to have my company and my assistance. I was delighted and proud that he saw fit not to speak English to me.

One day I found him far along the bush tracks where he had set his hīnaki in a dark part of the creek. He was waiting for me because the trap was so full of eels that he needed help to pull it out on to the bank. We cut some of the eels down from head to tail and opened them out. Aki lit a fire in his smoke drum and hung them inside it. We spent the remainder of the day delivering the rest of the eels to various families – all of whom it seemed were related to him, and me. There were those who had grown up with my mother and had stories to tell. It was an exciting day for me, the first of many.

On arriving back at the house I lit the kitchen fire and put water on to boil for making tea, not thinking that there would be any recording done that day, but Aki sat down at the table where I had left the recorder, pressed the button and began.

| Chapter 13 |
AKI

I'm going to talk about letters. Six months after Pearl Harbor was bombed I came home to find a note from Oriwia waiting for me. It told me that Chappy had gone away and had made no contact with them. He'd taken fright after learning that Britain and America were at war with Japan. She believed he was afraid of being arrested and put on Somes Island like Harry Krauss and his sons.

The silly fool. I thought of all the places he could have hidden and been safe: on the farm, in the bush, even as far as the foot of the ranges. Not even the people of the town would have had any idea where he was. As Oriwia went on to say, there was no one looking for him anyway. And what if he was picked up? Mrs Krauss and Dulcie had heard from Harry, and it seemed Somes wasn't such a bad place. Meals were good and prisoners were well treated. After the war they'd all be home to pick up their lives again.

I wrote back and told her not to worry because Chappy was good at starving and the war would soon be over now the Yanks had joined. Well, that's what everyone was saying – that the war wouldn't last long now the Americans were in it.

The ship I was on had formerly been a cruise liner but had now been fitted out as a troop carrier. Some months later we arrived in

Wellington to embark American troops who had been training in New Zealand and were headed for Pacific assignments.

Oriwia was there to tell me off, waiting in a nearby milkbar where she knew I always went for a milkshake. Don't ask me how she knew we were to be in Wellington as it was supposed to be all top secret. It was my words 'silly fool' and 'good at starving' which had got her temper up. I did regret my carelessness because really I was sorry that Chappy had done what he did, and sorry for the distress it had caused his wife and family. I should've said he was tough, he was a survivor, because that's what I meant. I couldn't comprehend Chappy's actions at the time, but certain realisations came later. Oriwia had a gift for Ela. I can't remember what it was, some sort of cake I suppose.

Once back in Hawai'i I thought more about what could be on Chappy's mind. I believed his daughters would not come to any harm in our small town, but I became aware of what was happening on the US mainland, where many thousands of Japanese were interned in relocation camps all over the country – Arizona, Arkansas, Wyoming, Utah, California – all those places you hear about in songs. The majority, though they were already American citizens, were suspected of espionage and plotting sabotage. It was thought that the United States was harbouring an enemy within, an enemy that included not only those Japanese born in Japan, but second- and third-generation Japanese born in America. All, it was believed, would turn against their adopted country in the end. It included whole families. It included orphaned children with any small trace of Japanese blood. All this, told to me by my wife's Japanese brother-in-law Ishy, made me think Chappy's fears were not so silly after all. It was happening there in Hawai'i, too, where there were four or five internment camps.

'Why haven't you been carted off to prison then?' I asked Ishy.

'Too many of us, that's what I think,' Ishy said. 'No place to put us and they couldn't feed us all, so they're just grabbing the important ones – leaders and lawyers and politicians. Anyway, Hawai'i would fall into ruin without our Japanese skills and our little businesses. We make up more than a third of the population you know.' Well I didn't know, only knew that in his business Ishy had contacts all round the Pacific, which included the United States West Coast.

Now the letter from Harry. Harry Krauss wrote frequently to his wife and daughter, and whenever I called in to the bakery Dulcie was always keen to show the letters to me. There was nothing Harry couldn't do when it came to cake decoration. He was known as the best in the district, the North Island – the whole country, some said. Any mother of a bride who didn't want to be outdone in matters concerning her daughter's wedding would know that Harry Krauss was the one to go to for the cake. At any wedding, a cake done by Harry was a talking point. He was aware of his reputation and proud of it, spending many hours perfecting icing roses. [Also bunches of forget-me-nots, lilies, cascades of mock orange blossom, leaves, lattice, scalloping, loops, knots and bows, bride and groom. O.S.] Now he turned his artistry to his letters, and it was his little drawings that Dulcie was always so pleased to share with me.

Bordering each page and meandering into each paragraph were intricate and detailed drawings of flowers, foliage, birds, fish and small creatures, as well as sketches Harry had made round the beaches and bush of the island.

I came from my watch one evening with time off until seven in the morning. I wasn't sure how I was going to get home from the railway station once I arrived as there was no taxi available now. Also petrol and tyres were in short supply. I thought I would go over to Oriwia's and borrow her horse.

However, as I came off the station platform, I saw Oriwia's horse tied up at the bakery. I went in to find Mrs Krauss, Dulcie and Oriwia bunched over a letter from Harry. Daphne and Binnie were there in their pyjamas, eating raspberry buns. They jumped off their stools, excited to see me.

At first the letter the women showed me seemed no different from others I'd seen coming from the island. As I read, the room became silent. The eyes of the three women were on me, and I felt as though I were undergoing some sort of test. I was not so good when it came to reading, writing or speaking English – but nor was Harry Krauss. No sentence was more than I could manage, no words were out of my range. I examined them – the vines and bees and butterflies, the trellises, hearts and flowers.

Then I saw it – a precise and elegant drawing of one of Chappy's baskets. I looked up. Eyes were making holes in me. I reread the letter. The little basket illustrated the sentence: 'A new Chap came Today.' Peeping over the edge of the basket was a little pencilled star. That was how we learned that Chappy Star had been apprehended and detained on Somes Island.

We didn't know the reason for Harry's secrecy, but found out later that when Chappy was taken, he had identified himself under a Japanese name, not the one given when he was born, but the one his grandmother gave him when she took him to the basket-maker. He was determined that nothing he did or said would lead the authorities to his wife and children. Fearing recognition, he'd managed, by turning his face to stone when he saw Harry, to convey to him that he didn't want to be exposed.

Oriwia had an idea what was in Chappy's mind at the time. She said that when Harry and his sons had been taken away, Chappy had told her that they should hide Daphne and Binnie. He wanted to send them to stay with Dorothea. 'I didn't understand his fears, and I still don't understand,' Oriwia said. 'Why would anyone want to take our daughters away, or hurt them?'

It was a relief to all of us to know that Chappy was safe and would be having the regular 'good meals' and 'good bed' which

Harry told about in his letters, but Oriwia was worried that he would be deported.

'They can't do that while the war's on,' I told her. 'Not while they think he could go home and take up arms against Britain and America.'

Oriwia was comforted by this. She told me to take the horse and said she was going home to write a letter to her husband, hoping there would be someone at the prison able to interpret it for him. I wasn't sure that this was such a good idea, since Chappy was trying to keep his Star secret, and I didn't think the letter would reach him in the first place. But, then again, he and Oriwia were husband and wife, which had to stand for something.

Chapter 14

ORIWIA

My grandmother was on the phone speaking to her friend Dulcie when I came into the kitchen for breakfast. The latest translation was on the table waiting for me.

After putting the phone down, she told me that Dulcie still had the letters written by her father during his imprisonment and had invited us to come and read them.

'And by the way,' she said, 'I had second thoughts about writing to Chappy. Instead I included a message in Dulcie's next letter to Harry: "We like the new drawings. Oriwia loves the little basket and the little star." Though Harry wasn't able to pass the message on to Chappy, from then on he included the basket and star in all his letters – Little Star eating an apple, Little Star fishing over the side of the basket, Little Star in a hospital bed, Little Star within a semi-circle of hearts. That's how I was able to keep up with some of what was happening to Chappy.'

———

One day about six months later, the Krauss family received a letter showing that the little star, having sprouted wings, was flying from the basket. The prisoners had all been moved to a camp in Pahiatua by then. It was a new camp built on what used to be a racecourse. Harry didn't like it there. It was cold in winter and, unlike the island, bare of trees. There were no more interesting walks and no beaches. They could not swim or fish. The worst thing of all was that it was too far away for his family to visit regularly. He was lonely, and felt his life was being wasted in idleness while his family and business suffered.

My husband's been deported, Oriwia thought, when she saw the fly-away star; either that or they've killed him. She found out later that by the time she received the message of the flying star, Chappy was already on his way aboard the *Kamakura Maru* to the Port of Marmagao in India. This was where most of the Japanese prisoners were evacuated to as part of a prisoner exchange agreement. Commonwealth and American civilians who had been interned in Japan and other parts of Asia were also exchanged at Marmagao.

———

When we arrived at Dulcie's that night, she was waiting for us in the driveway. She yanked open the car door and pulled my grandmother from the car; 'Oriwia, come, come. This is your grandson. This is Daniel.' Her eyes took in every piece of me. She kept on talking as she hugged and kissed us and led us into the house. 'Isn't he just . . . isn't he just It. His father's height. His mother's complexion. Dear Daphne . . . I can't wait to hear. Daphne, the darling, the princess, and the gown . . . The cake . . . We did three tiers didn't we? The bottom one, the biggest ever. It cut up into a hundred and twenty pieces, I remember that. Handed round. Everyone got a piece. Gave the middle tier to Dorothea, and the top one to Dad to take back to Auckland to Hermie and Kurt. Talk about "coals to Newcastle", giving Dad wedding cake. But it couldn't've been better, the cake or the decorating. Dad said he couldn't've done better.'

Dulcie had cooked a wonderful roast dinner. Her husband, who came in just as Dulcie was taking the meat from the oven, was as reserved as Dulcie was talkative.

After dinner, Dulcie brought out the correspondence between Harry and his family that had taken place during his internment. The letters were fascinating. While we were there Oriwia copied the 'flying star' letter, which I reproduce here, without the little drawings of course.

Dear Marion and Dulcie,

I received yesterday your letter. But remember please two pages. Two pages only were given to me by the senser. So I miss out on the rest of your news. Maybe other pages are returned to you. You can write on bigger paper but only two. It is very cold here and nothing to do, not like on the Island. There are good meals. But I should not be here. I have written my objections to the authorities. There are many arguments and fights here between the Nazis and Anti Nazis and we are separated in our barracks. I keep away from all the trouble not being a Nazi or a Socialist like others. For you my dear wife and daughter I am chosing paua shell broches made here by my friend Helmut. He has quite a business and wants me to join him. But I am pleased to work outdoors instead. A change from baking bread as I did at Somes. But still I help him with the drawings. Sometimes I do the cutting out for him. Only the sawing is done by hand. The grindstone and polisher machines are driven by electricity. He gifts to me broches in return. My selection are butterfly and seahorse. Also there is a ticky for Oriwia who is a helpful friend. The paua shell ornaments are sent out to Yewellers all over the country and go all over the World. I have written now three letters to my Mother. I have received no reply so I worry. Helmut's brother is missing on the Russian front.

So he is worried. His parents' house is bombed and most of the city is bombed also. Both are injured and now they live with his Sister. Please can you go to Buckle Street and get a permission to visit with him. His Uncle is in Auckland. Too far to come and his Uncle is old. His Uncle writes sometimes all the bad news. Our sons are well. They will write their own letters. But they should not be here. They are against that Maniak the same as me. I will try not to complain next time.

Your loving husband and father,

Harry Krauss.

But how did Chappy's deportation fit with what Aki had said, which Oriwia had been counting on? Why would they repatriate a man who could then take up arms against them?

Aki told her later that all those evacuated would be old men, or else too unfit to fight. This is what Ela's brother-in-law Ishy believed. Oriwia thought of the message contained in one of Harry's drawings depicting the little star in the hospital bed, thought of her husband's scars and his fevers. She waited, believing that Chappy would find some way of contacting her.

After a year, she wrote to Aki, asking him to go and find her husband for her.

| Chapter 15 |
AKI

Silly thing. She had this idea that I sailed the oceans of the world and walked through every country and spoke to every man, woman and child – just as we do at home – and that all I had to do was keep my eyes and ears open.

Anyway I didn't want to hurt her feelings, so although I was never in any place where I thought Chappy might be at this time of my working life, I wrote back. 'I'll look for him wherever I go,' I said. Then one day . . .

[I'm going to interrupt here. I'm inserting a little note into this translation because I want to mention that between where Aki has said 'I'll look for him wherever I go . . . ' and 'Then one day . . .' he skipped twelve years. What he tells next happened in 1958 and goes on from there. O.S.]

Then one day I was coming off one of the coastal boats when I caught sight of Mo, who had been my mate in past journeys and who had come back home for a brief time when I first took Chappy there. We had met again once or twice, but that was before the war. Mo was walking about the wharf as though looking for someone. The 'someone' he was looking for was me. My son Eric was waiting with the car to take me home, and I persuaded Mo to come with us, even if it was just for a few hours.

One morning Mo was leaving the docks in Yokohama when he heard someone call his name and turned to see Chappy coming towards him. They sat down together while Chappy wrote a message on a piece of paper and kept repeating 'Aki, Hawai'i.' At the time we met, Mo had been carrying the note for more than a year and had been twice to Hawai'i but not found me. I couldn't make anything of the Japanese characters on the note, but I knew who would be able to help me. On the way home, I called in to see Ishy, who told me that what Chappy had sent me was an address in Tokyo. Ishy knew the area well.

Though I had been to Tokyo twice, it was in the early days. Now I was in a settled job in Honolulu, working on the tugs and machinery of the inner harbour, which suited my family and me. No more roaming. I'd had enough of that.

However, if I was to make my way to Tokyo I'd have to find work on a ship that would take me there, which would mean leaving the convenient job I had. These were the matters on my mind as we walked along the beach that evening – Mo, Ela and me. It was Ela who kept saying, 'You have to go and find your brother.' But I was thinking of my comfortable life. Chappy was alive. The war had been over for thirteen years, so what was stopping him from returning to his wife and children, or at least finding a way of contacting them.

'You won't be happy if you don't go and find your brother.' I knew Ela was right, but I kept trying to think of other solutions. That is until Mo, fingering his chest, said, 'Chappy sick.'

All right, I had to go to Tokyo, even though I didn't know what I would be able to achieve by it. Japanese immigration to New Zealand was not possible at the time, and having a wife and family in New Zealand could seem a falsification if all he had to show was a marriage certificate bearing the name of Chappy Star. I wondered if it could even incriminate him.

Before driving Mo back to his ship, I wrote a note for him to deliver to Chappy saying I would come when I could. I don't know if he ever received it or, if he did, whether he was able to find someone to interpret it for him.

I'd first met my wife's brother-in-law Ishy on the day of our wedding. At the time he was struggling to set up his business and had been away from home seeking custom. Not long after my marriage to Ela, I began helping him in his enterprise by delivering packages to different Hawaiian destinations, and then further afield to marketplaces round the Pacific. Smuggled goods? I don't know. I didn't ask. Anyway, it was all harmless as far as I was concerned – watches, rings and the like. Not like these days with all this trafficking. Maybe Ishy didn't have a licence, or maybe it was just a cheaper or more convenient way of doing things.

Ishy wanted to pay me for the work I did, but I didn't want payment, being only too pleased to be of use to my wife's family. One Christmas, Ishy gave me a very nice jewelled watch for my mother, which I was happy to accept. My mother wore it to social gatherings, especially when she went out to play cards. She said it brought her luck. Its sparkle distracted others round the table while she spread out before them her pairs, three of a kind, queen high flushes, full houses.

After the war, Ishy obtained franchises in several of the best hotels in Hawai'i and trained up young members of the family – his Japanese family, Malia's Hawaiian family – who were interested in that kind of work. It wasn't long before he set up the first of several shops in the city. I'm very pleased to have been part of his success. As a journeyman it was easy enough to do. I knew that Ishy would help me now if he could.

I made enquiries about shipping schedules, and three months

later, after quitting my job, I was signed on to a cargo boat on a Pacific circuit, which would give me a little time in Tokyo.

Ishy, who knew Tokyo well, sent a message to Chappy with details of when I'd be there. I was excited, though hadn't yet contacted Oriwia as I was aware that this venture could lead to disappointment.

The docking port was at Yokohama. I needed to take a train to central Tokyo and was grateful for the map given to me by Ishy. It had instructions for me in English as well as directions in Japanese for the taxi driver who would take me to the railway station, the attendant who would sell me a ticket and the stranger who would show me my platform. I was aware of people. People everywhere as I boarded the crowded train that took us through a concrete landscape – factories, apartments, teeming shopping centres, temples, department stores. Here and there were little wooden houses sitting among it all.

I stepped from the train at Tokyo station, knowing that, despite the throngs, I would not be difficult to find. At the end of the platform, blocking my way while the hordes moved around us, was Chappy.

All I could do at first was wrap my arms round his emaciated body and let tears drip on him. It was like holding a bundle of his bamboo sticks that I used to carry for him sometimes, and just as rattly. We didn't speak.

Another taxi driver sped us through the town, where I expected to see evidence of the destruction of a city. I knew Tokyo had been bombed over a hundred times during the course of the war. What I saw was a new city, a rebuilt city, a modern city, alive, burgeoning.

We arrived at a public garden, a restful place of soft colour by a large lake where pathways went in many directions. After the noise of traffic and the bustle of people there was the quiet stillness of rock.

We sat.

The story Chappy told me, after we'd found our way back into our common language and common memories, was the story of his deportation from Aotearoa and his arrival in Japan. For two years he had lived in the ruins of Tokyo, working at shifting rubble, and was now living in the old part of the city, working in a factory making radios. When not working he would take a train to Yokohama and watch the boats come in, believing he would find me one day. He found Mo instead.

When I tried to talk to him about returning to New Zealand, he wouldn't respond. Although he had wanted to get hold of me it was not, I soon found out, with the hope of being able to return to his wife and children. I did my best to find out his reasons, but all he would say, in a roundabout way, was that it wasn't for the best.

We stood and walked for a while. Carp and turtles broke the surface of the lake. Different kinds of water birds cruised about. I spoke to him of home and family as we made our way out of the park and on to a little crowded restaurant where Chappy ordered bowls of seafood and vegetables that had been dipped in batter, deep fried and seasoned with black sauce and radishes. It was good. I hadn't eaten since I left the ship.

Once again I tried to discover the reason for my brother's reluctance to discuss a return to his wife and family.

'Japan is not loved,' he said. 'In Tokyo I have work. I must help rebuild Tokyo.' He paused. He smiled. 'But I'm happy to see you. You and your little brother.'

Where did that leave me? It was time to return to my ship. What was I to say to Oriwia? He gave me a parcel which I was to take to her.

| *Chapter 16* |
ORIWIA

My grandmother and I were breakfasting together one Sunday morning while she read out what she had translated from the most recent tape. When she finished, I put a cup of tea in front of her and, thinking this was an opportunity to keep her in one place to do some recording, I turned on the tape recorder and asked her how she'd first heard news that her husband was living in Tokyo. She didn't answer that question straight away.

'You know,' she said, 'even though I had asked Aki to find Chappy for me and trusted that he would, in my heart or stomach or somewhere like that, liver maybe, I believed my husband would come home the way he left – riding on his bicycle. Perhaps a new bicycle with a new tinkle. From the time the war ended, I listened every day for the ring and rattle, bike wheels churning the stony road. The sounds were in my dreams.'

Oriwia stood, her tea still untouched.

'Now the telegram. Come with me,' she said.

I pressed the 'stop' button and followed her into the bedroom, where she pointed to a cardboard box on top of her wardrobe and asked me to get it down for her.

We spent the rest of the morning going through the contents – photographs, letters, invitations and so on – but of most interest to this part of the story were the telegram and letter sent to her by Aki.

———

The telegram read: CHAPPY TOKYO LETTER COMING AKI

The first thing Oriwia did when she received the message was to hurry along to Dulcie's, where she flattened the telegram on the bench and asked her friend what it meant.

'It means what it says,' Dulcie replied.

'I'm going to Tokyo,' Oriwia said.

It was Dulcie who persuaded her to wait for Aki's letter.

———

I typed up a copy of the letter. There is a style and a cursive script that Aki and my grandmother, and others schooled in those times, seem to take much pride in and which I could only admire. I wish that I could've reproduced that elegance as well.

> Dear Oriwia Star,
> I hope this find you and your daughters well. You have received the tele gram by now. Chappy send his deepest love to you Daphne and Binnie. Send his love to all the family. Working in Tokyo at a place making electrics. The brother in law of Ela will try and bring Chappy to Hawaii. May be he can do it. You wait there. My wife's brother in law Japanese. You can write a letter for Chappy. Ishy will translate and send to your husband.
> Yours sincerely,
> Tiakiwhenua Morehu (Aki)

Back in the kitchen, I put pies in the oven to heat, and water on the stove to make fresh tea. I was not sure whether I should expect any more of my grandmother after a morning of reminiscing, but she began speaking without any prompting from me.

'I didn't just sit round on my backside waiting for him,' she said.

I reached over her shoulder, pressed the button and went back to my tea making.

'When Chappy and I got married, Paa gifted us this piece of land which had come from the yellow-eyed grandfather, and we set up our business. The first thing we had to do was clear people's bills and pay off my creditors. I'd already begun to do this, but it was slow. However, the war years were good years financially. There was a demand for meat and other produce and we were able to send all our goods straight to market. War was proving profitable in that sense. Also there was work available in the cities. There was more money around. It was all to do with the war effort, but Chappy left in the middle of that. Our land here was covered in fruit trees and vegetable gardens.

'Part of my dream after the war, Grandson, was that my husband would come home to high silky corn, tomatoes ripening, grapes hanging like jewelled bags. Daydreams. It made work light. I wasn't unhappy. I wasn't too lonely.

'The war ended. Harry Krauss returned, but his business as a baker of bread and pies and a decorator of cakes had dwindled. People now owned cars, and had taken their business away from the German spy and his family and gone elsewhere. The same was the case for Hermie and Kurt when they reopened the garage.

'I wanted to build a new house and I wanted a motor vehicle. Another part of what I had in mind for Chappy to come home to was a place with three bedrooms, a living room and kitchen, a bathroom and wash-house. But I had to wait. It was impossible for Māori to obtain finance for home building, and it wasn't until the fifties that a scheme through the Department of Maori Affairs enabled Māori to secure housing loans. Piki and Mina had already built a house this way. All electric apart from the stove. The electric stoves came later, and the refrigerators. Securing a loan was not a straightforward matter for a woman, especially one with an invisible husband, but after many months of to-ing and fro-ing, and having Paa as my guarantor and spokesperson, we received finance. I think Paa must have taken after his yellow-eyed father. He could be formidable. Also, though he had given the land to us, he was still the legal owner of it. I suppose that made a difference. We would inherit at the time of his death.

'Easier to obtain was a truck which I bought when my horse died. They're greedy things, these motors, and less reliable than animals. Some places they can't go at all. But when they're on a decent road and when they're well behaved, they can move you about no trouble. The girls were pleased with it, and I thought Chappy would like it too. Horses had no time for him.

'All this time my husband had been in Tokyo, but I didn't know it. The girls were growing. They worked alongside me. My ambition for them was higher education. Their father would come home, not only to a new house, gardens and good businesses, but to educated daughters. I was determined that they would go in to the professions, medical or legal. Either that or they would run their own enterprises. They would marry educated men, professionals like your father, Grandson, or men well on their way up the ladder.

'I had other ambitions too.' Oriwia stood. 'But right now I've got to go and get ready for tomorrow.'

Something I was used to doing by now was helping my grandmother to set loaves, prepare pies, and make myself useful cleaning down benches and wiping out ovens over at the bakery.

'I'll do these dishes and come over,' I said.

'Bring your notebook and follow me around,' she said. 'I want to keep on talking. About the ambitions. I have to be honest and say that all of what I've been telling you, about waiting for Chappy, wanting this and that for Chappy to come home to, might not have been quite . . . Well, maybe I really wanted these things for myself. Maybe it was nothing to do with Chappy, though I told myself it was. Not that I didn't miss Chappy. I did want him back. But I had plenty to occupy me in the meantime.'

I thought my grandmother was going off on a tangent when, once into the swing of dough making, she began talking about the Krauss family and their misfortunes.

———

Mrs Krauss died a few years after the war ended, Grandmother told me. She was Harry's second wife and Dulcie was their daughter. Harry and his first wife had come to New Zealand from Germany when Herman and Kurt were small boys, but the first Mrs Krauss had died as a result of a fall three years after their arrival.

After Harry and his sons were taken to prison, Dulcie and her mother shut the doors of the garage, the taxi disintegrated in the yard and, with Mrs Krauss in poor health, the two of them struggled to keep the bakery going. It was not just the absence of the men that made life hard; the people of the town had turned against them. Abuse was hurled through the bakery doorway, unfriendly messages were painted on the closed doors of the garage and its side windows were smashed by thrown rocks.

The situation didn't improve once the war ended. Harry took over the role of chief baker once more, Herman and Kurt reopened the garage and rejuvenated an old car to do a taxi service, but nothing was the same. A silence built up around them. They struggled on for three years then, after the death of Mrs Krauss, the men decided they needed a new start. They put the businesses up for sale.

Oriwia saw her opportunity. She bought them out.

Herman and Kurt changed their names to Henry and Kevin Crowe, though their father remained Harry Krauss. His sons went to work for motor firms in Auckland until they were able to start their own workshop again. Harry worked in a restaurant kitchen, planning to save enough money to return to Germany. However, he never did go back to his homeland because he had New Zealand grandchildren by then and didn't want to leave.

Dulcie changed her name by marrying a local farmer. The two met when the man and his fiancée came in and ordered a cake from her and asked her to do the catering for his first wedding. Dulcie was pleased to have the work and asked Oriwia to help her. But since the new wife didn't take to mud, pigs and early mornings, the cake lasted longer than the marriage.

Oriwia had never worked so hard in all her life. With Paa, Taana, Dorothea and the help of the girls, she was still growing and selling vegetables. Now she had a bakery, a garage and a taxi business to run. Paa came and helped with the bakery and soon decided that he could be the taxi driver as well, even though he didn't have a driver's licence. He didn't need one, he said, because he could drive very well. Oriwia thought it was probably true that his being without a licence wouldn't cause problems for anyone. Paa was kind of untouchable.

In the early days, Harry's sons had taken Aki's cousin Lou as a trainee, but a year before he completed his apprenticeship Lou left to go to war. When he returned, he went back to the garage but didn't last long. There was too much flak about how he had fought the Hun in the war and now he was their lackey in peacetime. He couldn't cope with it and just disappeared one day without a word to anyone.

Oriwia went looking for Lou who, once she found him, took over the garage while she looked after the books for all parts of the business. She was happy with that for the time being.

———

'Remember what Aki said,' Oriwia asked, 'about me coming to Wellington to meet him off his boat to tell him off about – ?'

'Silly thing and good at starving?'

'Yes. And that I had a present for Ela's family?'

'He didn't know what.'

'It was a Christmas cake. I'd spent hours on it, but just as well he didn't remember it. It was a show-off cake.'

There had been gift-giving going on between the two families ever since Aki had made his engagement to Ela known – even before that. Gift-giving stakes had been raised over the time, whether the exchange was in shell necklets, pāua ornaments, foodstuffs, lotions and potions, statuettes, cloth, pictures or mirrors.

The cake, now that Oriwia thought back on it, was not given with love but in order to impress. It was a wedding cake recipe, the size of a bottom tier. With the help of Dulcie, who was teaching her the art of cake decoration, she iced the top and sides, then began to decorate it with everything she had been taught. There were rosebuds and full-blown roses, lace and trellis and bells – which Dulcie had tried to talk her out of. 'There could have been red berries, green leaves and greetings. Christmassy. Joyful. There could have been kiwi birds and fernery, fish and butterflies, if there'd been more love,' she said. It seemed important for Oriwia to admit all this. 'The cake was meant to out-rival any gift the Hawaiians had ever given, as if to somehow show what Aki had given up for love.'

Oriwia was quiet for a while as she rolled out the pastry. Thinking we'd done enough talking for the day, I put my pen and notebook down so I could help her.

'We went to a tearoom in Cuba Street,' she said. It took me a moment to realise she was still talking about Aki and wartime. Oriwia had not been into a place like that before. There was such a display of large and small cakes, slices, marshmallow, marzipan, nougat and novelties that it hurt her eyes. That's how she put it.

There were small glass-topped tables and white china, metal jugs, sugar bowls, and teapots in two sizes so that customers could order tea for one or tea for two. There were individual strainers supplied for separating tealeaves. Chatter and light laughter of women dressed for a day in town.

Ever since that day she'd known she wanted to be the owner of a tearoom. Not in Wellington 'or any posh place like that', but in her home town where people knew her. It was years later that she set about making this dream a reality.

| Chapter 17 |
AKI

'His chest is caved in, his breathing shallow and he's the width of a rail,' I said to Ishy on my return to Hawai'i. 'But I couldn't persuade him . . . says he has to stay there and build Tokyo.'

'It's an excuse,' Ishy said. 'Also it's obligation. Citizens of Japan must remain and raise the country from its ashes. They must build the new Japan.' I was beginning to understand, but was concerned that Chappy had said very little about his wife and children. Apart from the gift that he gave me to pass on, it was as though he were a man alone and preferred to be that way. Yet he had contacted me. When I told him of Nunu's death, I could see that he was sad. When I talked to him about his wife and children, Paa and the rest of the family, he said it made him happy to know they were well.

'We have to bring him to the place of sunshine,' Ishy said.

'If we could.'

'What does he do?' Ishy asked.

'He's a basket-maker,' I said. 'And a businessman. He was in the army, in the Japan war against North China.'

'What business?'

'Buying and selling fruit and vegetables.'

Ishy's importing business was doing well by then. He was working long hours, many of them away from home visiting hotel shops and markets in tourist destinations throughout Hawai'i and the Pacific. He needed an assistant who could speak and write Japanese, who could liaise with Tokyo and do the documentation and warehousing of goods.

'What's his name, his own name?'

I didn't know the answer. 'He told me he was from a shamed family and that his true name did not exist any more.' I thought I should tell Ishy that. 'It was something to do with his father being against war.'

'I'm going to Tokyo,' Ishy decided.

I don't know everything Ishy did to get Chappy to Hawai'i. I understand that, after some weeks of negotiation, he was able to engage this 'family member' to assist him in his importing business, the part of it which was to do with bringing souvenir items from Tokyo to Hawai'i. But the same thing that worried me also worried Ishy. Chappy, without exactly refusing to come, was reluctant. Yet we knew he could die if we left him in Tokyo. Oriwia would never have forgiven me if I'd allowed that to happen, nor would I have forgiven myself.

In the letters I sent to Oriwia, I didn't mention the state of her husband's health, nor did I mention his languor, his hesitation about leaving Tokyo, his unwillingness to give good reasons.

'Why?' I asked Ishy.

'Hmm. You ask me why?' Ishy said, pausing for a long time before he continued. 'What you want to think about, Aki, is Chappy's words: "Japan is not loved."'

I was away at sea for two days after that, with plenty of time to put thought to 'Japan is not loved.' Up until then I had dismissed all Chappy's fears about his safety and the safety of his wife and children. They were silly thoughts, especially now that the war was more than a decade behind us.

But I had to remember. As a seaman during wartime, I was on the boats that landed and evacuated troops from the Japan-occupied islands. I knew about the enslavement by the Japanese of native people on those islands, who as a consequence became hungry, homeless and sick, who were beaten and stoned, who died, were beheaded, or killed in other despicable ways. I had heard stories of prisoners being starved and subjected to hard labour as well as to prolonged interrogation and torture. I knew of men, now at home in New Zealand, ex-prisoners of Japan, who had lost their minds because of the treatment they'd received. My own cousin Noddy was one of them. There were those who reviled the Japanese and would have been pleased if the whole race had been exterminated. I had never in any way associated any of this with Chappy, my brother, nor had I thought about how he might feel because of it.

At the time, these atrocities were worse than anything we had heard of before. We were not aware of what we were to find out later regarding camp conditions, ovens and experimentations in other parts of the world. We did not know that, in our own country, more than forty Japanese war prisoners in Featherston had been fired upon and killed. And we did not understand, at first, the force of the two bombs that ended it all.

I tried to put myself in Chappy's place in the hope of better understanding, and decided also to keep my war experiences to myself. What good would it do to share what I knew with Oriwia? It was over, the US occupation of Japan had ended, and we were all buying things from each other now. We were supposed to be friends. That didn't mean that in my far-off homeland there wouldn't be resentment, ill will, and even hatred. I had to remind myself that to many at home the Japanese were despised. Indeed, not loved.

Chappy did come to Hawai'i, and began work two days after his arrival. He had been given a limited work permit with possibility of renewal, and would have an opportunity to apply for immigration to Hawai'i. What I had in mind, and what Oriwia would have had in mind too, was eventual immigration to Aotearoa. We believed this wouldn't be difficult once she and Chappy were together in Hawai'i. I wrote telling her to come. There'd be time for fish and kalo to get meat on her husband's bones before she arrived, I thought.

One day, there they all were – Oriwia, Paa and the girls, in clothes and shoes all wrong for the climate, coming down the gangway with so much baggage I thought I might have to make two trips. But we packed everything in to the car, squeezed them all in and off we went, windows open and furnace air flowing through. Paa was so excited, full of talk about the journey; Daphne and Binnie were exclaiming about this and that along the way; Oriwia was not saying a word. Every so often, Paa would stop talking and, though it was full daylight with no moon in sight, he'd sing 'Sail Along Silvery Moon', or his version of it.

As we walked towards the house, we saw that my wife's family was lined up with Chappy, holding loops of flowers to place round the necks of their visitors. Chappy stood unmoving, apart from his non-stop tears. Paa and I had to hold Oriwia up. She was stumbling. She kept blacking out.

We had done up one of the empty houses for Chappy, Oriwia, Daphne and Binnie. Paa came to stay with Ela and me, but spent most of his time fishing from the beach with Ela's father, or out by the reef in a canoe. They were all to stay for a month while my mother and father and Dulcie looked after the businesses at home.

In the meantime Chappy and Oriwia became husband and wife again, the daughters became their daughters. Fish and kalo put flesh on Chappy's bones and sun gave him back his shine.

Chapter 18

ORIWIA

'Start again,' I said to my grandmother. It was the busiest part of a day when the small town was crowded with people on their way to a big agricultural show. My grandmother, in preparation for the day, had been up most of the night baking. It was not my intention to do any interviewing on that occasion. Instead, I would help her out in the tearoom.

The fact that she'd been working most of the night hadn't stopped her from writing up the translations of Aki's latest recording, and I was sure that there was something she'd found in there that was firing her up. But customers were queuing for cakes and pies and the little tables were full. She was out in the small kitchen at the back of the tearoom, flipping back the hinged lids on the metal pots, spooning in tealeaves, filling them with boiling water. Out she went smiling, in she came talking.

'There were people waiting for us in the bonfire air,' she said.

'Not now,' I said.

'A bubble bubble of words . . .' I took the tape recorder, put it down on the bench and sat her on a stool.

'I'll do the orders. I'll see to the customers,' I said. 'Sit there. Start again. Five minutes. That's all.' I pressed 'record' and took over making the teas.

'There were people waiting for us in the bonfire air, adults and two narrow boys, a bubble bubble of words fluctuating, with a sickening scent of flowers. People were moving apart, coming together, not real. Kind of luminous. There, and not there, like cloud people dropping and fading. I was borne along by arms and shoulders, feet not touching the ground, then sitting, held up, being fanned by large leaves, sipping lime.

'Paa had his arm across the shoulders of Chappy. He and our daughters were seated cross-legged, opposite me. Daphne and Binnie were glancing sidelong at their father, who was the same wisp, the same ghost he was the first time I saw him. I don't remember anything else about that day except that I woke in a little house that had been prepared for us. It was smaller than the first house Chappy and I built at home in New Zealand. It was without a stove or fireplace. Chappy had already gone to work in the city. Daphne and Binnie were out somewhere with Aki and the family.

'Once up, I felt myself floating about in the heat on swollen feet, washing, dressing, eating, drinking, trying to talk but wanting to sleep. I can't sit here speaking into this thing all day, Grandson. If you can't take notes you'll just have to remember.'

Oriwia had come to Hawai'i with the intention that she and Chappy would return home together, but though Chappy listened with interest to what she had to say about the businesses she had developed, and with delight when she described the house to him, it was soon evident that he didn't see himself as part of it. She was undeterred at first and questioned him about his doubts. They were husband and wife, after all.

'I can't be a stowaway any more,' he said, 'or a runaway, or an illegal alien. Can't be an outcast, bringing shame on you and the family in a country where Japan is not loved.'

Oriwia wouldn't take what he said seriously. She'd be able to persuade him. Maybe he'd had some bad experiences as a fugitive that he hadn't told her about. But love would surmount all. She told him this.

'I have to be a true citizen with a name and work,' he said.

When Chappy was taken as a prisoner to Somes Island, he had given the Japanese name that his grandmother had told him to use. This was the name he was known by in Tokyo as well.

'Got to have my true name, Chappy Star. Got to have work and be able to look after my family. My family mustn't be hurt.' And he said again, 'In a place where Japan is not loved.

'I shouldn't be in Hawai'i,' he added. 'And can't be in Aotearoa. I should be in Tokyo where my situation can't affect my adopting family, my wife, my daughters.' He paused for a while before saying, 'One day, when the world has changed. One day when there is a new Japan.'

But Oriwia knew that Tokyo was no place for her husband, where he had been sick and alone in the world.

Not long after that, when Oriwia was giving Chappy a more detailed insight into her business ventures, he said, 'It means you will not come to Hawai'i to live? Just for a few years? Until things get better, until I get my papers, until I can have my name?'

———

'I was stung, Grandson,' Oriwia said to me. 'Live in Hawai'i? I actually couldn't stand Hawai'i, wouldn't have dreamt of living there, even for a few years. The heat made me feel sick and swollen. I felt boiled there. And had this sense of having stepped back in time. I mean, you have to move on in life, don't you?'

———

For Aki to give up his family and his land, Oriwia thought he must be living in paradise. She'd imagined an airy, spacious villa on extensive lands amid palms and large red and orange flowers, facing out to sea. In her mind were crystal waterfalls and deep, clear pools.

Well, some of this she found to be true, but not in any romantic way. There was also dust, rough tracks, insects, a choking atmosphere and a beating sun. Though there was one larger house, with rooms, in the place where the family lived, the other living places were no better than the little house she and Chappy had built when they were first married.

Oriwia loved Chappy with all her heart. Should that have been enough to make her uproot herself, give up what she'd built, give up the work that she thrived on, to go and live in a foreign land even for a few years? The answer had to be no. She didn't know whether love would have survived it.

Should love have been enough for Chappy to leave Hawai'i, or Tokyo, and come back with her to a piece of land that had been given to both of them, and where they had both been happy? She believed it should.

———

'I didn't understand, Grandson. Even if I'd known what Aki talked about on that last tape, I still wouldn't have understood. I believed my husband should have come home with me, that there was nothing we couldn't have faced together. As for "Japan is not loved", what was that supposed to mean? Germany was not loved either, but that didn't deter the Krausses, even though they had difficult times at first.'

———

As for Ela, Oriwia had expected her to be beautiful, not so dark, not so fat, not so bushy haired. This woman, with her large upper jaw and spaced-out protruding teeth, her fleshy nose and little black eyes, had got hold of a father for her children. She'd found herself a husband fool enough to provide for her whole family. And nothing Ela said or did on Oriwia's first visit caused her to change her mind about any of that.

Chappy did have a plan, one which he and Ishy had worked out together, but it was too drawn-out for Oriwia, who immediately dismissed it. The idea was for Chappy to gain citizenship in Hawai'i where he had work and could save the money he would need. He would change his name and re-register as Chappy Star, then enter New Zealand as the spouse of Oriwia Star.

It would take years.

Oriwia argued that he must come with her right then and they would sort everything out once they arrived home. However, Oriwia's time in Hawai'i was cut short. Her stay there still had two weeks to go when she found out something that had her heading home with daughter Binnie in tow. She discovered that Binnie had fallen in love with Lani, who, before they all arrived in Hawai'i, she had known only as one of the bad boys. Falling in love at eighteen was not on Oriwia's agenda for her daughter, and falling for 'some kind of green-eyed sand prince who did nothing but float about in a canoe all day' was certainly out of the question. When she caught the two of them walking hand in hand along the beach, she snatched Binnie by the arm and hurried her home to pack. It was January, near the end of the summer holidays, and her younger daughter was soon to begin university studies at Victoria College. Her older daughter, Daphne, despite her mother's wish that she study medicine, was in her second year of training to be a nurse; she had returned home earlier in the month.

———

'Your mother could have become a doctor, you know, Grandson,' Oriwia said to me, 'but at least she did the right thing and married someone with ambition and a secure future.'

My grandmother became thoughtful, sad. 'But then, of course, she left me, they left me, and there you all are living on the other side of the world.' She paused again. 'Anyway, why should I complain? I have you here right now, don't I?'

———

Oriwia and her daughter left Paa behind in Hawai'i. He was having a great time.

Chapter 19

AKI

C happy endeared himself to Ela's family right from the time he landed in Hawai'i. The same couldn't be said of Oriwia, though the family was too polite to say anything about that. During the first visit, they didn't come to know the real Oriwia, the gutsy, loyal, big-hearted girl and woman we all knew at home. I could see they thought her dissatisfied and snobbish. Disappointment and heat had a lot to do with her frown and her silence, at times her absence from our company. Now she's going to listen to what I've said on to this machine here and she'll have a go at me. But, too late, the words have already flown out of my mouth. There's more to come.

Even though Paa laughed his head off when he found Oriwia had gone home dragging her love-struck daughter, it was no laughing matter to me. I was insulted. Ela and I had been married nearly twenty years by then, and during the first year of our marriage I had filled out adoption papers that made me the legal father of Eric and Ke'alohilani. Though we had expected to have more children, and I had come off my ships in those early days hoping to be given a very special piece of news, this had not happened. But we were content with our family as it was.

Eric and Lani are my true sons, the most loving of boys. When I was home, they came everywhere with me; they waited for hours on the road when they knew I was coming; they clung to me. They called me Father.

Now they were young men in their early twenties. I found work for Eric on the boats. He became a journeyman, travelling the world as I had, and was home about once every three months. He had married the previous year. Lani didn't have paid work but stayed home to help his grandfather and make sure there was a daily supply of vegetables, wood and fish. It may have seemed an idle and idyllic life to an onlooker, but Oriwia should have known better. He was a quiet, home-loving young man. This didn't mean he was useless. What he did was important to the family. Two young people walking hand in hand didn't seem to me a reason to insult my wife's people. Though he never said so, I know Chappy was embarrassed that his wife and daughter had gone off in the way they did.

'Don't worry,' Paa said. 'She'll be back.'

'With an apology,' I said.

'And without her daughters. Ha, ha.'

My poor Lani. Personal experience had taught me how consuming new love can be – how it can sting, bring you out in a cold sweat, how tender and crushed you can feel. Yet, though I had known uncertainty in love, which was like a grab to the throat, unlike Lani I had not known rejection or been forbidden. Oriwia must have known what it was like, too, as she waited for me to return from the sea to put her proposal to Chappy all those years before.

My son lost all his exuberance and spoke of joining a ship. I asked him to wait until I could get harbour work again, as on returning from Tokyo I'd been unable to go straight back into my old job. This meant that I was away at sea much more than I wanted to be and Lani was needed at home. 'But don't give up on love,' I said, though to be truthful I thought the situation impossible.

Oriwia was a determined woman and little Binnie's heart could change once she made new friends and saw more of life.

A letter arrived for Ela two or three months later, in which Oriwia attempted to explain that she had certain careers in mind for her daughters and was determined they would complete their training and education before thinking of love, marriage and children. She said she had acted wrongly in leaving the way she did and was sorry for the hurt this would have caused. She explained that the hopes she'd had for the visit had come to nothing and that she'd been feeling unwell most of the time. In the last part of her letter, she had words to say about Lani – to do with his fine looks, his manners, his good nature and kind disposition, his good humour.

It infuriated me. Why bother to apologise when the message between the lines was saying that Lani wasn't good enough for her daughter?

Anyway, there was something Oriwia didn't know about my Lani and her Binnie – but that's getting ahead of the story.

Chapter 20

ORIWIA

'**F**or a month after I returned,' Oriwia said, 'I went about murdering my pots and pans, mistreating fruit, vegetables and loaves of bread, and threatening my daughters. But what good did that do me? You have to get on with life. I settled down, thought about my situation and decided there were things I needed to do, some things I needed to find out.'

———

First of all, Oriwia went to the Department of Immigration armed with her marriage certificate. She wanted to end this nonsense once and for all and get Chappy home as soon as possible. But it was a mistake to go there with the truth. She should not have told the story of how her husband had disappeared during wartime, been imprisoned and deported. She should have lied, she said.

The woman behind the counter twisted her mouth sideways, breath blowing out of a gap in the corner of it as though she were avoiding blowing smoke in Oriwia's face. Her eyes went in the opposite direction to her mouth. Oriwia thought that behind the counter at floor level, hidden from view, could've been a pair of shoes two sizes too small, twisting the woman's feet and making her face screw. The woman asked if Oriwia had married an illegal immigrant, an enemy alien. 'Did he jump ship?' she asked, pouncing. 'Plenty of them around those days. Pommies. Portuguese.'

Afraid that if she took this matter any further it could lead to an investigation, Oriwia left there biting her tongue. She decided to turn her attention to 'Japan is not loved.'

While Oriwia was in Hawai'i, Chappy told her the story – written down earlier under the heading of 'Chappy on the Run' – of his going off and finding himself in a market-gardening region south of Auckland. After he had cycled away from that first town followed by thrown rocks and Ching Chong chanting, he was like one of the itinerants of earlier years, a roadie seeking work. The weather was becoming cooler.

However, he was given employment here and there in exchange for a meal or a coin, though he wasn't given accommodation – not that he had asked for it. He was always sent on his way before dark, often with dogs at his heels. He'd look for a place to spend the night – in bush, under a bridge or in a doorway of an unused building – always knowing that he could be discovered and imprisoned at any moment. He was not afraid of being arrested now that he was away from his family, and thought that if his situation became too bad he would present himself at a police station. But he was determined to remain free for as long as he could, because what he did fear was deportation and never seeing his wife, his daughters and his family again.

What Chappy didn't know at the time was that the words Paa had called to him on the night he left were true – that people would think he was a China Man. It was this mistaken idea that people had about his origins that was helping him to evade custody. Chows were all right in their place, people said. Just leave them alone. They worked hard and didn't need much pay because they lived on the smell of an oily rag.

Going from one place to another became his life for the next year and a half. Chappy knew nothing about the progress of the war, but in his journeying witnessed the comings and goings of uniformed servicemen and army vehicles.

During the next summer harvest, he was able to mingle with migrant workers and find paid work. He spoke to no one and nor was he spoken to. He bought a blanket from a surplus store, which helped him to survive the next winter but didn't save him from beatings. In the following cold season, he became ill and unable to work. One day he woke to find himself in a hospital bed wearing a pair of striped pyjamas and wondering what had happened to his bike. There were people observing him, questioning him, voices getting louder and louder with each repetition, as if decibels would aid his understanding. Though he guessed what they wanted, there wasn't any information about himself that he felt like giving. He was too sick for that.

The hospital authorities decided to bring in an interpreter, so went to Mr Lee to ask for assistance. Mr Lee was a Chinese man, owner of several stores in town. He mingled with other business people and attended town meetings. Chappy didn't know the name of the man or why he was there in the hospital. All Chappy knew was that there was an exchange at his bedside, between a Chinese man with gold in his teeth who was dressed in a three-piece suit and clutched a bowler hat, and the hospital sister. At one stage the Chinese man had folded himself in half, laughing. After this folding there was confusion and further exchange.

Not long afterwards, Chappy found himself in the local lock-up, before being taken under escort to Somes Island as a prisoner of war. That's all he had told his wife about the time between pedalling away from name-calling stone-throwers, and the time of his arrest.

Was there more to know? Instead of bad-mooding round the place, Oriwia decided to leave others in charge of the bakery and go and find out. She thought she'd be setting up a tearoom by this time and had worked out how she was going to finance it, but there was too much else on her mind. She went on a journey.

———

'Grandson, I took notes. I'm going to find them and write the story for you.'

Chappy the Legend
By Oriwia Star

I bundled my daughter off to Wellington where she would stay with her Aunt Ti and do her studies. I muttered my unhappiness to Mother Dorothea, who, witnessing the crashing of saucepans, thought she'd better stay a while with me. My marriage was over, thumping down dough, slapping pastry, my daughter was stupid, salting and peppering mince for making pies.

'You're no good here,' Dorothea said. 'Go to Auckland and see your sister.'

'Sister.' Thump and bang.

'All that temper mixing in your buns and pies. Customers'll get the stomach ache.'

'Stomach ache.' Knuckle knuckle.

'How long since you saw Moana-Rose?'

'Moana-Rose.' Sigh.

'I enjoy running the bakery for you.'

'Ten years.'

On my way to Auckland by train I thought about Chappy's journey along this same route in 1941, nearly twenty years earlier. After many hours, when the train stopped at the station where Chappy had left the guard's van and cycled away, I wanted to get off and somehow find him. I put that thought out of my mind as Moana-Rose was expecting me in Auckland, but decided I would return within the next few days. Chappy had not only arrived in this place, but had later been hospitalised and apprehended there, before being taken under guard on a return journey. What could the town tell me?

As the train moved out into the countryside, spread out on either side of the railway line and stretched to the horizon were the market gardens, an enormous patchwork of tilled soil, cabbages and carrots, but at this time of the year it was mostly acres of onions, already harvested, laid out to harden before packing. These were places where my husband had found work, the kind of work not unfamiliar to him. The scattered homesteads were places where he'd been given food or had dogs sooled on to him.

Three days later my sister and I arrived back at that same station. Though I had no plan, I'd brought a notebook and pencil with me. There was a sky of hectic blue, like medicine bottles, as we headed towards the main shopping area.

To do what?

I was dressed in a wool suit – charcoal grey, with a lighter grey hat and gloves – and black shoes with small heels. My sister had on a cream suit, also wool, the jacket trimmed with brown piping. It was the outfit she'd worn to my wedding, but now without hat and gloves. She'd had nothing new since my wedding day from what I could tell. She never went out anywhere as far as I knew.

My brother-in-law, now a watersider in Auckland, provided well for his family. They had a good house to live in and the cupboards were always full. What I didn't like about Benjamin was that he kept my sister poor. The older children were away working and only the youngest was at home. Times were different now, I thought. Moana-Rose could have work of her own, modern conveniences for the house.

New clothes. I noticed that her husband had several pairs of shoes and a good gabardine coat. And why were they living in Auckland? He could just as easily have been a wharfie in Wellington. I had this idea that he wanted to keep my sister away from us.

What I was starting out to say before I sidetracked on to my brother-in-law was that though summer was coming to an end and birds were already clubbing together above the fields, it was a warm day and a dusty trudge from the railway station to the shopping centre. It was a relief to arrive on to the concrete slab footpaths under the verandahs of Farmers Trading, Haberdashery and Wool, Glass and China, Newsagents, Furniture, Tobacconist, Butcher, Fishmonger, Department Store – where I could've gone in and bought for my sister a new hat or shoes, but we kept walking.

It was the picture theatre that stopped us. We lingered by the billboards showing advertisements for *Desk Set*, starring Katharine Hepburn and Spencer Tracy. Katharine Hepburn with her high round cheeks, her red hair lifted in rolls away from her face and her red mouth laughing, had her arms round the neck of Spencer Tracy, whose raised eyebrows and 'O' shaped mouth showed mock surprise. Behind them were little scenes of love and laughter.

'We could see it this afternoon and get a later train home,' I said.

My sister frowned. 'We'll still be back in time to get Benny's tea . . .' but she looked doubtful.

'Yes let's, let's,' I said, 'after we've . . .'

Now that we were in 'Chappy's town' I wasn't sure what we were going to do.

'Maybe we'll find the police station and ask if they know the whereabouts of the Chinese man who was at the hospital when Chappy was taken there. But we'll get a drink first,' I said.

We crossed the road to a dairy, where the headline on the news-stand announced the disintegration of Sputnik Two. 'A drink, and a newspaper to read on the train.'

The woman behind the counter was chatting, full of smiles, to her customers, but her expression blanked when we came in. This wasn't a new experience for us. The woman had a floured face, orange lips and a dusty frizz of hair tied back. A large brooch studded with glass rubies assisted green buttons to tighten the stretched cloth over her cabbage breasts. At the grim sight of her, my sister dodged in behind me, pulling at my clothing as a signal that we should leave, but I knew that I was going to make this woman speak to me no matter how long it took for her to dawdle with the other three customers, no matter how long she chose to ignore us.

Eventually I ordered a lemonade and an orange squash, which were provided to me without a word, my change pushed across the counter.

'My sister and I are in town enquiring after a Chinese gentleman who we believe lived in the district in the early 1940s,' I said in my snottiest voice.

A customer on her way out stopped and turned, took another look at these strangers in town, overdressed and brown.

'Mr Lee,' she said.

This name was echoed by others who had their ears tuned from other parts of the store and who then converged towards us.

The blanked shopkeeper couldn't help herself. 'Is he a friend of yours?' she asked through a slitted mouth, her eyes averted.

'I would like to know his whereabouts, please, if you can help.'

'Nineteen forty-two. That was when,' someone said.

'That was the time.'

'In the paper.'

'Our town.'

'Mr Lee.'

'Unmasked this –'

'Jap spy.'

What my sister and I discovered was that there was a whole legend which had built up around the Japanese spy who had mysteriously appeared in their midst disguised as a China Man.

Spy.

The word cut deep into me, but I remained calm and allowed the stories to come, told by gossips who, except for one, had never set eyes on Chappy.

This Jap spy had been put ashore from a spy submarine which had entered the Hauraki Gulf undetected.

'Town became famous.'

'In the paper.'

'It wasn't until after the war was over that people found out New Zealand was a hair's breadth away from being invaded by Japan.'

'Could all've been speaking Japanese by now ha, ha. Haw, haw.'

Anyway, this Jap fellow had infiltrated the country, mixing with the migrant workers, all the time gathering information and drawing up maps and charts which he rolled up and hid in the handlebars of his bicycle. Alby and his mate were the heroes.

'He lives just down the road these days. Alby.'

'Wait on, we'll ring Alby.'

Alby turned up, only too pleased to tell how he and his mate Kev had been playing round the ditches when they came across this bashed up dead man with a bike on top.

That was up in Runciman in their farming days. The boys ran off to Kev's place and told his parents. Kev's old man thought he'd better go and have a look.

Kev's dad had a poke around, realised the fellow was still alive, bundled him into the back seat of his car and brought him back to the hospital, a whole hour's drive. Kev's dad reckoned if he knew then what he was to find out later, he would've left the Jap where he was. The boys could've had the bike.

Alby and Kevin were interested in the bike, which they said rightfully belonged to them. Finders keepers. But by then it was in the hands of the police. They went down to the police station a few days later to lay claim to it only to find that the bike was in many pieces, having been thoroughly searched in all its tubing for proof of espionage. Successfully searched, all the talkative ones in the dairy believed, otherwise why would that chap have been taken away and locked up.

Although the two boys failed in their bid to get the bicycle, they were given a cake of chocolate as a reward, and there was a story about them, with a photograph in the local paper of them holding up the chocolate. Spy-Catchers. Alby offered to nip home and get the newspaper cutting, which was in his mother's photograph album – gone all yellow but you could still read it.

I told him we had to go.

'Mr Lee, too. In the paper.'

'They called him up to the hospital to be the translator but that spy fella wasn't giving anything away. I know. I was there. I was a nurse at the hospital those days.'

'Owns half the shops round here, including this one, Mr Lee does.'

'Is he a friend of yours?' Ruby Brooch wanted to know, pasting on a smile just in case.

We left there almost at a run. I was holding back anger and sorrow as we hurried along under the verandahs away from the shoppers, workers, kids running – to the dusty road where I cleaned out with tears and huffs and snorts and misery. We'd left our fizzy drinks on the window ledge.

My sister steered me off to the railway station, where she tried to calm me down with drinks of water collected in paper envelopes provided at the water dispenser. 'We'll go to the pictures,' she said. 'Come on, come on, Katharine Hepburn. Have a good look at her, won't we? Get home and do our hair up like that.'

I had to snap out of it. Moana-Rose was already walking along the platform, almost running, giggling. 'We used to? Hairdos like . . . you know . . . like Greta . . . Greta G . . . Garbo.'

'*Flesh and the Devil*,' I said running after her shouting with laughter, catching up to her, collapsing against her, wobbling along, hooting and crying until we neared the pavement and the verandahs. 'Cut our hair off, to be G . . . Greta.'

We straightened our faces, straightened our legs, walked a straight line to the picture theatre without looking at each other. We wobbled and giggled again at the sight of Katharine Hepburn's wide open laughing mouth, gathered ourselves and went in.

That town. That town. I'd never been in a place like that before.

We went inside to purchase tickets, asking for seats downstairs in the mid-section just as we often did in our little theatre at home.

'Gallery only,' the boxed ticket seller said.

I didn't understand at first. There were patrons already making their way in through the downstairs entrance.

But Moana-Rose knew. She'd heard of this. She was standing behind me speaking our language. We only ever spoke our language at home, not in public places, but now she was whispering into my neck that this must be one of those segregated theatres where Māori were barred from downstairs seating.

There was fury going on inside me. I thought of standing my ground, allowing the queue to lengthen behind me until I got what I wanted, but I became too dispirited. We left and returned to the railway station. 'If Chappy and I had come to the theatre together,' I said, 'he would have been allowed downstairs but I would not.'

I stayed with my sister for another week, but I regretted that I hadn't spoken with Mr Lee. Now that I knew his name, I was able to look up his address in the phone book. I rang and made an appointment.

The next day I went back to the town, on my own this time. I think my brother-in-law's patience was wearing thin with his wife spending so much time with me. I took a caraway seed cake.

Mr Lee was a man in his eighties, kindly and hospitable. I explained that I was trying to find out as much as I could about the circumstances of the man I had married, the Japanese man whom he had been asked to be interpreter for at the hospital back in 1942.

He told me of that day when he'd been asked to find out the name and details of the man in the hospital bed. 'A very sick man. Cuts, bruises and broken bones,' Mr Lee said. 'I would've helped if I could, but the man in the bed was not Chinese. I didn't know his language. When I told the hospital authorities this I think it made them suspicious of me. I told the sister, whose pen was poised above the information sheet, that I thought the man was Japanese. So I was very largely surprised, Mrs Star, when the good sister turned and spoke to me in a most impatient manner saying, "Mr Lee, if you don't mind, would you *please* at least ask this man his name and his place of abode?"'

It was then that I witnessed something that Chappy had described to me: Mr Lee bent right-angled laughing.

At that moment all the anguish I had felt since my last visit left me and I began to laugh, too. We sat there, two strangers facing each other, laughing until tears gathered and ran and poured, and we gasped and choked and hiccupped, the two of us.

It was all to do with sorrow.

A darling girl brought us tea in fine cups, and I found myself telling Mr Lee the story of my life, about Chappy and me and our children, our lives together and apart.

'You have suffered in your life, Mrs Star,' he said.

'I've known great happiness in my life, Mr Lee,' I said.

It was a wonderful day. My soul was rinsed. I was looking forward to my return home, the conversion of the bakery into a tearoom, the letters I would write. One day my Chappy would join me.

End

| Chapter 21 |
AKI

It was a year before I was able to get shore work again, another six months before Lani took employment on a trans-Pacific cargo ship.

Oriwia wrote to Chappy frequently. I would read the letters for him, translating from English into Māori. Although Oriwia could easily translate spoken Māori into English and write it down, she was unable to write the letters in her first language. She hadn't been schooled in it. None of us had. We had never seen the written form of our language. If I wasn't home, Ishy would translate the letters into Japanese. Though Chappy could speak English by then, he couldn't read or write it. Ah, the fun we had with our languages.

They were newsy letters about the progress of their daughters, the health of Paa and the family, her work and business, the house and garden, the state of the roads, the railway and the government. I looked forward to these letters, which always ended by mentioning Chappy's return. Chappy himself was silent on the matter.

'Ah, love,' said Ishy after reading one of Oriwia's letters. 'Love gave Chappy to me, now love will take him away to New Zealand at some far edge of the earth, just when I wanted to take him into my business.'

'I'm not so sure that he'll agree to go,' I said.

On my mind was what Oriwia had said about love overriding

everything (except if it came to her living in Hawai'i). Was there more to Chappy's silence than the belief that his presence among his family in Aotearoa would harm them?

It wasn't the right way to ask but it seems to be the only way I know. 'Do you still love your wife?' I asked. There are times when Chappy can tolerate my manners, but this wasn't one of them. He faced away from me, unmoving and silent for so long I thought he would ignore my question altogether. Did that mean he secretly wanted an end to his marriage? My stomach dropped to my feet as I thought of Oriwia, my sister; Chappy, the great love of her life.

'Duty,' he said, and walked away from me.

But what was I to make of his answer? It was no remedy to the fear that had settled in the empty space my gut had left behind.

'One word, "duty", is all I can get out of him,' I said to Ishy. Ishy laughed, which in the mood I was in made me wish I was away at sea.

'Ha, ha. He's not like us cosmopolitan Japanese,' he said. 'No, no. Different talk. Different head.'

'Look, he's my brother . . .'

'Your brother must look after his New Zealand father, look after his wife, look after his family, provide for them.'

'He can do that at home.'

Out of politeness Ishy didn't respond, which gave me cause to reflect. At home in New Zealand, Oriwia was the owner of small businesses which kept her working from early morning until dark, but which I knew would barely be providing a living for the family. I didn't know how she had afforded to buy the businesses from the Krausses in the first place. If Chappy did return, though he would be able to lessen Oriwia's workload, it would be unlikely to make a difference to their income, the town being too small for business expansion. Added to that, I had to admit that Chappy would find it difficult to find work of his own. I thought he should have explained all this to Oriwia, but she wouldn't have listened anyway.

['Kore taringa,' he said on tape, Grandson, about my not listening, implying that I had 'no ears', which is insulting. How would he know? And what a cheek to talk about my enterprises in that way. I was doing very well. Anyway, I won't let myself get sidetracked. I just wanted to express my objections. But since it has come up, I might as well make a confession as to how I afforded to buy the businesses. It was all my own doing, financed by the sale of my mother's land. Yes, I sold your inheritance, Daniel. Thinking back to what was reported to me when I was a child – that my mother had told my father to sell some of the land to build a store because he was a trader, not a farmer – I felt she would have given me permission. All that's left now is my sister's share. But this land given to Chappy and me by Paa, I will never sell, and I'll never move from here. O.S.]

'And duty to his country,' Ishy said. 'In the work he does here, he's helping rebuild Japan.'

'He always said he didn't have a country,' I said.

'This is the *new* Japan,' Ishy said. 'It's a different story.'

'And I don't know why there should be more bad feeling against your race in my own country, which is so far away, than there is here in Hawai'i whose harbour was blasted to matchsticks, people along with it.'

'It's not all peace and love here either,' he said. 'Not by a long way. But what you have to remember is that Japan has been paid back by America.'

'The two bombs?'

'After that, we all had to start again.'

'But the little countries of the Pacific?'

'Their hearts are still burning.'

There was something Oriwia didn't know about my Lani and her Binnie.

Chapter 22

ORIWIA

One Sunday, Oriwia was preparing to cut pattern pieces from material that she had laid out on the table by her front window when she saw three people coming from the morning train. She was making summer frocks for Daphne and Binnie from dress-lengths she'd bought at a sale. The dress she'd made for Daphne was hanging on the door with the hem tacked ready for hand stitching. She'd pinned the paper pattern on floral print for the frock she was about to cut out for Binnie.

Coming towards her house with something on their minds were Aki, Binnie, and she didn't know who else. Up until then she didn't even know Aki was in the country. The other, she soon saw, was 'that son of his'.

The moment she recognised Lani she knew what scene she was looking at. What was before her was a daughter with a ruined career, three years of study and money down the drain, a lifetime of poverty and drudgery ahead of her, disgrace, shame, and their reputation as a family in ruins.

'So what have you come to tell me?' she spat out of the flung-open door as they arrived at the end of the path, and without even a greeting. Aki was walking ahead as a kind of shield, as though he thought she might take to them with scissors. No one spoke, only began removing their shoes, Binnie in tears. 'Why wouldn't she be crying? And that other one with his eyes scraping the ground in front of him.'

All this happened three years after Oriwia pulled Binnie from Hawai'i. After many tears, she settled in to begin her university studies. She was living with Aki's sister, her Aunty Ti.

Binnie's sister Daphne had graduated from nursing school and was working in Wellington Hospital, where she met 'the great Dane', who was visiting this country before taking up a position in a bank in Switzerland. He'd been brought into the hospital following a skiing accident, and by the time he returned to Switzerland Daphne had a ring on her finger. A year and a half later they were married.

———

'A girl with some sense, a man with some ambition in life,' my grandmother said. 'But then . . . but then of course . . . then she left me, after the wedding they left me – which they had to do. Grandson, you all left me to go and be born and live on the other side of the world.'

———

After Oriwia had pulled her daughter from Hawai'i, she thought that was the end of whatever there was between Binnie and Lani. So it was, for more than two years. In the meantime, seeing Lani so unsettled and despondent, Aki found work for him in a ship's galley, hoping to divert him from sadness. Maybe it did, maybe it didn't. What the ship did do was put him ashore one day in Wellington where he and Binnie met by chance in Cable Car Lane.

Everyone was to blame for the condition that Binnie was now in on this Sunday morning – Aki, Ela, Ti, Daphne, all of whom must've known what was going on, according to Oriwia.

'Out of my sight,' Oriwia ordered. 'I don't want to see any of you ever again.'

Binnie and Lani left, but Aki did not, despite Oriwia's 'You too. Out. Out.' He sat in an armchair and picked up a *Woman's Weekly*.

At the table by the window, Oriwia tore fabric and pattern pieces from top to bottom, stamped off into the kitchen and began cleaning out cupboards and scrubbing the floor – not usual tasks for a Sunday.

Late in the afternoon, she looked in on Aki, bringing tea and cake.

'He'll do anything for her,' Aki said. 'Anything except –'

'Except leave her,' Oriwia said.

'But if he did leave –'

'She'd go with him.'

'You think he's not good enough. I'm insulted on behalf of my son,' Aki said. 'You and your stuck-up ideas.'

'Go and get them,' she said. 'Take my car.'

‎———

'He can marry my daughter,' she said when they returned, ignoring the couple and speaking to Aki, 'if he comes here and learns to fix cars.'

‎———

'What if they'd refused, Grandson?' my grandmother asked me. 'What if they'd left me?'

‎———

Binnie was twenty-one, had money of her own and could easily have gone and made her home in Hawai'i. Oriwia planned that they'd go to Wellington the next day and make a booking at the registry office, but she hadn't got all the words out before she was interrupted by Aki.

'Our children will have a proper wedding,' he told her, 'at the marae, with a minister, followed by a feast in a large marquee, all witnessed and celebrated by their elders and families. Your daughter will have a proper wedding gown. My son's –'

'Your son, your son,' Oriwia said with her voice rising. 'Your son has ruined my daughter –'

'Your daughter is not ruined, she's having a baby. A baby, Oriwia.'

'Wedding gown? Wedding gown, with a bump in front you mean?'

'Not a bump, a baby.'

'Shame.'

'Not shame, a baby.'

———

'Well, you can stick in one place or you can get on with life,' my grandmother said. 'If I was to hold on to my daughter I would have to listen to what Aki was telling me. And yes, of course when I calmed down there was a baby already reaching out its arms, whose breath was already on my neck, who was already sitting in front of me on an ambling horse, although there was no horse by then.'

———

They decided on a summer wedding, which gave three months for everyone to put their minds and efforts to wedding preparations and the reception of visitors from Hawai'i. In the meantime, Binnie returned to her studies with just a month to go before completion.

The wedding dress, Oriwia thought at first, would have to announce her daughter's sullied condition by being blue, pink or apple green. Then she decided it would be white, virginal. If she was to do a turnaround with this wedding, let it be a full turn. Aki's sister Ti agreed with her. Ti was to be the dressmaker.

When Ti left home at fifteen, she'd found work as a machinist making shirts and trousers in a clothing factory. During the war, she made army and air force uniforms, and later went to work for a tailor where she learned pattern-making and fine stitching. It was Ti to whom the family turned for bridal wear, bridesmaid's dresses and presentation gowns.

'I went to see *Funny Face*,' Ti told Oriwia. 'Come down in the weekend and we'll go and see *Funny Face*. Little Binnie's the dead spit of Audrey. We'll make her an Audrey gown.'

Binnie did resemble Audrey Hepburn in some ways. She had the same slight figure and the same quickness. Her hair was dark and cut short, her skin pale and clear, her face elfish and bright. 'She doesn't have Audrey's large, sweepy eyes, nor her wide mouth,' Oriwia said. 'My Binnie's eyes are watchful and they show her heart. She has a gentle smile.'

But Oriwia thought Ti was right, Audrey's *Funny Face* gown, with small adjustments, would be perfect for Binnie. However, they thought cap sleeves and a ballerina-length skirt a little too modern for their home town and went for long, fitted sleeves and a full-length skirt. All in white satin, it would have a fitted bodice, rounded neck, a V waistline in front and a sheer organdy overskirt. When they arrived home from the theatre, Ti drew sketches, took Binnie's measurements adding 'room for expansion', and soon had a pattern drafted.

It was not only a perfect gown that Oriwia wanted. Everything else had to be perfect too, for the people coming. She had to show the visitors 'we weren't "nobodies"'. The Hawaiians had to realise they were privileged to have Aki and Chappy living among them, even though temporarily.

'That was how I thought. That was how I felt then, harbouring resentments as I did.'

The rest of the family were more generous in their thoughts. They wanted to give of their best to Aki and his Hawaiian family. They wanted to honour Chappy's return, and left nothing undone that could possibly be done in order to make the 'visitors from afar' welcome and comfortable. Oriwia didn't have to ask for anything. The wharenui was renovated and painted, and the grounds attended to. The interior was scrubbed and polished, mattresses were aired, linen was rewashed and ironed, and women spent their evenings embroidering new pillowcases. Closer to the time, food on the hoof arrived and eel traps were set. Their more southern relatives lowered crayfish pots from their dinghies, gathered kina and pāua.

A workforce arrived with bags of potatoes, kūmara, onions, carrots, cabbages and corn. Vehicles came in, unloading a large marquee as well as additional crockery, chairs and tables borrowed from other marae in the area. Oriwia knew she didn't have to worry about any of those arrangements and she was able to put her mind to finishing off the hand sewing on the bridal gown and to making cakes.

There was a collective sigh at the sight of Binnie coming across the marae towards the wharenui in her Audrey gown – 'as if the old building itself drew in and noisily expelled air'. Though the V waistline and fullness of organdy were not quite enough to disguise impropriety, nobody cared. They all had tears to look after. For Oriwia it was not only the sight of her daughter that started up her own flood, it was also seeing her husband by her daughter's side, wearing his dark blue kimono. He was home. He would understand now that this was where he belonged – despite what was to happen later.

| Chapter 23 |
AKI

There was nothing that could have made me happier than to have my son marry the daughter of Oriwia and Chappy. If all our lives had been a generation earlier, when taumau was still a custom in some families, this joining would have been what I wanted to arrange for my son – or, to be exact, it's what I would have wanted my elders to have arranged for my son. Also, in my lifetime I've had no finer duty, no greater honour, than that of bringing my Hawaiian family on to my marae to be formally welcomed by my home family.

We assembled at the gateway on the day before the wedding. I knew this was a big, important occasion for the home people, as important as the wedding itself. I could see from where I stood the effort that had gone into the repair and painting of the meeting house and the upkeep of the flower gardens in preparation for this day.

Though my own return was not significant, what was important was who I brought to my home family. First was their loved and remembered adopted son, Chappy. Then there were the 'visitors from afar', 'birds of a single flight'. These were my wife and in-laws – Ela and her parents and my son Eric and his wife. Also, there was 'A'makualenalena, the old one. To have such a respected one as Ela's grand-uncle travel with us was something which I knew would dignify our visiting group in the eyes of the people at home. They would have glimpsed him already as they waited, full of curiosity, in front of the meeting house, ready to call us across the time-honoured ground.

I want to talk about 'A'makualenalena, the sage.

My own wedding in Hawai'i was a day and night of singing, dancing, laughter, gift-giving, feasting and speechmaking. But it was when the old man spoke that everything stopped except for the sun, which by then was quitting the flaming sky and silhouetting the black mountains.

Hearing the genealogies was something I was used to when I was growing up. As a boy, I would become impatient with these recitations because I was made to sit and listen to them for hour upon hour while other children were outside playing. It was Paa who would sit me beside him, holding my ear to aid my hearing, and who wouldn't let go until all was done.

As I grew, I came to understand that it was through the genealogies that important links were made. At a wedding, there was often a genealogical joining between the bride's and bridegroom's families. It was a matter of those who were experts knowing the connections and going far back into whakapapa to describe the links down to the present time. At a funeral, the aim of the genealogist would be to describe the connection of the visiting groups to the one lying in state. These are the moments when all time becomes present and you understand that you are merely a bead on an unbroken necklace which is without beginning or end.

I realised as we sat in the fading light of my wedding day, my ears attuned to the language that I was becoming more and more familiar with, that the old man was reciting whakapapa. And as he continued I realised that what I was hearing, there in Hawai'i, was my own genealogy – the names from before the earth was made, the names from before the earth was peopled, the names from after the earth was peopled, the names before the sailing and venturing, the names to do with the sailing and venturing.

My heart was bumping against its walls. I was hearing the same names that I had heard from the lips of my elders when I was a child with a held ear.

Now, to return to our visit. We were called on to the marae and, once seated, the speech-making began, alternating between hosts and visitors. Paa, the ear-holder of my boyhood, was the final speaker for the host side. As it happened, the sun was sinking on this occasion, too, beyond the valley, the town and the distant ocean. My Hawaiian family were at once alerted when they heard the names that connected them in time and place with my home family, we of Aotearoa being junior to those left behind in 'the great, far-distant, etched-on-the-heart, longed-for homeland of Hawaiki'. Beside me, so still it was as though he didn't breathe, was old man 'A'makualenalena.

Though Paa had been the ear-holder when I was a child, this was the first time I had ever heard him doing the recitations himself, ranging far and wide, down, out and along the many branches, to connect our home family to my Hawaiian family. He was the only one left of my home family who could do this now.

'*Except for you,*' said Moonface into my heart. '*You had your ear held, remember?*'

In the field next to the meeting house, the big marquee had been erected. We were taken there for a meal after the formal proceedings, and then back to the wharenui for further speeches and opportunities for the two families to get to know one another.

Something unexpected happened during that time.

I want to talk about Noddy. This cousin was three years older than me, someone I looked up to as I was growing. At fourteen, he sheared his first sheep, and a few years later he was as good a shearer as anyone I knew, including his father and mine. He knew how to kill, skin and butcher a sheep at an early age, how to hunt pigs, for which he trained his own dogs. During the first years of the war, when many others left the land to find work in the cities, and other young men enlisted, he put his back into the land and the market-gardening ventures. He, too, spoke of going to war, but was persuaded that he was needed at home – not so much persuaded as told.

Finally, however, he did enlist, going off to fight in the islands of the Pacific. I met up with him once in Suva, but it was not long afterwards that he became a prisoner of war and I didn't see him again until he came home.

But this Noddy who returned to us was not the same man who had left us a year earlier.

Near to the end of the circuit of speeches in the wharenui that day, there was a commotion at the door. It was Noddy, screaming the devil's name into the house, kicking off his boots to come in, chopping down hard with his hands as if defleecing a slaughtered sheep. His eyes were fireballs. His bare chest was quivering and sweat ran down his dark skin as though he had become molten. My father, who was seated near the door, and Noddy's sister who had come running after him, took an arm each, turned him and led him away. He calmed down once hands were on him.

After they had gone, the mihimihi in the house continued. During the course of these remaining speeches, and for the sake of visitors, Noddy's plight was explained.

The next day, after the marriage ceremony, everyone was assembled in the marquee to sing the bridal party to their seats at the main table. The sides and ends of the tent had been done out in ponga fronds and flowers, the tables were covered with white cloths. As we seated ourselves, a chain of helpers was formed, and bowls of food were handed along from the outside cooking tents to be placed on the tables. There was everything you could think of in the way of food. Noddy was one of those who had been out back all morning helping to put the hāngi down, and I know he would've been there helping to unearth it and carry the baskets to the tents where the food was served into bowls.

The meal was interspersed with speeches, and it was when Chappy stood, as father of the bride, that there was another incident.

Chappy had just begun to speak when Noddy stepped in through one of the marquee openings behind our table. He put his hands round Chappy's neck, throttling him. It took all my strength to prise his fingers away. Once I'd done that, I wrapped my arms around Noddy so tight that he couldn't move, and talked him down. Instead of taking him out or allowing him to be taken away, I called for a chair and sat him down beside me.

In the meantime Chappy was having a drink of water while my mother and Oriwia fanned him and frowned into his face. He was pale and there were marks on his neck, but after a while he stood and continued: As I was saying, he said. At this there were barks and whoops and tin-pans of laughter. The marquee billowed with it as I wiped tears, sweat, ash from Noddy's face and put food on a plate for him. He picked away at it.

Before he ended his speech, and before the toast that he was to give, Chappy said that he never wanted his presence to disturb anyone, not this cousin Noddy nor any other member of the family, not any person of the town nor anyone at all.

This incident was talked about over the weekend. People spoke of Noddy, who screamed and rampaged at night, who in frenzies of digging made holes where holes were not wanted and sometimes hid himself inside them, who wandered off in any direction in any weather, who cried and scratched deep marks across his chest – but who always allowed us to calm him and bring him home. This was the first time we had known him to try and hurt (maybe kill) another person. We would make sure it never happened again. There were enough of us to see to it.

Noddy had been given back to the family after the war. He was someone whose past life and work would not be forgotten and whose presence would be a reminder of what can go on in the world. People wanted to reassure Oriwia and her husband that when Chappy returned there would be nothing to fear. He would not be harmed, and neither would his family.

A year later, Chappy came back for the marriage of daughter Daphne. When it was time for him to return to Hawai'i and all the relatives were gathered to farewell him, Paa spoke about the time when Chappy would come home for good.

He began by speaking about my mother – his daughter Dorothea – and her two brothers. Though Dorothea and her husband Taana had raised their family on the land, her two brothers had become officials of the Mormon church. They married in America and were now living with their families in Salt Lake City. He spoke about each of them.

He also spoke of children he and Nunu had fostered for a time. They'd come and gone. Sometimes they would return to visit. He remembered all of them and spoke about each one.

Because of the length of time Paa was taking, and because he was explaining all in detail, people knew that he had an important message he wanted to impart. No one was sure what he was getting at until he began speaking directly to Chappy.

'You are our true son,' he said. 'In taking you as our son, we had the agreement of everyone. Your sister agreed that you should be her brother. Your cousins and elders all agreed that you would be our whāngai to whom we would all have obligations. They understood you would be treated the same as children born to us. You would inherit land in the same way on behalf of your children. War and separation cannot change that. Your children are our grandchildren and that will never be different.'

As he sat down the discussion was picked up, going round the house in the customary way. The talk was all in support of what Paa had said, with a few anecdotes and songs thrown in to lighten the occasion. I changed my seating position so that I could be the last speaker. I needn't have done so as I had every right to stay silent until everyone had had a say. It was expected that I would speak for Chappy as it wasn't protocol for him to speak for himself. I could have stood from anywhere in the house.

When my turn came, I told what I knew of family circumstances in Japan, the disintegration of a Japanese family, the annihilation of a name. I spoke of war experiences and Chappy's fear of outrage towards his family in Aotearoa and possible injury. I told of my visit to Tokyo and meeting with a dying man.

Following that, I was able to tell of love and hope. But it wasn't until I put all these thoughts into words that I finally realised the depth of Chappy's fears. He wasn't a 'silly thing'. He was a selfless and brave man, and based on what he understood, he had done what he needed to do to protect his family.

Two or three years later, Noddy went missing and though searches went on for several weeks, he was not found. He'd gone with the mountain folk, people said.

| *Chapter 24* |
ORIWIA

When the 'marriage of local bride Daphne Dorothea Star and Arni Lars Knudsen of Denmark' was being planned twelve months after Binnie's wedding, dressmaker Ti was keen to make a Grace Kelly gown for the bride. It would be less elaborate than the princess's, and made in the dressmaker's choice of materials. Because Daphne was smaller in build than Princess Grace, and therefore in danger of being overwhelmed by fabric, the skirt would be more trim. Ti drew it up – lace bodice with long sleeves, high collar and tiny covered buttons; full-length skirt in brocade with a fitted cummerbund. The article in the local paper included a full description of it.

The dress wasn't what Daphne had wanted, but although the plain, shin-length, sleeveless sheath she had in mind would have suited her, her mother and aunties couldn't agree to it. It wasn't possible to have the older sister looking skimpy as compared to a younger sister married just a year before.

Business had improved at the garage. There were more vehicles on the road, and Lou now had a position for a trainee. This place was what Oriwia had offered Lani on the dress-ripping, cupboard-scrubbing day, and which he accepted – or which Aki quickly accepted on his tongue-tied son's behalf. Lani was settled in at the garage. Binnie was keeping the books for both businesses and helping with the baking. And there was a 'delicious baby' who was 'all of life' to Oriwia.

Though she was still impatient to see Chappy back with the family, business, weddings and a baby were all distractions for Oriwia as Chappy's applications for Hawaiian residency and citizenship made their slow way forward.

Despite the near-throttling Chappy had undergone at the hands of Noddy, he'd felt greatly moved by the warmth and love shown to him by the people on both wedding occasions. It convinced him that he should be at home. But still he needed papers. He had to be a person, one with a name, a country and a livelihood, who depended on no one else. He was prepared to wait.

'Forever?' Oriwia asked.

But then something happened which caused Oriwia to think she shouldn't be in too much of a hurry to bring Chappy home.

In the winter of 1964, two years after Daphne was married, Paa died.

As soon as they were able, Chappy and Aki boarded a plane for home, coming in to Wellington through a bank of cloud. This broke around them as they made their way, coatless, across the tarmac. A numbing wind, whipped up from southern oceans, accompanied the downpour.

They were met at the airport by relatives and driven first to Ti's house, a short distance from the airport, where Ti was waiting for them with hot food and dry clothes. But the cold had already made its way into Chappy's bones.

In the early afternoon, Aki and Chappy arrived in the doorway of the house of mourning. From where she sat, Oriwia could see the mottled, bruise-coloured hue of her husband's skin. It was because of a plane journey, which elongated time and stretched out his insides, she thought. It was because of cold. It was because of sorrow.

The sounds of weeping and wailing broke in waves as the men made their way to the open casket – arrayed as it was in fine cloaks and precious ornaments – but it was the sorry sight of her husband more than Paa's death that brought deep sounds from Oriwia at that moment. She moved aside to allow Chappy in next to the casket and sat, holding him.

Dorothea, on the other side, moved so that Aki could sit there. The lamenting subsided, the speeches of welcome began, after which those gathered came in a line to share their sorrowing with these latest arrivals.

When all of that was done, Chappy lay down on the mattress next to Paa. Oriwia covered him with a blanket, and he went to sleep. Groups of mourners came throughout the afternoon as Chappy slept on.

It was when Oriwia tried to wake him so that he could go for an evening meal that she realised something was wrong. Her husband's skin was moist and he wouldn't stir. She loosened his clothing, and Aki helped her shift him to a mattress by the open door, where she attempted to cool him down with dampened cloths. He stirred but didn't wake.

At midnight he was helped to the car to be taken to hospital. Bird bones, a bird. By morning he could have flown. 'Hurry,' Oriwia said.

'Take care,' people said.

'We'll wait the burial until you come back.'

Aki returned for the interment the following day. Oriwia went to stay at Ti's house while Chappy remained in hospital for the next six weeks. 'He's good at surviving,' Aki said as he left, and Oriwia took strength from this as pneumonia brought Chappy near to death.

It was during the weeks of Chappy's illness that Oriwia first asked herself whether Aotearoa was the right place for her husband after all. With the weather the way it was, she now felt she wanted to get him back to Hawai'i as soon as possible. She decided she would go with him and stay until he had fully recovered.

––––––

'Turn on that machine, Grandson,' Oriwia said. 'I'll just finish what I'm doing. There's something I want recorded. I want you to play it to Aki. He has to hear this.'

Once my grandmother was settled, and though there were still questions I wanted to ask about the return to Hawai'i and my grandfather's citizenship, I turned on the tape recorder. It was the first time she had asked me to do this. I pressed the 'record' button.

––––––

They called the baby Noelani after Ela. I don't know why young parents these days take the naming of their children into their own hands. I walked out of the hospital that day and burst into tears.

'It's a pretty name, Mother,' Binnie said after she came home with the baby.

My two daughters began calling me 'mother' after they decided, when they were eleven and twelve years old, that they were going to speak English all the time. With Chappy away, and because of living in town and all the trading I had to do, English had become a habit with me also.

'I didn't say it wasn't,' I said to Binnie, trying to keep the edge out of my voice. I had not said anything about the naming and was determined I never would, but Binnie, and I suppose Lani, noticed that after several weeks I'd only ever called my granddaughter 'Baby' and 'Baby Girl'.

'Well, I feel sorry for my mother-in-law,' Binnie said. 'She has three grandchildren. Two in Las Vegas and one here. She never sees any of them. Nor does their grandfather. Neither of the grandfathers see much of this one.'

I held my tongue.

'We have to use the full name,' I said after a time, 'not just take out the middle bit. She can't be just Ela.'

It's true it is a pretty name, and Noelani is a beautiful and brilliant child. Her parents have been most generous towards me with all the children, but especially with their first-born.

Binnie and Lani had three children by the time Lani had completed the apprenticeship, and they didn't stop at three. This life wasn't what I'd wanted for my daughter, but at least ... well ...

———

At least, Daniel, they've never left me. They lived with me for six years, which was long enough for me to change my mind about my son-in-law.

To tell the truth, Grandson, offering him the trainee position in the garage was a test, even a kind of punishment, for both him and for his mother and Aki. Maybe I didn't really think Lani could do it. He'd been spoiled all his life was what I thought then. He had, has, this perfect skin, you know, which turned me against him. Teeth too. On the other hand, I couldn't get used to seeing him covered in all that grease and oil. You're right, Aki, about my snobbish tendencies. Besides, I was soon to find out what a very good cook he is. I pride myself on breads, cakes and pies, but have to admit there's nothing tastier than meat, fish and vegetables cooked by son-in-law Ke'alohilani. And the children are angels. Angels to look at, I mean. Otherwise ... But the main thing is ... they didn't leave me except to move up the line a little ... Well, not until later.

When they said they wanted to take over management of a grill room in the next town, I didn't stand in their way, though I didn't like the idea of my grandchildren being brought up in a restaurant, and when I suggested Noelani stay with me and return to them in the weekends, they agreed. It was Noelani's wish also, to remain with me. Now all five kids are doing well in life, despite being spoiled by their father.

Once they'd gone, I sold the garage to Lou, who was the manager at the time and who had seen Lani through his apprenticeship. I could've moved my business closer to them, but I loved my old bakery, just as I enjoy my old-fashioned tearoom now, in this old-time town. There are all these fancy cafés around these days, but the tearoom suits me fine.

Anyway, this is what I want to say on this machine here. It's what I've started to say to you, Aki, on different occasions but you always cut me off, call me a silly thing and change the subject. This is for you.

―――――

I want it to be clear that I have never harmed Ela. I wouldn't and couldn't. Jealousy can kill, I know that. It can eat away at the one who harbours it. It can be the death of the one who may be on the receiving end of it. It can damage their offspring.

In the past, I had unkind and unwarranted thoughts regarding Ela. I've been uppish and righteous, but I have to tell you that hard jealousy didn't come in to it – neither the deep, affecting kind which can knock people down in their tracks or damage a family lineage, nor any lesser kind. No. I have never knowingly harmed others, never ill-wished anyone, never uttered a swear word in all my life, never called anyone a bad name. Though I've experienced dislike, I've never experienced hatred.

There's a cousin on my father's side, named Hariata. You remember her. She was one of the chosen ones, like you, Aki. From the time she was a baby, she was taken to every meeting and gathering by the old people. She was like one of those old ones herself. Once she turned five, she was regularly taken out of school to attend tangihanga, land meetings and other important events. As you were, Aki. She stood behind the old women when they called visitors on to their home marae, and walked directly behind them when they crossed other people's domain as visitors.

Like you, Aki. She was made to sit through all proceedings, whether they were for a day, two days or longer. She didn't play with other children during these times. As she became older, she didn't help with food preparation and was criticised by her age group because of this. Instead her work was confined to preparing the wharenui for visitors. It involved sweeping, dusting off cobwebs, laying out mattresses and placing pillows in exact positions.

She had an aunt, twenty years older than her, who was particularly jealous, venomous in her criticism. This aunt had never been encouraged to learn the art of karanga from her elders. In fact, she was probably thought unsuitable because of her belligerent manner.

One early morning, there was a crowd of us going on to a marae for the opening of a newly renovated meeting house. Hariata was in her late forties by then. As dawn broke, our large group made its way across the marae, the calls from the old women sounding out one after the other. Hariata had been positioned among the kuia as usual but, on this occasion, halfway across the ground she felt a sudden prod in her back, by which she understood the time had come for her to use her voice.

Though it was unexpected, because the duty of kaikaranga was usually reserved for much older women, her mouth flew open and her karanga sounded out over the marae. I was walking several rows behind her. Beside me was the jealous one whom I've already mentioned. As soon as Hariata began her call, this one cursed and muttered strings of vile words against her.

As a result, just as Hariata was concluding her karanga, she fell to the ground unconscious and was carried to a shelter to recover.

I didn't go straight to Hariata to tell her what I'd overheard. I went to the old ones, but they already knew. Some of them had heard the bad words, too. When Hariata recovered, they told her that she must rise above ill-speaking. What had happened was a good lesson, they said; and they told her that she should be grateful for the experience. It would help her to know what her gifts were and to understand that she had power within her to counteract any such evil. They said nothing at all to the one who caused the trouble. It was as though they were leaving her to stew in her own bitter juices.

———

Of course I've been carried away telling all this, Grandson. If I'd written it down it wouldn't be so jumbled. All I want Aki to hear is what I've had to say about Ela. Never mind the rest. That's the trouble. It's all stuck here on this gadget. You can't take it back. And it should be in a different order. Anyway, as long as he knows that what happened to Ela was nothing to do with me. My ungenerous thoughts disappeared as I came to know her. She was kind. She was lovely. She married for love, as I did, as Aki did. Just play those bits for him, Grandson, and never mind the rest.

| *Chapter 25* |
AKI

I didn't want to hear that from Oriwia. Silly thing. Listen to me, Oriwia. This is for you, my sister. You and I grew together and we are inside each other's hearts. We don't have to explain. We know. We understand. You changed towards Ela over time, just as you have changed towards my son. I knew you would. Eventually you took time to look into their faces just as you had to look into your daughter's face in the days before her wedding, and in so doing you remembered about love. Ela's illness was nothing to do with you. Of course not. It couldn't be. Let's hear no more of that.

But now, since the subject of Ela has come up, I'll speak of her.

There are reasons we become ill or dispirited. It's what Oriwia was referring to. There's always a cause. Sometimes we bring sickness or punishment upon ourselves through carelessness, distraction, transgression, or failing to dedicate the day or the task. Weak moments may invite wrong forces.

Sometimes sickness is caused by a vengeful person such as Oriwia describes. I have seen those affected by the spite of others become ill, go mad, become lame, turn black, drop dead, die slowly. I have seen their children born with ailments and deformities.

It was natural for me to dwell on these matters when Ela became ill.

But what I knew was that my Ela had never hurt anyone and had not broken any old laws. So far as I knew, there had not been any curse from way back put on the family which could now be affecting her.

What I did not put enough thought to at the time were the effects of underlying anxiety or hurt – the invisible distress that people live with every day. This is grief and loss, or the threat of it, which works its way through whole communities down through decades. It's a communal distress, which lodges somewhere in the communal mind. It hides unnourished until somewhere, in someone or some people, it dislodges to live in the physical body. Once there, it is fed. It has roots within it which begin to seek out their own life blood. It has tendrils which branch in every direction in search of light. Everything, everything, is a search for light.

In listening to myself speak like this, I hear the voices of my mother and elders. I tell it their way because there's truth in it.

For me, it was a beautiful life we led, with enough of everything – that is until it all changed. There was work for money that some of us did. Plenty of work for enough money. Then there was work that everyone did, such as hunting, fishing, growing, gathering and preparing food. This is the work I looked forward to whenever I was ashore. It was working with the family, being with the family, being with Ela and our sons that kept this sailor sparked. But there are times when, in order to be better prepared for adversity, we need to upend satisfaction and unearth what lives beneath.

Sometimes I felt my life to be a self-indulgent one. I had been brought up in a certain way to be the keeper, the guardian for a future time of certain knowledge, histories, genealogies, stories. Though unaware of it at the time, I'd been trained as an orator. Held by the ear. When my mother sent me away from home, though it was never said, everyone knew that it was with the intention I should return and take my place among my own people. But for now I was still a young man in that regard. There were many years when I didn't have to think about this at all. There was Paa. Between Paa and me there were men and women of my parents' generation who, in the meantime, were the keepers of stories.

Ela.

I discovered that intrusion myself, that trespasser, that assailant. It was larger than a walnut and equally as hard.

The most unforgettable moments of my adult life are the times I came ashore in Honolulu, and after a cold-water sluicing and the discarding of dungarees and shirt for a pair of shorts, I could be alone for a few moments with Ela. I could come behind her, put my face in her bundled salt, smoke and nut-oil hair, and reaching forward, cup my barnacled hands under the heavy hand-sized moons.

Just that.

It was joy. It was love. It was home. These were moments more tender, more aching, more memorable than any to follow then or later.

During one of those occasions, my fingers came across that walnut, that bulb, which felt to me as though it should be on a dish or in a garden. I didn't mention it right away.

'What is it?' I asked, the next day.

'What is what?'

I put her fingers on the spot.

'It's nothing,' she said, lifting and poking. 'No, it doesn't hurt at all.'

'That's all right then. Is it?'

'Nothing of anything considering this wonderful life I have,' she said.

These were words I was happy to hear. I went out into the kalo field to work my heart into the ground. That was before life changed.

The old stories of Hawai'i were similar to that of my own country, except that in ancient Aotearoa we were not ruled. My wife's people had reigning chiefs once. They had divine queens and kings. They had divisions of land, gifted territories, which flowed from mountaintop to ocean. The ordinary people could not be removed from these lands though the chiefs sometimes could.

Because these territories went from mountain to sea they included everything needed for life in the way of food, water, medicines, timber and stone. People built irrigation systems, and there were sacred waters for every kind of use. They had knowledge of winds, tides and weather, and they travelled on land or oceans taking direction from the stars.

All this was told to us by 'A'makualenalena as we fished or pounded kalo, preparing enough for the following weeks. He had his own memory of events, but added to that were the memories he had of all those who had gone on ahead of him. It was a familiar story in many ways, told in a manner familiar to me.

'There came a wisp of smoke,' he said one day. 'It was barely noticeable to the sovereign people living on their lands. It was a thin line, as though it issued from a small opening. As it came closer, this line was seen to be made up of smoke-coloured insects which came down and began to chew at the edges of the land, soundlessly.

'If you haven't got everything you need in your own territory, you contact your neighbour and they tell you to come and get it. One day they will come to you for something and you will tell them where to find it.

'This time there was no asking. The insects came and they chewed.

'And after a time the thin line became a heavy cloud, blocking the sky from every horizon. An impenetrable crust formed over all the islands of Hawai'i, suffocating the sovereign people, altering their lands and removing their waters.

'But never mind about that, the land was given to the sovereign people by the deities, which is why the sovereign people will not be lost. They are from a seed that was put into the ground at the time of creation. There we were, along with all other seeds of plants and creatures who are our older brothers and sisters. There we were enduring. Here we are, enduring.

'During the time when the world was at war, our water was diverted from our kalo gardens. It was taken many miles away from here for the sugar plantations. People had to give up their kalo gardens. Fish didn't survive in the remaining streams and the shores were also affected.

'Our watering systems fell apart. Sovereign man became destitute. People moved to the cities. Those of us remaining lived on the front portions of our lands and kept our old ways as much as we could. But the land didn't belong to us any more, we were told. It had been stolen from us because the sovereign man failed to pay taxes, we were told. We were told there were going to be roads and other people's grand houses.

'The next war of the world came. More people had to leave the land to find work so they wouldn't die. They had to go to war in order to survive. You live, you survive so you or your child can have life. Often you live in darkness, crushed and creeping about in search of light.

'I won't be here when the new roads come. But you will be here,' the old man said. 'Our grandchildren will be here. I won't be walking the roads, or riding on them in cars, but you'll all be here. As for me, I'll be out there beyond the reef, listening to the wisdom of my turtle relatives. Or I'll be sleeping in a rocky shelter in the cave of my ancestor.'

'What's happening?' I asked Ela one day.

'Lumps and bumps,' she said. 'They come and go, it's change of life.'

What a coward I am. Though I ride high seas and face ghosts or go through bombings and fire, mention such things to me as 'change of life', 'time of the month', 'womb', and my insides shrivel. Ela's words shut me up for some time. I think of my stupidity every day.

| *Chapter 26* |
ORIWIA

Since Oriwia's disappointing visit to Hawai'i seven years earlier, Chappy had taken an apartment in the city. He was running his own franchise now, and though the enterprise had suffered during his illness and absence, it had been kept afloat by Ishy and Malia's daughter, whom he'd employed six months after taking over the business.

Oriwia was comfortable in the new place, which had electricity and plenty of water and ceiling fans to keep it cool. Unused to being surrounded by so much concrete, bitumen and heat, she seldom ventured outside except to shop for daily needs or buy postcards to send to the family.

Comfortable – yet they were long days, days of waiting for Chappy to return from work, filling in hours until he came home sniffing the aromas of special dishes she'd prepared for their evening meal.

Oriwia was not good at being alone. She missed her grandchildren, she missed Dorothea, the family and Dulcie. She missed her customers, the town gossip, and the Country Library Service van.

Though she occupied herself with business books, writing postcards and looking after the apartment, there just wasn't enough work to keep her mind off her sense of isolation. She talked to herself, telling herself that she wasn't a child, she was a wife, mother, grandmother, who ran her own businesses. She was in Hawai'i living in a fine apartment with her husband. But silence made her neck prickle. Silence made space for ghosts.

Every morning, when Chappy left for work, Oriwia turned on the television, grateful for the sound of voices. She'd turn it up loud enough to be heard in every room as she went about her tasks. If she went out shopping, or to post her cards, she'd leave the television on so that on her return she wouldn't walk in to silence.

Although she had brought library books with her, she couldn't settle to read. Again there was too much quiet, a kind of noiselessness which left her alone in the world. However, when she could think of nothing more to do, and it was too early to begin preparations for the evening meal, she'd turn the television down just a little and read for an hour, rereading passages which pleased, puzzled or intrigued her, discussing with herself what she liked and didn't like, taking her time, afraid she would run out of books to read before it was time to go home. She put aside one book for the plane journey, telling herself that if she ran out of material before then, she'd read the other books over again.

As evening neared, Oriwia would find herself drawn to the front window, looking out for a man on a bicycle, which would eventually materialise as a man driving a sedan. She would listen for the tinkle and squeak which would become instead motorised sounds slowing and halting, the graunching of a handbrake, the shutting of one door, the opening of another.

All was well. She belonged in the world again. Her husband was home. They could exchange the news of the day, though there was not much to tell in her case unless there had been a postcard from home or Aki had called in.

Chappy had emigration documents to discuss with her. Now that his United States citizenship had been granted, he was eager to talk about the next stage of his return and would've wondered at Oriwia's reticence when he brought up the subject. All she would say was that she would be concerned for his health should he return to Aotearoa. Cold and damp was something she hadn't taken into account when she'd been so adamant that love was paramount.

'I'll put on warm socks,' he said.

'You were right down.'

'Before I get off the plane.'

'And your business?'

'Our.'

'Leaving behind a going concern.'

She'd earlier dismissed the latter as unimportant. Now, in mentioning it, she felt as though she was making up reasons for her husband not to come home.

'Doing okay. Keep on working for us if we keep a share, or just appoint a manager.'

'You were low.'

'I'll talk it over with Ishy, Malia and their daughter. Janet did a good job while I was away.'

'There in the hospital.'

'I saw myself.'

'You were leaving me.'

'I saw. There I was, afloat, my back bumping up against the white ceiling of the hospital ward. Looking down there was my other self on a stretcher, stretched, dressed in white as though for my own funeral, skin as blue as maomao. Leaving that self. But there was a voice, Paa's of course, yelling at me to get back, you can't come with me, get back home.'

'To the warmth of Hawai'i, maybe?'

'To the warmth of my wife and family, to the warmth of the land. The voice didn't say that, but I knew what it meant. I knew it was Paa. There was a scent of flowers. Those ones which smell lovely by the door.'

'Stock. Carnations and roses.'

'I breathed them. Stole every breath, used it and let it go, slow, slow. Had to. Took another, slow, and let it go. All the way back.'

Home.

So, home was where Chappy wanted to be, and working on the land was what he wanted to do. He thought he could have their stall again, where motorists could stop for fresh fruit and vegetables and drop a few coins in a box. Just a small stand. They wouldn't need a real income from it.

Oriwia didn't want to return to the days of roadside vegetables, not for herself anyway. There was time to think about it, still a process to go through before Chappy could come home to live. Until then, she decided she would return every winter to Hawai'i to be with her husband, provided she could make a suitable arrangement for the shop and bakery.

In the meantime, how good it was to have evenings together, and what a relief to be sleeping with her husband again, coiled, uncoiled, or lying back with covers folded down, his cool skin, his bony frame. She imagined his ankle and wrist bones incandescent in the dark.

Sleeping alone was an abomination. From ever since she could remember, until Moana-Rose had married at nineteen, Oriwia and her sister had shared a bed where, at the end of the day, sitting on the edge of it practising hairdos, brushing down, pinning up, plaiting or curling, they would spell long words, sing rounds and duets, stop and make faces at their hair achievements. They'd giggle on and on because their teacher had tube legs and no feet and there was a woman at the market with lipstick missed by miles.

In bed side by side, back to back, front to front, back to front, top and tail, Oriwia would tell her sister what she'd read in newspapers or love books. She described giant, beautiful heroes with lightly furrowed brows, and heroines with cream skin and lovely eyes. Sometimes they talked about what the men they would marry would look like, and when Moana-Rose reminded Oriwia that she was going to marry Aki she'd say, 'I know. I'm just talking about my pretend husband.' They discussed movies they'd seen or what they'd like to see when certain pictures came to show at their hall. On and on they chatted until the hour came when Moana-Rose said what Oriwia was waiting for her to say: 'Tell me about our mother.' The comfort of the telling would send them to sleep. In the morning, neither would remember at which point talk had ceased and dreams begun.

'Get up. Hurry up,' Oriwia would say in the morning, in English, to Moana-Rose, as though English was the language of urgency. They would hear Jimmy out in the kitchen lighting the stove.

'Why are you always snooty in the mornings?' Moana-Rose would ask, also speaking in English.

After the loss of Moana-Rose, whom she had never been parted from even for a day, there was an empty half bed that she could never bring herself to occupy, and a whole night stretching out in front of her like an expanding beam of dark light.

Oriwia retired later and later as time went on, working until overtaken by the necessity to sleep, which she would do for three or four hours before daylight. Although she found companionship in her daily contacts, those empty places, the feeling of abandonment – especially after her father died – remained until she married Chappy. After four years of marriage, Chappy had ridden off on his bicycle.

But she had children. She had businesses to run, a house to build and land to attend to.

After a time there were weddings to arrange and babies to care for.

When Noelani was eighteen months old, her brother Tiaki was born. Oriwia was pleased to take over the night-time care of Noelani, bathing her and putting her to bed. If her granddaughter was unsettled, Oriwia would put her in her own big bed and lie down beside her until she went to sleep. She'd leave her there for the rest of the night, where Noelani, who had often been wakeful in the past, would sleep until morning, occupying that yawn, that space, that empty place.

While Oriwia was away, the bakery and shop was being managed by Binnie with the help of Marianne, who was friend Dulcie's granddaughter. Her parents lived on the property and were part owners of the farm. Marianne was fifteen years old and had often come in after school to help. As the weather improved, Binnie had to return to her work at the restaurant, and since it was school holidays Marianne managed well enough with help from her grandmother.

On her return Oriwia went to see Dulcie. Farm work and the outdoors had thinned her friend and reddened and toughened her skin. Her hair was turning grey but her black-crystal eyes hadn't changed. She was wearing a cotton skirt and a fisherman-rib jersey with the sleeves rolled up. She was barefoot. Dulcie embraced Oriwia, seating her at the table while she made tea and hacked fruit cake.

'Talk to me. Talk to me, Oriwia. You're tanned. You're so rested and healthy. Tell me, tell me.'

Oriwia told her friend all about her stay in Hawai'i and the decision she had come to.

'I want to ask about Marianne,' she said. 'I know she's still at school, but I need someone for the winter months. Before I approach her parents, or Marianne herself, I want to know what you think. She enjoys the shop. She's capable, bright. People like her. At the same time, I hesitate because . . . because it wouldn't have been what I wanted for my own daughters . . .'

'She hates school. Her parents want her to stay on and do her exams, but she can't stand it.' Dulcie poured tea, brought the cups to the table and sat down. 'Like her grandmother. No great scholar. Begging her parents . . . She'll help out on the farm, she says.' Dulcie broke a piece off her slice of cake and examined it. 'All those years ago, when I told my parents I wanted to leave school, they didn't stop me. I was twelve. I loved the bakery. Talk to me, tell me . . .'

'I want to train someone to take over for two months during the off season, and of course I'd keep her on after that.' Oriwia blew steam across the surface of her tea. 'You know, the climate here. For Chappy? It's no good. But Marianne . . . the farm?'

'In the busy season there's work for her on the farm, but I don't know if farming's the life for her. As you say, she's chirpy. Needs to get out among people. I reckon she'd . . . And winter? I'd keep an eye on her, have time to do the baking if you think . . .' Dulcie's eyes prickled. 'I love the baking. We'll talk to her parents.'

| *Chapter 27* |
AKI

When my Hawaiian family spoke of new roads, they were talking in general terms about roads to accommodate high-cost housing and the expansion of private beachfront properties along the coast. Homes for the wealthy. Planning was advancing. Road construction would see Ela's people removed from the remainder of their land.

I'd heard this talked about for many years. Every so often there would be activity, meetings and visits by various authorities. Men with instruments would signal to each other from beach to hillside. When they'd gone there'd be silence for many months, as though it had all been forgotten. This silence was the void, but a void is never truly that. A void is always a hatchery.

We took Ela to the hospital. It was a lonely, haunted and frightening place where treatment caused suffering, so we brought her home again. I helped my mother-in-law go up the mountain to collect leaves, roots, flowers and a variety of barks for making medicines and poultices. These had a good effect on Ela. Pain lessened. She put on weight. But one day my mother-in-law said, 'We're taking her to Lili.' We were living in town by then.

The roads were near completion and grand houses continued to be built. Knowing what was to come, many people had already left the land. That meant that there were not enough young people to work the gardens and catch fish. Some moved into public housing in large suburbs where they had to buy disagreeable food and pay rent, but the only work they were able to get was poorly paid.

Ela, my mother-in-law and I took a run-down beach house just outside Honolulu. It had boards missing, some broken windows, a leaky roof and was due for demolition. But it had plenty of rooms and some space around it. Other places we had looked at were crowded in on all sides, and expensive. We couldn't see ourselves in any of them. Chappy helped us patch the house before leaving his apartment to come and live with us.

My father-in-law, who had refused to move from the land, was living in his beach shelter under threat of being arrested. Every so often, while I was at work, Ela and her mother would go and visit him – now trespassers on their own territories – taking food and bringing home fish. They found him dead there one day. That same night, we carried him up the mountain tracks in his old canoe and placed him in the cave of secrets.

Lili, I knew, had special healing powers. She and her husband had also refused to move from the land. Instead they hid themselves high on the mountain where they made a little house and lived off forest foods. Lili had chants and prayers and potions to drive out illness and torment. She had advice to give. Her husband was a healer of a different kind; he was my tooth puller of many years before.

We arrived at Lili's house with gifts and sat among the trees while she talked of many things, other things. After a time, without asking why we had come, she stood and put her hands on Ela's temples, then on her back.

No one spoke. She beckoned Ela to follow her.

Lili took Ela along a forest track to a deep pool. Whispering her incantations, she immersed Ela several times, pressing her head under and stroking her hair down so that not one strand floated on the surface.

On a special fireplace to the side of the house, with utensils kept aside for the purpose, she made tea from laukahi flowers. 'This will be your drink now,' she said to Ela, and she told us how to collect the flowers and prepare the tea. She had advice to give about foods and their preparation; and finally she instructed Ela to take kalo, which she was to prepare herself, and present it to her ocean guardian.

'She's well now,' she said as we left.

What I can say about those words of Lili's, 'she's well now', is that I found them to be true. To be well in spirit is the most important health. Ela was the song of that run-down house. She was its roof, its walls, its windows, its doors. She was its song.

To be well in spirit is the most important wellness. To be well in spirit lifts the physical and mental state to an extraordinary level. All are affected by it. Dark thoughts disappear.

I'm not sure of the reason for it, but during those days of caring for Ela, my thoughts would often return to the time of my childhood when I would hear the old people say that we earthlings are related to the stars. The stars are our flesh and blood. I came to understand that this must be true in the deepest sense. We come from the dust of stars.

Chapter 28

ORIWIA

Oriwia made preparations to go to Hawai'i the following New Zealand winter. Marianne would manage the shop and bakery while Dulcie helped out with the baking. Also, the shop was to close for two weeks while Taana made the alterations needed to change the premises to a tearoom.

———

'We were all into nylon in those days, Grandson,' Oriwia said to me. 'I packed three nylon frocks, two Crimplene skirts, four nylon blouses and a pair of leather sandals. The clothing was lightweight, took up little space and needed only the minimum of ironing. But it was all a mistake. You heat up and drip inside synthetics, nothing absorbs. Also, the sandals became a size too small.'

———

A week before departure, Dorothea called in on her way home from town. Over a cup of tea, Oriwia once again expressed her doubts about Chappy's return. Now that he wanted to get home as quickly as possible, she thought it unwise. 'He almost left me in that hospital,' she said to Dorothea. 'He watched himself slipping away.'

Dorothea had heard all this before.

'But he pulled himself back,' she said, and she reminded Oriwia that Chappy had acclimatised once and would do it again. 'If he comes home in summer, he'll be able to get used to the colder weather through autumn and be prepared for winter.'

'But the immigration process is so complicated. I'm worried he'll be investigated somewhere along the way.'

Oriwia had already explained to Dorothea what had happened when she'd gone with her marriage certificate to make application to bring Chappy home, how afraid she was that enquiries would lead to trouble.

Dorothea stood, put on her coat, then sat down again. 'There's something', she said, 'that's been trying to get out of my mouth for some time.'

'What is it?'

'You could take care of all that . . .'

Oriwia waited.

'By marrying him again. In Hawai'i.'

Oriwia was shocked by the suggestion. Never, she thought. No, never.

'I married Taana twice,' Dorothea went on. 'That's what made me think of it. When I brought Taana home to meet the family, my elders wouldn't accept him. He was a city boy who was landless and couldn't speak his native tongue. Though it was true that he was brought up in the city and wasn't strong in his language, it was not correct that he is landless. Taana's family has land shares all over the place.

'But that was beside the point really. I think the truth was that he's from an iwi that were our enemies way back in time. That was the problem the elders had with Taana. My parents had no voice in the matter.'

Taana and Dorothea eloped and married in a registry office in Auckland. They stayed there for two months before Dorothea wrote to her parents to let them know where they were, and to tell them she was married.

'Paa and Nunu came all the way to Auckland to bring us back,' she said. 'They told us we were to get married properly at home and that the old ones would have to get used to the idea. It's not as though my parents or elders had anyone else in mind for me, thank goodness. That would have been a different matter.

'That's what we did. Everyone came, even those who had opposed our marriage. And they're not sorry. Taana's a worker who quickly learned to be a farmer, learned to shear sheep and keep the fences in order. That's how he was judged. He'd done a building apprenticeship when he left school, so he brought new skills to our family. As the old ones died, former enmities were forgotten. No one could find anything to complain about with my Taana.'

'But which was your true wedding?' Oriwia asked.

'The second one,' Dorothea said. 'The one that everyone came to celebrate.'

Oriwia had no more to say. Her husband would come home one day, but in the meantime she was the wife of Chappy Star, as witnessed by a large gathering of family and friends. No matter how many oceans parted him from her, there would be no other wedding.

In suffocating air, she was driven through the evening streets until they came to a jaded villa where slashing had been going on in the overgrowth. A cool bath had been prepared for her, cold drinks, light food, a soft bed. She fell asleep under a wobbling ceiling fan and woke many hours later – husband gone – in a billowing room. Lengths of coloured material hung from ceiling to floor. They bellied and backwashed like dancers.

Oriwia, dressed in one of the nylon dresses, went out through the back door to where she could hear voices. Ela and her mother were under an open lean-to at the back of the house where there was a leaping washing machine, suds flowing down its sides.

'Hula mai 'oe,' Ela sang, dancing with the machine as Oriwia came to the doorway. Ela was thin, her eyes and smile large. She could dance like nobody's business. It was a Saturday, a no-work day for Aki and Chappy who, soon afterwards, came carrying fish in a bucket which they had bought from a fisherman at a jetty somewhere. With them were a young man and his two younger sisters who had come to live in the house, too; Oriwia hadn't met them when she arrived the day before.

When the men came in, the language changed. Oriwia didn't notice it at first – reo Māori, 'ōlelo Maoli – as English dropped away. 'They'd been speaking English for *me*.'

Aki and Chappy busied themselves cleaning and cutting up fish.

Ela's mother went inside for lime water, plates and glasses. They spent the morning there washing clothes, putting them through the wringer which, every so often, would slip out of its lock and swing. Oriwia helped hang the clothes, cloths and covers over lines. All could be dry within an hour she realised. They chatted as they worked, Aki being the negotiator between the two languages.

As the day went on, they helped themselves to marinated fish, sliced fruit, kalo and cool drinks.

'So you wouldn't notice the holes in the walls,' Ela said of the drapery in Oriwia and Chappy's bedroom. Everyone laughed. The state of the old house was a source of great amusement to them. Oriwia, who had been asking herself why Chappy would give up a convenient and well-manicured apartment for such a dilapidated old place, felt a jolt of guilt. The family had made special efforts for her because . . . She looked at Aki. Because of certain perceptions they had of her. This is what Aki's amused look confirmed.

'It's lovely,' she said. 'I had a wonderful sleep, and, and . . . welcomed the ventilation.'

They all laughed.

There was no loneliness.

'And the roof is very good,' Chappy said. 'My mate and I patched it up after the last rain.'

'The big room is all waterproofed too,' Aki said. 'When the rain comes, we drag all our bedding in there to sleep.'

'Had to put buckets everywhere,' Ela said, 'to find out where the water's coming in.'

But they'd done Chappy's room first because Oriwia was coming. Aki was watching her. She thought of Jimmy's old shop. 'I'm familiar with leaky roofs,' she said, 'and shifting bedding around.'

'Well, couldn't have you and Chappy changing your bed about, hey Chap?' Ela said. 'Better things to do now that your wife's here.'

'Make up for lost time,' was what she thought Ela's mother said. 'Hey Chap? Hey Oriwia?'

When they woke to rain two nights later, she was grateful not to have to move to communal sleeping. Lights came on, mattresses were shifted. Chappy put his hand over hers, with his thumb hooked under her palm. She slid back into sleep. The rain beat down.

Ela and her mother took Oriwia in hand while Chappy was away at work. They persuaded her out of her synthetic clothing to try on loose cotton frocks and sarongs. She liked the dresses. They were airy and comfortable. The colours, the wide fit, made her feel as though she were a different self, one not so fierce, so on guard – a melted version. The sarongs she couldn't manage except as waist wrap-arounds to be worn with a cotton shirt. Dressed in bright and unfamiliar clothes, she accompanied Ela and her mother to the stalls and food markets and gradually adjusted to a more leisurely and companionable way of getting through the day's chores and routines.

By afternoon, Ela's strength was low and she'd sleep for an

hour or two. Oriwia would help Ela's mother prepare a meal, the two of them all the time trading languages. Every few days, she'd purchase ingredients and bake biscuits, small or large cakes and ginger loaves for snacks and suppers to take to Ishy and Malia's, or for when the sister and brother-in-law came to visit. In the weekends, she'd make scones, pikelets and fry bread.

'I like it here,' Oriwia said to her husband one day. 'I could come more often, or stay longer. And you could come home during spring and summer.'

'I have to return to my family and my father's land,' he said. 'I'm grateful for the work I have here, but someone else can do it. A good garden and a small stand where people can drive in for vegetables . . .'

Those days are gone, Oriwia thought to herself, though she could see that Chappy needed to return. But what did it mean for herself, her tearoom, if they were to go back to working the land? Chappy drove off to work, and she was left questioning herself about what was more important – her husband's health or his peace of mind? His health or his happiness? Her own peace of mind?

Most evenings, whether at the old house or at Ishy and Malia's, began with card-playing but ended up late at night with singing and dancing – songs Māori and Maoli, learning these from one another. In all her life, Oriwia had never felt so free, so unburdened, and if it hadn't been for thoughts of the grandchildren, Dorothea and the family, and for wondering how Marianne and Dulcie were managing, she could have extended her time in Hawai'i.

Oriwia was not a real card enthusiast, though cards had been part of her upbringing. Whenever people came together, hands would be dealt and she would be obliged to join in. She could enjoy this for an hour or two, after which time she'd want to hand over to someone else so she could get back to the shop and read the weeklies. But reading was considered unsociable when people were together. Euchre and 500 were rowdy and funny in those days, just as they were now.

One night, they were singing a love song that compared love to flowers, carnations in particular, held close to the heart:

Putiputi kāneihana e
Māku koe e kato e
Mehemea ko koe
Taku tau pūmau
Piri rawa i tēnei uma e

After they'd been through it a few times, Aki, Oriwia and Chappy had everyone stand to learn the actions, before going on to another old favourite. It was in the middle of this next song that Chappy stopped singing, held carnations to his heart and said, 'Flowers which smell lovely by the door.'

Conversations had already taken place on other evenings, where Chappy had told of his desire to return to Aotearoa and work the land. Oriwia, who had now decided that his happiness was what mattered most, had put other alternatives out of mind. Though there were no markets for small-time veggie growers any more, what did it matter? Chappy was coming home. She could have her tearoom, he could grow and sell vegetables.

But when?

And now, flowers.

The patch where they'd grown their vegetables, now taken over by lupin and scrub, suddenly burst into bloom – gladioli, stocks, pinks, sweet peas, sweet william, spring bulbs. Roses.

'Baskets,' he said.

Baskets, long and open-ended for gathering blooms, round and open for display, tall with collars – high at the back, low in front – for special floral arrangements, small and pretty for flower girls strewing petals in church parades.

Incense and roses.

Their land would be covered in colour and fragrance. They would provide blooms and baskets to florists who would do them up into bouquets, posies, sprays and corsages for weddings, or wreaths for funerals. Or maybe they wouldn't sell flowers at all, but just have beautiful gardens. They'd belong to a garden society and win cups for prize blooms.

But?

Her tearoom?

Aki, on guitar, moved on to a new song, 'Me he manu rere' – if I were a bird I'd fly to your bed and hold you in my arms. Or should that be wings? Oriwia wondered.

The singing didn't continue for very long after that. Ishy and Malia made moves to go home. Ela's mother told them to wait. She was cutting up cake and putting biscuits on a tray. Oriwia went to help her. Aki and Chappy were talking about gardens and rotary hoes and a small tractor.

Flowers.

———

'I was handing round biscuits with my head full of flowers when my mouth said something, Grandson, but I didn't get the words right.'

———

Oriwia stood there holding a plate of chocolate coconut clusters.

'I want to remarry,' she said. Her worried look wouldn't have helped anyone understand what she was getting at. 'Gee whiz. You should've heard the silence. You should've seen the faces. They were all at once wired stiff,' she said.

Chappy's straight black hair looked as though it had been electrified. His wavy eyebrows went up, his eyes widened and his lips were tucked back under his teeth so no sound would come out. Aki, who was standing leaning the guitar against the wall, swivelled and straightened. Oriwia could see he was boiling, all muscle and eyes, heat rising through his body, arms hitching and bulking his shoulders as though he could tackle a bull. Ishy halted the biscuit that was going towards his mouth and stared with his lips poking towards her. The Hawaiians became statues, except that their eyes were flickering from face to face to see what story was written on them.

It was guilt that gave her the worried look. She'd had the answer all along to Chappy coming home, but hadn't shared that solution.

'My husband,' she said.

There was a letting out of breath from Aki deflating and from Chappy's lips untucking.

'Remarry. And take him home.'

Aki crashed, laughing, onto a wicker chair, which broke and deposited him on the floor. Big men that you read about in books have big laughter, according to Oriwia. They boom like waterfalls in canyons. Aki's laughter was high pitched and it flopped him all over the place.

Ela pushed the crashed chair aside with her foot.

'Here,' Oriwia said, 'in Honolulu and –'

'My sister . . . my sister . . .' Aki said, getting up from down there, shoving his big head sideways at her and explaining to the others what he knew she was trying to say. Chappy, who also understood, was trying to make himself heard. 'Whenever do I get to make my own marriage proposal?' was what he wanted to know.

The Hawaiians were up dancing. Malia gave Oriwia a crack with her hip.

———

'You have to watch these Hawaiians, Grandson,' Oriwia said. 'They can cut you in half with their hips.'

———

There was clatter and shrieking. Aki opened another bottle of something, and they stayed up all night singing and laughing. They made breakfast. Ishy and Malia went home. Chappy went to work, and later so did Aki.

Ela and her sister arranged the wedding, which took place in Ishy and Malia's garden three weeks later. Oriwia, who for so long had resisted the idea of another wedding, put herself in their hands.

———

'The Hawaiians do nothing by halves, Grandson. It was a wonderful celebration, with singing and dancing, gift-giving, lei exchange and beautiful food. We all wore colourful clothes. Though I hadn't wanted a second wedding, it now felt right to me. I knew it was right. I became Mrs Chappy Star over again.'

| Chapter 29 |

AKI

We were the last family to move from the land. While most had gone to live in the outer suburbs, I wanted to take the family into Honolulu, close to Chappy, Ishy and Malia, and near to the harbour. In our new lives we needed money and I was the only one with employment. As well as Ela, her mother and me, there were three of Lili and Puna's grandchildren living with us – two granddaughters and a grandson whom the old couple had brought up. They were now in their late teens and early twenties.

When Lili and Puna decided to stay behind, we asked if we could take the children to live with us. We would find work for them. This was a relief to the old couple, who had known no other life than one on the land and in the forests, where they wanted to stay and continue making their medicines and doing their healing work. They could see no future for their grandchildren on the land, as their old way of life had been pulled from under them.

As we prepared to leave, Chappy set about finding a house for us. This brightened him. He'd had tears pouring down through his insides ever since Paa's death. In an attempt to drive through this inner cloud, he'd put his head down and worked every hour of every day. He'd travelled, finding more and more outlets for goods, widening his networks. Though his heart wasn't in it, his business was thriving as never before.

I, like Oriwia, doubted whether Chappy should move from Hawai'i. On the other hand, I thought he'd die of regret if he remained. I kept my mouth shut on that subject, remembering that he was a survivor.

Every so often, I'd go and get Chappy and take him with me to stay for a night, and he'd talk of his sorrow at not getting home before Paa died. After the war, he believed that his wife and daughters would be better off without him, and it was only when he thought he was dying in Tokyo that he wanted to make contact to tell us what had happened. He never thought he'd see his wife and daughters, his parents, his family again, but wanted us to know he hadn't forgotten. As for the land, and the old life, he hadn't considered being part of it again.

Convinced that he was soon to die and would never return to Aotearoa, he went along in a languid way with Ishy's proposals for him to come to Hawai'i as a first step to going home. He was disbelieving. But Hawai'i gave him the opportunity to see his wife, his children and his father again, which was more than he had dreamed of. And Hawai'i made him well.

It wasn't until Binnie's wedding, despite hands around his throat, that he began to realise that returning permanently might be possible. Back in Hawai'i, he completed his application to become a resident of the United States as a first step. At the same time, he legalised his name as Chappy Star – not a problem, because many Japanese in Hawai'i were changing their names at the time.

After the wedding of his second daughter, when Paa expressed his strong desire for the return of this 'true son', Chappy knew that he must come home no matter what the consequences might be.

'Now, I think,' he said, 'I could've stayed home, right then after the wedding and taken the risk that my wife was asking me to take.' He paused. 'So that he could see me there. Paa.'

'He knew you'd return,' I said. 'Death, to Paa, was not much different to life. Time didn't mean a lot. You would come during his lifetime, or you'd come later, but you would come. And in his manner of thinking, you were already home because your grandchildren were there. You are your grandchildren. They are you. And the land waits. "Toitū te whenua, whatungarongaro he tāngata", as they say.'

We'd been living there for about three months, when Chappy said he wanted to give up his apartment and come and live with us until he could return to New Zealand 'so we can all cook together'. It made sense, and of course he would've known this would help us out financially as well.

It was a great get-together when Oriwia came. I'd never seen her so relaxed. One night, when we were fooling around, Chappy stood with his eyes phasing to three quarters and announced he was going to grow flowers. Another string on the guitar pinged. You can't eat flowers, I thought, as I gave up on the now three-stringed guitar. I was putting it away when Oriwia announced she wanted to get married again. Hey. It took me a moment to catch on. Floored me. Well, I was drunk anyway. It all ended in a wedding.

About a year after Chappy and Oriwia returned to New Zealand, we thought of giving up the old house, believing that a convenient apartment might be more comfortable for Ela, but Ela didn't want to move. It proved to be the right decision to remain where we were because it meant there was plenty of room for family coming to stay. Eric and Mele, Lani and Binnie arrived at different times to help look after her. Others came and went through open doors, relieving us of cooking and washing and shopping so that we could care for Ela in the final stages of her illness (which I would've taken for my own if it were possible.

Let me have it instead. Let me have it was my unanswered plea to the unknown).

At the last I had to give her permission. 'It has to be you,' my mother-in-law said. So I did. I gave it. 'You have to go now, my sweetheart,' I said to Ela. 'It's all right. We're all here, but we have to let you go.' In the room with me were Ma, Malia, Eric and Lani. There were others in the house, asleep, or just waiting.

Though Ela gave no sign, I know she heard me because soon after that she died.

In the days that followed, I thought of her alone on that pathway where I would willingly have been her companion. Or maybe she was not alone. The way could've been full of friends, I thought. There could've been singing, laughter and dancing on the journey to join the stars. That's what we do at such times, I guess. We find comfort in any thought or imagining, or in any old-time musing, or in any way we can. The old house became dispirited after the song had gone.

Ma went to live with Malia and Ishy, taking the young ones with her.

So much death. My father, Taana, died suddenly in the same week as Ela. My mother, Dorothea, died not long after Chappy came home.

I had to leave off crying, become once more a rover, finding work that would take me across the world's oceans, douse me in salt spray.

Salt cures.

Sea washes. It cleans.

Expanse enlivens the spirit, frees the mind.

There was no need now to work for money, and somewhere along the way I began to think about other responsibilities.

'*Go on home,*' Moonface said.

'*Take me with you,*' said my Ela, '*now that you've shown me the world.*'

| *Chapter 30* |
ORIWIA

'**T**here was no explosion,' my grandmother said. 'Except for the one in my head.'

———

Oriwia returned to New Zealand while Chappy spent the next six months in Hawai'i arranging a management partnership with Ishy and Malia's daughter. There was also the matter of sponsorship to be organised by Oriwia at home.

By the time she arrived, Taana had finished building a kitchenette in a corner of the bakery. He'd opened up a wall to form a servery and enlarged the shop space to make room for tables. Oriwia set about painting the walls, laying linoleum on the floor and making three sets of tablecloths for each of the ten small tables.

Because her day began at three in the morning when she baked her breads and pies – which in the meantime she served to customers from a side door of the bakery with the help of Marianne – much of the work in the new tearoom was done after she had closed for the day.

———

'Of flowers. Eruptions, all colours, like fireworks, Daniel. All the time while I was painting, tacking lino, sewing, shifting tables, there were spouts and blooms, stars, fountains, shooting off in my head.'

———

Dulcie went with her to make purchases. Dishes, teapots, jugs, a fridge – which turned out to be too big for the kitchen and had to be put out in the bakery. Oriwia decided to paint the house as well. Brown was the wrong colour to go with all the heady blooms.

Dulcie tried to persuade Oriwia not to paint the house, advised her to wait until Chappy came home, knowing that there was still so much that needed doing before the tearoom could be opened.

'Greeny-blue, or bluey-green, with white facings,' Oriwia told her friend, and went off to buy paint.

Oriwia also had letters to write and sponsorship forms to send to Chappy for his temporary visa. Residency would take much longer. Proof had to be given that she and Chappy had been together for more than a year so that the application could be dealt with more quickly. About their earlier marriage and the children they'd had together in New Zealand she said nothing, instead attaching letters of guarantee obtained from one of Ishy's business contacts and a ship's captain of Aki's acquaintance.

Lani and Binnie came over in the weekends to help her paint; but there was something she didn't know, to do with Lani and Binnie, which the couple had been discussing during her time away.

It was while she and her daughter were working side by side, standing on boxes painting windowsills, that Binnie broke the news that she and Lani were going to move to Auckland.

'Definitely not,' said Oriwia, letting paint drip.

'We've had an offer and we've accepted,' Binnie said.

'You're not taking my grandchildren to live in that rat-race.'

'A big new place, a new restaurant. Lani as cook, second in charge, me as goods manager.'

'People get murdered there.'

'Oh, Mother.'

'Oh, Mother, oh, Mother. Who's going to look after the kids?'

'I'll work days, Lani'll work nights.'

'And what sort of life is that?'

'A working life, Mother, just like your life.'

'The children? What life for the children?'

'And Father will be –'

'Without his grandchildren . . . Anyway, how can Lani be second in charge? To hold that job you have to boss people around. He wouldn't say boo to a goose.'

'Mother.'

'Mother, Mother . . . You're not taking Noelani,' she said.

'Noelani can stay with you if she wants to,' Binnie answered, 'but we want to have her back in Auckland for her secondary schooling. We're sending her to Queen Vic.'

Oriwia wondered if it was her own ambitious nature which sent them all away.

Noelani, who was ten years old at the time, stayed with Oriwia for three years before going to Auckland to complete her schooling. Oriwia couldn't argue against it, as in her opinion the local high school had little to offer such a brilliant girl. She didn't see much of Noelani, or any of them, from then on. Noelani spent her holidays with her parents as she was able to earn pocket money waitressing at the restaurant. At the end of her secondary school years, she went south to Otago University. Now Noelani was down there living her own life. That was Oriwia's complaint with education. That was the price you paid.

Lani, Binnie and the children had packed and moved by the time Chappy returned from Hawai'i and were at the airport to meet him when he landed in Auckland. He stayed overnight with his daughter and son-in-law before making the last part of his journey. By the time he arrived, Star Tearoom had had its sign up for a month, and Oriwia had welcomed her customers through the new front door, treating them to tea and cake on opening day.

'We had a big homecoming celebration for Chappy,' Oriwia said. 'Ti and I went to the airport to get him while all our relations crowded into the tearoom to wait. I could've done without the celebration, which went on until it was time for me to switch on the ovens. What I really wanted was to be at home with my husband, in our own house. But first things first. We celebrated. I knew there would be many happy days ahead of us.

'And truly, they were good days. We had each other. I had my tearoom. He had his garden, a much different garden to the one I'd imagined. Chappy did grow flowers, he just didn't grow ten thousand of them. The rainings and pourings were all in my head.'

Oriwia and Chappy would go to the bakery and tearoom early in the morning. Oriwia would put the bread and pies in the ovens while Chappy went out front to arrange chairs and lay the cloths. The bread and pie part of the business was declining because of competition from large bakeries, but Oriwia was not sorry about that. Now she could concentrate on serving tea and cakes. Once the loaves and pies were in the ovens, she would begin icing and decorating the cakes which had been baked and set to cool the evening before. She would cut and ice lamingtons from the previous day's sponges and whip up mixtures for slabs, small cakes and fruit loaves.

At nine o'clock, Marianne would arrive and dress the shop window and the glassed-in counter with a display of chocolate, ginger and Neapolitan cakes, Swiss rolls, melting moments, cream puffs and éclairs, peanut brownies, ginger crunch and a variety of scones, pikelets and sandwiches. At ten o'clock she would open the door and return to the counter to serve the first customers of the day. Some wanted cakes and sandwiches to take away. Others would give their orders and take their seats. For these customers, it was Oriwia who would make the teas, prepare the trays and bring them to their tables.

When Marianne arrived, Chappy would hang up his apron and go home. On days when the weather was unsuitable for gardening, he could have stayed and helped through morning teas, but he didn't want to interact with townspeople. He was a ghost who disappeared in daylight. After the tearoom door had closed at five, he would return and help with the washing down while Oriwia baked and prepared for the next day.

While the last cakes were in the ovens, Oriwia and her husband would sit among the fragrance of spices and essence, drinking tea. She felt a deep contentment at such times. All her dreams had come true. Her husband was home, her daughters and grandchildren were all doing well somewhere in the world, she was running her own little village tearoom where people gathered and gossiped, enjoyed company and exclaimed about what she was able to set before them. She'd taken over the reputation, once held by Harry Krauss, of being the best maker and decorator of special cakes for miles around. Unsigned notes, maligning her husband, his race and his family came into her letterbox from time to time. Oriwia read them, burned them, and told no one.

———

'The flowers?' I asked.

'I said to your grandfather, "Poor husband, you're starting everything from scratch."'

———

Oriwia was aware that the grounds around the house had been neglected. The house and veggie stall that she and Chappy had built when they were first married was close to the road. In two narrow borders, either side of the front step, Dorothea had planted bulbs and flower cuttings from her own garden, scented, 'lovely by the door' – stock, carnations, roses. Freesias creamed out on the tail of winter.

When Oriwia decided to rebuild, she had chosen a site well back from the road where it was quieter and away from dust. For this purpose the old house and stall sites were cleared and some of the fruit trees had to be chopped down. Once the new house was built, she'd thought of gardens – vegetables at the back, flowers in front, for her husband to come home to. 'Bursts, both sides of the drive, shrubberies and borders, yellow hot pokers, red hot pokers. Don't know which is hotter – red or yellow. Often wondered about that, of fire, I mean. But it was all in my head. It all went to pot. Poor husband – not even a proper lawn. Nothing but paddock grass out front, humps and bumps.' Though the remaining fruit trees still bore fruit, the orchard had become overgrown. The paddock had given way to scrub and weeds.

Chappy cleaned up the orchard and manicured the trees. His heart was right in it. He fixed the fences and put a goat in to mow the sheep paddock. Then he asked Oriwia what sort of garden she wanted.

Flowers.

What kind of? Where?

Let it be you, Oriwia told her husband. Let it be you.

For the next seven or eight years, they were fourteen-hour days for Oriwia from the time she left home until she returned at night. In the town, there were only a grill room and a dairy that sold any kind of prepared food. The grill room was open in the evenings only, and the flat pies and curly sandwiches put out by the dairy were no competition. Regulars to the tearoom included travelling salesmen and truckies who were keen on Oriwia's pastries. They'd take lunch in a bag and be off on the road again. Oriwia made tea for them to take away if they had their own tea mugs. Orders were made up for workers round town. But what Oriwia enjoyed most were the customers coming in, placing their orders and putting their feet under the tables, ready for a chat. The really big days were show days, twice a year.

However, custom declined when a new café opened on the opposite side of the street, serving new kinds of coffee and plated food. Road improvements, and the fact that people all had good cars now, meant that they would bypass the tearoom, driving to the next town where a food market and chainstore had opened, advertising low prices.

| Chapter 31 |
AKI

I was at the woodpile sawing stove-lengths from mānuka trunks I'd brought down from the slopes. About mid-morning. There was mist soft-footing about the hills, grey like old photos. Earlier, I'd heard Chappy drive up and knew he was over at the bamboo grove getting canes for the garden he was making. I had a few woodchips and scraps burning behind me in a ring of stones. In a minute or two, I'd boost the flames with a few sticks and put the billy on to boil. Before Chappy went home, we'd have billy tea and a yarn. I was thinking this when I looked up and saw him coming towards me, slow, slow, slow. He stopped and stood a way off with nothing to say. He was inside himself, ghosting.

'What?' I called, straightening, leaving the saw stuck in a half-cut piece.

He came towards me.

'I found him,' he said, whispering, turning away.

His ghost feet led me to the mid-section of the bamboo thicket where he'd been cutting. There were tied bundles on the trailer, loose sticks on the ground. I pressed my way in behind him while he held back a section of canes for me, and in there, deep, was Noddy – bones, old cloth, gumboots – still standing because of the tightness of vegetation which now grew through and about, binding him.

We came out from there and sat in silence for a long time. I said, 'Make him a casket while I go and arrange his tangihanga.' I went home to use the telephone and on returning saw that Chappy had the bamboo casket well under way. Noddy's older brother arrived not long afterwards, and together he and I untwisted Noddy from his standing death.

'Do we notify anyone?' I asked his brother, meaning doctors, police, authorities.

'The ones who matter to my brother have all been told,' he said.

So we took our crate of bones to the marae for the ceremonies, and the next day buried Noddy by his mother and father.

Some time later, I was pacing out by the bamboo grove searching my soul. For several days I'd been backwards and forwards between there and the spring where, nearly fifty years before, as a fourteen-year-old, I had drawn water and allowed my attention to stray. It's a distance of fifty impossible yards or more. Impossible yards. A four-year-old could not have, in that time, gone from one place to the other without my knowing. Could he? While we searched in other directions? But, no. He would've answered our calls, come running, his hiding game over.

The bamboo grove, which in the early days had begun as runaway shoots from my mother's garden but which was controlled to some degree by animals, had taken up and thickened to a wide belt in an unused paddock. Other unwanted plants – scrub, thistle and blackberry – struggled against it as it broke fences, jumped ditches, clogged waterways.

Since the tangihanga of our cousin, Chappy had come to see me every day. On this day of my wandering, he told me he needed help with his garden, but I suspect that he was attempting to move me away from my thoughts. Tomorrow, I told him.

He went away and came back the next day with tools – secateurs and little saws, hand forks and trowels, which he used in his own garden. There were no slashers, axes, shovels, spades. Nothing big like that.

'Take it down, piece by piece,' he said. 'Examine every leaf, every stem and every dab of soil, and then we'll know.' He paused, looking away from me. 'Do you want to know?' he asked, becoming my other voice.

In reply, I took up a pair of secateurs and cut the nearest cane. We examined the length of it and put it aside, next scratching the earth round the root, which we then extracted. We worked there until it was time for Chappy to go back to the tearoom. 'Come and have a cup of tea with Oriwia and me,' he said. 'Then we'll go home and cook up a feed – bacon bones, cabbage, swede . . .' I hadn't eaten since we buried Noddy.

The next morning – it must have been a Sunday because Star Tearoom was closed – Oriwia came to help with removing bamboo, and in the afternoon Noddy's brother and sister came. Others joined us from time to time.

Day after day, we inched through the grove, cutting, scratching, scraping, sifting and examining throughout the area of what we called the 'old bamboo'.

'Nothing,' I said, at last.

'*Away with the fairies*,' said Moonface. '*Believe it.*'

We put the area of new bamboo under the control of goats, which Chappy and I, with the help of a nephew and his brave dog, picked up from the side of the gorge road. I watched over the old area, taking out and burning any new shoots that came up.

To me, a garden means food – potatoes, kūmara, pumpkins, cabbages, carrots, corn, kamokamo, tomatoes, melons. It means growing and harvesting and storing enough to see the seasons through. My mother grew flowers because she took pleasure in it, but I hadn't learned to call that a garden. So I couldn't figure out what Chappy was doing with his rocks and stones, his digging and shaping and making of crooked pathways that led nowhere.

What I could see once I came home from my travels was a few doctored trees, collections of flat-topped stones that had been taken from the river mouth, and large rocks that had been delivered from the quarry out on the coast. The stones were not only collected, but also selected, Oriwia told me, one, two or three at a time and tried out for suitability. They were used to form stepping stones, not across water – a use I was familiar with – but embedded in soil so that only the flat tops showed – stepping to nowhere. There was a pile of shingle, littered through with shell, which came from the shore of the estuary.

However, by the time of Noddy and the bamboo, I had begun to see what was taking shape out front of the Star house: mounds and hollows, bridges across shingle, paving, bamboo shelters and ornamental screens protecting shrubs. Not much in the way of flowers, I thought, as I kept up my supply of lettuces, cabbages etcetera from my own garden. Rock you cannot eat. But my eyes did eventually open up to Chappy's garden. That was after he died, when I would go there and sit with Oriwia.

There isn't much more to tell. They were brotherly days with Chappy in Hawai'i and at home. I've been fortunate in life and love and the work that's been given me. Chappy believed himself lucky, too, to have reached his seventieth year and to have the life and love that he had. I miss him. I miss them all in different ways.

But, not to worry, there's singing in the mountains, laughter in the trees, dancing in the light of evening fires. There's whispering in hearts and minds and shadows. That's enough for me.

That's enough from me.

| Chapter 32 |
ORIWIA

'Star Tearoom was saved by Chappy's garden,' Oriwia said. 'I'll show you.' My grandmother, requesting that I bring a stool, led me to her bedroom where, though the window was open to its last notch, there was a heaviness of late summer air, a woolly weight, a smell of baked wallpaper, hardened polish, forest, sacks, church pews, camphor.

'Dusty butterflies,' my grandmother said of the atmosphere, rushing forward, unlatching the window and flinging it outward.

A quilted counterpane of old-gold nylon covered the bed and flounced down to touch the floor like a large gown. Under the cover would be all those trappings my mother had spoken to me about.

Eighteen months before, as a new arrival and having decided I must follow all my mother's instructions, I'd asked my grandmother to enlighten me as to the mysteries of making this kind of bed. She explained and demonstrated the spreading of sheets and blankets, which had to be folded back at the top end and tucked in all the way round under the mattress. The bed cover cocooned the pillows and concealed all this art underneath. It took effort, but my skills improved after a few days.

On arrival, wanting to do nothing but sleep, I wondered how I would get into such a tight bed, but I stepped up onto it and managed to slide myself in so as not to disturb the tucking. It was like being in an envelope. The next night I pulled out some of the tucks and made myself comfortable, though it was still not easy to unravel myself when the night became hot.

Grandmother's bedstead was of dark brown wood with matching bedside cabinets piled with books. Dressing table, tallboy and a free-standing wardrobe left little space to move about. On top of the wardrobe was where Oriwia kept albums, framed photographs wrapped in old sheeting, and boxes of other memorabilia.

'It has a scenic cover,' she said of the album she wanted me to find. 'Yachts in a harbour and the hills behind. There's no wind. They're becalmed. They won't get anywhere.'

She asked me to bring water, and together we went outside to sit in the shadehouse. Sensing an opportunity, I took my tape recorder with me.

It was a warm evening of high light, which is the way light is in this country – high and spread and unfiltered, even in this season. From where we sat, we had a fine view of the forward portion of my grandfather's garden: the stone patio at the front of the house, stepping stones which emerged from there, mounds and banks where shrubs had been trimmed into boulder shapes. Some of these 'boulders' remained a glossy green, others were tight with red, white or pink flowers. In other places, flowers spiked up, blue, purple, yellow, but even so the impression was of muted colour. 'In their own contexts,' my grandmother said, 'flowers to enhance or surprise but not to overtake, some varieties which smelled lovely by the door.' They were plants I'd seen in other parts of the world, most of which I couldn't name in English until informed by my grandmother.

Others I'd never seen before coming here. There was a harakeke bush which I took an interest in because it was the plant the old ones had used for their basket-weaving, watched by

Grandfather Chappy that long time ago, inspiring him to make and add his bamboo containers to their collection. These bushes grew prolifically on farmland and roadsides, and the plantation was still thriving round the spring at Uncle Aki's. The garden one kept its strong, green blades throughout the seasons. Thick, black stalks emerged in spring, tipped by bulging encasements. These opened into bright orange flowers as the weather became warm, later forming black, rattling pods that curled and split, dispersing seed in late summer.

There was a cluster of three ponga trees, all kept at different heights. Easy to grow, my grandmother explained; a matter of cutting sections of black trunk to the required lengths and placing them in the ground. With plenty of water, the trunks take root at the base and ferns spread outward from their tops to form wide umbrellas.

Three and five were numbers that belonged in the garden. Large rocks of different heights and shapes were positioned in threes or fives, sometimes in screened areas, sometimes in the open where they had the appearance of large animals at rest on the twinkling shingle.

The most natural aspect incorporated into the garden was the small creek coming from the back through to the front of the property. My grandparents' first house had been on the other side of this, close to the road. Spanning the narrow waterway was an arched wooden bridge. Bulrushes, stone areas and grasses were built into the creek's banks.

The most formed features were the bridge itself, the screens and fences, the shade-house, and two elegant structures of carved stone. One of these was a lantern made of rock shaped and piled in sections. A flat-topped base supported a pillar, which gave height to a platform. On the platform sat the 'firebox' and its cover.

The other was a low basin to the side of one of the paths, cylindrical in shape and indented at the top to hold water. The stepping stones leading to it, the placement of stones about it and the thick planting of greenery to the rear made it cool and inviting. My grandmother would go to it, dip her fingers in the water and touch her forehead and temples. Without asking why, I did the same.

Though there was much to see, the garden didn't impose, didn't assume. And though it was man-made and structured, you could have the same feeling of peace there as you did up in the bush where Aki set the eel traps and where your brain and your being became heady with the steam from mulch, green vapours, the damp of moss and lichen, fungi, breezes, running water. And isolation. Or at the beach and river mouth where we fished, speared flounder with a three-pronged wire spear, where we could see for miles in any direction, and where we were the only ones.

Our companions there were the sea birds. Each time we visited, there were plenty of them, plonking themselves down into the water and coming up with fish.

'Serene and understated,' I said to my grandmother as we sat looking out, sipping from our glasses.

'And planned to be so,' she said, 'every inch planned. In consultation. My Chappy looked to his master. I'll show you later. There's a boxful. But now . . .'

Oriwia opened the album. On the front page she had pasted a newspaper item showing a photograph of the garden with a caption describing it as 'an oasis of peace in our busy town'. It was one of a series of photos over a double-page spread, depicting local gardens. Although to the family it was known as Chappy's Garden or Father's Garden, after the newspaper item it became described by the people of the town as the 'peace garden'.

It wasn't long after this publication that a woman came from Wellington to talk about mystery tours for the elderly and an arrangement was made. This was timely.

In the album were photographs of seniors, all chiffon, chairs and paraphernalia – snapped in the parking area, snapped in various parts of the garden, or enjoying afternoon tea at the tearoom. In the background of some of the pictures, Chappy could be seen with his back to the camera.

'All full of twitter and exclamation,' Oriwia said. 'Collapsed eyelids and smiles of unfitting teeth. Dusty face powder. Bandages. I lowered my charges. Bought new teacups with saucers and sideplates, gold-rimmed, country rose. I loved my senior citz. And the teasets.

'This is Nettie,' my grandmother said, showing a photograph of a startled woman in a neck brace, lips drawn back displaying long, colourful teeth with gums in retreat. 'She reminded me of my old horse when I first saw her, so I had to be extra nice to her after thinking things like that. She had no one, no one in the world, so Chappy and I went to get her in the weekends – picked her up on Saturday and took her back to the old folks' home on Sunday. Those old things wrote to us, you know, sent us all these cards and photos. I went to their funerals if I could, and if I knew.

'The buses kept us going for a time. They were not always full of old people. Some were chartered coaches on their way up north, calling in because the tearoom was considered a good lunch stop. We still had our salesmen and drivers, and some of our old faithfuls kept coming and putting their feet under the tables. We were ticking along but could've gone under if it hadn't been for the oldies.'

Leaving our water jug, glasses and the photograph album on the seat, we walked, as we often did, along the paths and stepping stones and over the bridge to the front of the section. We sat together on a large concaved rock, which still held its warmth though the garden was being swallowed by fading light.

'When your grandfather became ill in the winter of 1980, his spirit drifting and fluttering here and there filling all the rooms,

I closed the tearoom. He survived that first year but not the next. Flew. I didn't think I'd ever open the tearoom again.'

Oriwia kept the doors shut for two years. She spent a month of each year visiting her family in Auckland. While at home, she did little but sit in the garden, or walk about in it, 'poking here and there, interfering'. But she wasn't a gardener, she was a trader.

One morning, she crossed the road, walked to the tearoom and went about cleaning ovens, shelves and floors, because you have to get on with life.

'It kept me going, and makes enough money to employ a gardener. Do you want a tearoom, Daniel? You could turn it into one of these cafés doing all kinds of coffees – mochaccinos, cappuccinos, every other kind of cino – all-day breakfasts, hot-food cabinet, salad and chips. It would need a refit.' Then she answered her own question. 'Of course not. Of course you don't want a tearoom. That's just me trying to keep you here. No. There's no future for eating in this place now. It's turned into a retirement town – wheelchairs and crutches, shopping trolleys. Land Rovers, station wagons and BMWs do their shopping elsewhere.

'Anyway I might die, you know, just drop dead, and you'd be left. No, you have your whole life ahead of you and need much younger company. Your mother's right, you should complete your studies, get something solid under your belt so you can have one of these high-falutin' careers. If you remain here, sticking with the elderly you'll never get married.'

We stood, pulled to our feet by bird silence, a deepening brown, dense smells that mingled marsh and leaf-mould with night-scented plants.

EPILOGUE

Thoughts about my future were on my mind, too. What now? In all my life I'd never been as engaged as when recording the stories that somehow bound me to them. It was not only the collecting, but the life and learning that went along with it – which I haven't recorded – which captivated me. Anyone reading what I've written could think that the taping and note-taking took place on consecutive days over a short period of time, whereas recording was spasmodic. I took opportunities as they arose because in between times there was a life to live.

Fortunately, the sulking boy made the decision to lift himself out of disgruntlement to listen to his mother's advice – he learned to make a bed, sweep and clean floors, bake pies, wash out cabinets and wipe down benches.

Muck in.

The most invigorating days of all were those spent with my uncle by double adoption, when we went bush, bringing out dead wood to be cut and dried for the fire, when we fished at the river mouth, went eeling up the creek or walked over the hills shooting rabbits. Twice during my stay, I helped catch and kill a sheep, which we then hung up in a tree. The fleece had to be dragged down, the front had to be opened up and the stomach pulled out. We trimmed it, cut it up and put it all in my grandmother's freezer.

I didn't relish killing and butchering. It made me feel sick. Aki was aware of how I felt, but he didn't say anything, didn't let me off. Nor did he make it easy for me when it came to his language; he spoke to me in Māori all the time after the first day. His only concession was that he used his hands and other body language to aid my understanding. My grandmother had something to say when she found out what he was up to, but changed her mind when she discovered how interested I was. Being conversant and literate in English and Danish from my parentage, German and French from my environments and schooling, I was now becoming familiar with the rhythms and cadences of another tongue, whether this was during recording or while down at the marae where all of life went on.

It was on the marae where I noted that, of the many fine orators, Uncle Aki was the one whom people were most attuned to. I could see how he amused, entertained and informed, how attentive people were to every word he spoke, how they exclaimed, laughed, and at times became completely silent. Though there was no boy with a held ear sitting at his elbow, Uncle Aki did have his protégés. These were the adult children, now in middle age, of his two sisters Aunty Mina and Aunty Ti. One of them, Uncle Toby, was planning to bring his family on to the land to live with Uncle Aki.

Anyway, I spent hours listening to the kōrero, days on end; went to sleep immersed in the language as the talk went back and forth. I would wake to it when one of the elders, draped in a blanket, tapped his walking stick against the pou in the early morning and recited the karakia before showers – usually cold by the time I got to them – and a hot breakfast. It didn't matter to me that I understood little (at first). I was borne along on mood and emotion, laughing when everyone else laughed, silent among the silent, fascinated by the whispering and mutterings and body language, wracked by the wailings of sorrow.

I began to recognise patterns, understand words here and there, and eventually came to get the gist of the kōrero. I was able to augment learning by mulling over and comparing the recorded language with the translations my grandmother provided me with.

However, I couldn't indulge completely in what took place out on the marae ātea or in the wharenui. I soon learned that the talking that continued throughout the hui belonged in the domain of the elders. That was their duty. For my age group, there were piles of dishes to be washed, watercress to be collected, potatoes to be peeled, meat and pumpkins to cut up, tables and chairs to be arranged, toilets to be cleaned. I got the idea, became part of the picture.

But as we worked, there was language also, sometimes Māori, sometimes English, sometimes a mix of the two – stories, small talk, conversation, gossip, argument, laughter. I'll miss the laughter. It turns you inside out and gives a good clean. I'll miss the heart of it all.

The talk, more than anything else, was of genealogy. Family connection to this one, that one, the other one from here and there, and it seemed I was a person of special interest when it came to whakapapa. Well, I was certainly treated as such, whether this was on the paepae or in the wharenui where my relationship was explained, or outside where I'd be taken by the elbow to be introduced to yet more people with whom I shared ancestry.

Attachments, because of Oriwia, because of Chappy Star, because of an uncle by double adoption. To find these connections was one of the reasons I had come in the first place, initially with a quest to find out about my grandfather, Chappy Star.

So how successful has that been?

What I can say is that I have been able to trace fascinating aspects of Chappy Star's adult life. I have not sat at his knee, so to speak, or drawn in close to him in the way I have been able to do with Grandmother Oriwia or Uncle Tiakiwhenua and others. I have come to understand that he was loved by his family and his community, and it was a love that was mutual. Though I have been able, many times, to glimpse his heart, Chappy Star, without being a sphinx or a Mr X, remains an enigma.

That's all right. It's good.

A mystery solved is no longer a mystery. Like my grandmother, I can enjoy a conundrum for its own sake. Not everything in the world has to be understood.

I'd been with Grandmother Oriwia for eighteen months. My question now was what to do next so that I wouldn't be merely taking up space in the universe. My mother expected me to return to Switzerland in time for the next academic year, something I'd put off for twelve months already. But, home to do what? Hide in the dark and read?

Home to be what? A boy who displeased his father, who soft-shoed about after his mother whenever there was an opportunity, hoping she would play in the snow with him again, a malcontent left in the dust by a younger sister who had achievements and a social life?

I'd run out of time to be a boy. I'd run out of the desire to be one. That a man must find his own feet sooner or later doesn't mean he stands alone. According to Aki, you have to have a people in order to know you are a person.

'We'll always be here,' my grandmother said, as though she'd read this last thought. 'Even when we're dead, there'll always be a place, there'll always be someone. You can be anywhere in the world, but you have a tūrangawaewae that cannot be denied you.

'At the same time, it doesn't mean you have to hang around here in the company of the disintegrating. I already have a watery eye and scaly shins. No, we must share you with the whole world.

What you've done already, putting down the stories, is a big thing for all of us. It's your contribution, nōu te rourou, nāku te rourou, ka ora te manuhiri.'

It wasn't unusual by now for her to speak to me using her mother tongue. The conversations in te reo we sometimes had enlivened her, I thought, made her smile.

'Like Taana the builder and Chappy the weaver, you bring new skills to deposit in and withdraw from the shared basket – languages, new ways of telling stories. But you have to keep it up. It can't just be a oncer.'

In the meantime, there was one immediate task ahead of me, and that was to put together what I could of the life of Chappy Star, framed, contextualised, peopled and humanised by the lives of others. The material that I had gathered originally for my mother, Janny and myself, I now intended publishing for the whole whānau. I decided that, with the exception of some rearranging and minor alterations for the sake of clarity, I would not edit.

And I'll have to work on some kind of introduction, some words about what pushed me. The wimp will have to confess.

I'd never thought before, and it amuses me now to think that 'introduction', 'foreword', 'prologue' coming at the beginning of a book are probably done last, their time already gone.

When it's all done?

If I want to stay on in Aotearoa, I'll need to attend one of its universities and qualify in some useful field, otherwise my presence here will be prodigal.

In some ways, my financial independence embarrasses me, but I am who I am. I understand that now. I'm not about to chuck it all away and go barefoot, and don't wannabe a wannabe. So, no matter where I go or what else I undertake, I'll continue to increase my understanding of this part of myself that I embrace with all my heart. I'll keep in touch, work back and forth from wherever I am in the world and contribute whatever I can from the depth and core of me.

This brings me to the point. (I believe I've learned from my grandmother and uncle to ramble along a few pathways before getting to it.)

The reason I'm intruding myself into this text is to answer the question concerning what I may add to that basket, which can be taken out and shared for the benefit of all, 'nōu te rourou, nāku te rourou', etc. And how does that continue? How does it not be a 'oncer'? This is how the answer came to me:

After Grandmother Oriwia and I finished looking through the photographs, we returned to the house and, while I was standing on the stool returning the album to its place on top of the wardrobe, Oriwia asked me to pass down a cardboard shoebox tied with green ribbon. I found it – though the only green left on the ribbon was in the knot where the bow was tied – and handed it down to her. 'We'll look through it when there's time,' she said. 'Maybe it'll be of interest if you can make head or tail of any of it.' She placed the box on the cabinet beside her bed.

A week or so went by, and one Sunday morning we took the box out to the garden, where my grandmother opened it, explaining to me that all the time Grandfather Chappy had been making his garden, he'd been communicating with a landscape professional in Japan. It was someone he'd known, who had grown up with him in his village and who was from a family that was expert in the making of gardens. 'Apparently you can't just make gardens any old how in Japan,' Oriwia said. 'I had told Chappy "let it be you, let it be you", thinking of flowers.' She flung her arms. 'So all this is what he came up with. It's himself, his expression of love. For always. His secret self, a discretion of flowers, perfumed and not perfumed. Some of it is his own interpretation, depending on what trees were available.'

During the war the garden-maker's family had been displaced from their village. Chappy met his friend again in his travels after the war and so knew how to contact him. That's all Grandmother knew.

In the box was a pile of letters and addressed envelopes interspersed with drawings. The drawings, I could see, were of the garden or sections of it, with little notes written here and there. It was the notes and letters, none of which I could decipher, which gave me heartbeats in my head as I realised they could be the link to the early life of my grandfather.

Standing, with a bunch of pages clutched so tightly in my hand it's a wonder they didn't disintegrate, I experienced a moment of self-definition, epiphany. I knew right there, right then, that I would make contact with the master gardener or his family, that I would spend time learning the Japanese language, and that I would continue to research the life of my grandfather. It could take years, but I knew I would return at intervals to present my findings to the people. I would discover the origins, find a life, the first half of a life of a man who would nevertheless remain in the shadows. Kei te pai.

'You look like a stunned mullet,' my grandmother said. 'Sit down before you conk.'

'I'm going to Japan,' I said.

'I'm coming,' Grandmother said to me next morning. 'It's my turn to see the world,' she said. 'I'll stop off in Hawai'i to see who there is left to see, and meet those who've taken over the running of the business – changing everything – but I suppose that's the way of the world.

'After that I'll pay a visit to Switzerland before trotting about Europe while I've still got my trotters. That'll fill up my days, save me from sitting round here outliving everybody. What a fate that would be. I'll take Binnie with me, your mother too, once we reach Switzerland.

'And when you're settled, my dear grandson, we'll come and spend time in Japan. While there I intend visiting Japanese gardens. There must be books on the subject. There must be tours. If you find my Chappy's birthplace, we'll go there.

'I'll get Toby and his family to come and live in the house while they're preparing to move on to the land with their uncle.

'I'm going to rent out the tearoom space. It'll probably become a second-hand furniture shop, maybe an op shop, or a place that sells local crafts – you know, wooden toys, hand-painted trays, baby clothes, knitted slippers, net bath cleaners, sack oven cloths, covered coathangers, paper roses. Pre-loved clothing maybe? Or antiques? They could have all my metal teapots and sugar bowls. Maybe your wife will be Japanese. Daniel, Grandson, I mustn't die. There are things . . .

'And, Daniel, what about Father Jimmy's questions?

'Ko wai tōna maunga?

'Ko wai tōna awa?

'Ko wai ōna tīpuna?

'Ko wai tōna ingoa?

'Ko wai ia?

'I know my husband had his own reasons for secrecy, but there are children, grandchildren and a whole whānau who would be intrigued if answers were found after all these years.

'All time becomes one,' she said. 'Everything's a search for light.'

| Acknowledgements |

Thanks to friend Susan Najita of the University of Michigan for sending me her paper entitled 'Annexation and the Environment: Reading, Writing, Reanimating 'Āina', and for time spent answering my emailed questions. I am grateful to Captain Mike Pryce, Regional Harbourmaster at Greater Wellington Regional Council, for an enlightening telephone conversation regarding working conditions aboard ships in the 1930s.

Various institutions were important to my research: the National Library of New Zealand: Te Puna Mātauranga o Aotearoa, the Alexander Turnbull Library, Archives New Zealand: Te Rua Mahara o te Kāwanatanga, Porirua Public Library, Pataka Museum in Porirua.

The following books proved very helpful to me during the writing of this novel. *Island of Secrets: Matiu/Somes in Wellington Harbour*, David McGill; *The Penguin History of New Zealand*, Michael King; *Rescue at Sea, Maritime Interceptions and Stowaways*, UN High Commissioner for Refugees; *Stowaways by Sea: Illegal Immigrants/Refugees/Asylum Seekers*, B. A. H. Porritt; *A Century of Style: Great Ships of the Union Line 1875–1976*, N. H. Brewer; *Dark Sun: Te Rapunga and the Quest of George Dibbern*, Erika Grundmann; *Na Kua'aina: Living Hawaiian Culture*, Davianna Pomaika'i McGregor; *Pearl Harbour: An Eye-witness Account*, Blake Clark; *Tokyo: The City at the End of the World*, Peter Popham; *Tokyo*, James Kirkup; *A Guide to Tokyo and Environs*, Nihon Kōtsū Kōsha; *Japanese Gardens in a Weekend*, Robert Ketchell; *The Art of Japanese Gardens*, Herb Gustafson; *Creating a Japanese Garden*, Peter Chan.

Thanks to Debra Millar and the team at Penguin, including Tessa King, Harriet Allan and Megan van Staden. Thank you also to editor John Huria and cover designer Keely O'Shannessy.

| Also by Patricia Grace |

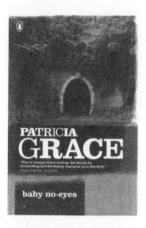

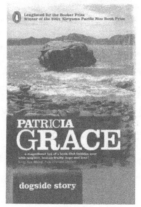

Also available as eBooks.